'Twas the Night After Christmas

Sabrina Jeffries

'Twas the Night After Christmas

**SIMON &
SCHUSTER**

London · New York · Sydney · Toronto · New Delhi

A CBS COMPANY

First published in Great Britain in 2012 by Simon & Schuster UK Ltd
A CBS COMPANY

1 3 5 7 9 10 8 6 4 2

Simon & Schuster UK Ltd
1st Floor
222 Gray's Inn Road
London
WC1X 8HB

www.simonandschuster.co.uk

Simon & Schuster Australia, Sydney
Simon & Schuster India, New Delhi

A CIP catalogue copy for this book is available
from the British Library.

Hardback ISBN: 978-1-47111-370-3
Ebook ISBN: 978-1-47111-373-4

Printed and bound by CPI Group (UK) Ltd, Croydon, CR0 4YY

To the Biaggi Bunch—thanks for always having faith in me!

And to the love of my life, who lost his parents at a young age.
This one's for you, babe.

'Twas the Night After Christmas

Prologue

April 1803

No one had called for him yet.

Eight-year-old Pierce Waverly, heir to the Earl of Devonmont, sat on his bed in the upper hall of the Headmaster's House at Harrow, where he'd lived for three months with sixty other boys.

Today marked the beginning of his first holiday from Harrow; most of the other boys had already been fetched by their families. His trunk was packed. He was ready.

But what if no one came? Would he have to stay at Harrow, alone in the Headmaster's House?

Mother and Father would come. Of *course* they would come. Why wouldn't they?

Because Father thinks you're a sickly weakling. That's why he packed you off to school—to "toughen you up."

His chin quivered. He couldn't help that he had asthma. He couldn't help that he liked it when Mother showed him how to play the pianoforte, which Father called "dandyish." And if he sometimes hid when Father wanted to take him riding, it was only because Father always berated him for not doing it right. Then Pierce would get so mad that he would say things Father called "insolent." Or worse, he'd start having trouble breathing and get panicky. Then Mother would have to come and help him catch his breath, and Father *hated* that.

He scowled. All right, so perhaps Father *would* leave him to rot at school, but Mother wouldn't. She missed him—he knew she did, even if she didn't write very often. And he missed her, too. A lot. She always knew just what to do when the wheezing started. *She* didn't think playing music was dandyish, and *she* said he was clever, not insolent. She made him laugh, even in her infrequent letters. And if she didn't come for him . . .

Tears welled in his eyes. Casting a furtive glance about him, he brushed them away with his gloved fist.

"What a mollycoddle you are, crying for your parents," sneered a voice behind him.

Devil take it. It was his sworn enemy, George Manton, heir to the Viscount Rathmoor. Manton was five years older than Pierce. Nearly *all* the boys were older. And bigger. And stronger.

"I'm not crying," Pierce said sullenly. "It's dusty in here, is all."

Manton snorted. "I suppose you'll have one of your 'attacks' now. Don't think I'll fall for that nonsense. If you start wheezing with *me*, I'll kick the breath out of you. You're a poor excuse for a Harrovian."

At least I can spell the word. You couldn't spell arse *if it were engraved on your forehead.*

Pierce knew better than to say that. The last time he'd spoken his mind, Manton had knocked him flat.

"Well?" Manton said. "Have you nothing to say for yourself, you little pisser?"

You're an overgrown chawbacon who picks on lads half your size because your brain is half size.

Couldn't say that one, either. "Looks like your servant's here." Pierce nodded at the door. "Shouldn't keep him waiting."

Manton glanced to where the footman wearing Rathmoor livery stoically pretended not to notice anything. "I'll keep him waiting as long as I damned well please. I'm the heir—I can do whatever I want."

"I'm the heir, too, you know." Pierce thrust out his chest. "And your father is just a viscount; *mine's* an earl."

When Manton narrowed his gaze, Pierce cursed his quick tongue. He knew better than to poke the bear, but Manton made him so angry.

"A fat lot of good that did you," Manton shot back. "You're a pitiful excuse for an earl's son. That's what comes of mixing foreign stock with good English stock. I daresay your father now wishes he hadn't been taken in by your mother."

"He wasn't!" Pierce cried, jumping to his feet. The glint of satisfaction in Manton's eyes told Pierce he shouldn't have reacted. Manton always pounced when he smelled blood. But Pierce didn't care. "And she's only half foreign. Grandfather Gilchrist was a peer!"

"A penniless one," Manton taunted. "I don't know what your father saw in a poor baron's daughter, though I guess we both know what she saw in *him*—all that money and the chance to be a countess. She latched onto that quick enough."

Pierce shoved him hard. "You shut up about my mother! You don't know anything! Shut up, shut up, shut—"

Manton boxed Pierce's ears hard enough to make *him* shut up. Pierce stood there, stunned, trying to catch his bearings. Before he could launch himself at Manton again, the servant intervened.

"Perhaps we should go, sir," the footman said nervously. "The headmaster is coming."

That was apparently enough to give Manton pause. And Pierce, too. He stood there breathing hard, itching to fight, but if he got into trouble with the headmaster, Father would never forgive him.

"Aren't you lucky?" Manton drawled. "We'll have to continue this upon our return."

"I can't wait!" Pierce spat as the servant ushered Manton from the room.

He would probably regret that after the holiday, but for now he was glad he'd stood up to Manton. How dare the bloody bastard say such nasty things about Mother? They weren't true! Mother wasn't like that.

The headmaster appeared in the doorway accompanied by a house servant. "Master Waverly, your cousin is here for you. Come along."

With no more explanation than that, the headmaster hurried out, leaving the servant to heft Pierce's trunk and head off.

Pierce followed the servant down the stairs in a daze. Cousin? What cousin? He had cousins, to be sure, but he never saw them.

Father himself had no brothers or sisters; indeed, no parents since Grandmother died. He did have an uncle who was a general in the cavalry, but Great-Uncle Isaac Waverly was still fighting abroad.

Mother's parents had been dead for a few years, and she had no siblings, either. Pierce had met her second cousin at Grandfather Gilchrist's funeral, but Father had been so mean to the man one time at Montcliff—the Waverly family estate—that he'd left in a huff. Father didn't seem to like Mother's family much. So the cousin who was here probably wasn't one of Mother's.

Pierce was still puzzling out who it could be when he caught sight of a man at least as old as Father. Oh. Great-Uncle Isaac's son. Pierce vaguely remembered having met Mr. Titus Waverly last year at Grandmother's funeral.

"Where's Mother?" Pierce demanded. "Where's Father?"

Mr. Waverly cast him a kind smile. "I'll explain in the carriage," he said, then herded Pierce out the door. A servant was already lifting Pierce's trunk onto the top and lashing it down with rope.

Pierce's stomach sank. That didn't sound good. Why would Mother and Father send a relation to pick him up at school? Had something awful happened?

As soon as they were headed off in the carriage, Mr. Waverly said, "Would you like something to eat? Mrs. Waverly sent along a nice damson tart for you."

Pierce liked damson tarts, but he had to figure out what was going on. "Why did you come to fetch me home? Is something wrong?"

"No, nothing like that." Mr. Waverly's smile became forced. "But we're not going to Montcliff."

A slow panic built in his chest. "Then where are we going?"

"To Waverly Farm." He spoke in that determinedly cheery voice adults always used when preparing you for something you wouldn't like. "You're to spend your holiday with us. Isn't that grand? You'll have a fine time riding our horses, I promise you."

His panic intensified. "You mean, my whole family is visiting at Waverly Farm, right?"

The sudden softness in his cousin's eyes felt like pity. "I'm afraid not. Your father . . . thinks it best that you stay with us this holiday. Your mother agrees, as do I." His gaze chilled. "From what I gather, you'll have a better time at Waverly Farm than at Montcliff, anyway."

"Only because Father is a cold and heartless arse," Pierce mumbled.

Oh, God, he shouldn't have said that aloud, not to Father's own cousin.

He braced for a lecture, but Mr. Waverly merely laughed. "Indeed. I'm afraid it often goes along with the title."

The frank remark drew Pierce's reluctant admiration. He preferred honesty when he could get it, especially from adults. So he settled back against the seat and took the time to examine the cousin he barely knew.

Titus Waverly looked nothing like Father, who was dark-haired and sharp-featured and aristocratic. Mr. Waverly was blond and round-faced, with a muscular, robust look to him, as if he spent lots of time in the sun. Pierce remembered now that his cousin owned a big stud farm with racing stock.

Most boys would be thrilled to spend their holiday in such a place, but Pierce's asthma made him less than eager. Or perhaps Manton was right, and he really was a mollycoddle.

"So I'm to stay with you and Mrs. Waverly for the whole holiday?" Pierce asked.

The man nodded. "I have a little boy of my own. Roger is five. You can play together."

With difficulty, Pierce contained a snort. Five was practically still a baby. "Are Mother and Father not coming to visit *at all*?" He wanted to be clear on that.

"No, lad. I'm afraid not."

Pierce swallowed hard. He was trying to be strong, but he hadn't really expected not to see them. It made no sense. Unless . . . "Is it because of something I did when I was still at home?"

"Certainly not! Your father merely thinks it will be good for you to be at the farm right now."

That made a horrible sort of sense. "He wants me to be more like the chaps at school," Pierce said glumly, "good at riding and shooting and things like that." He slanted an uncertain glance up at his cousin. "Is that what he wants you to do? Toughen me up?"

His cousin blinked, then laughed. "Your mother did say you were forthright."

Yes, and it had probably gotten him banished from Montcliff.

Perhaps it would get him banished from Waverly Farm, too, and then his cousin would *have* to send him home. "Well, I don't like horses, and I don't like little children, and I don't want to go to Waverly Farm."

"I see." Mr. Waverly softened his tone. "I can't change the arrangement now, so I'm afraid you'll have to make the best of it. Tell me what you *do* like. Fishing? Playing cards?"

Pierce crossed his arms over his chest. "I like being at home."

Settling back against the seat, Mr. Waverly cast him an assessing glance. "I'm sorry, you can't right now."

He fought the uncontrollable quiver in his chin. "Because Father hates me."

"Oh, lad, I'm sure he doesn't," his cousin said with that awful look of pity on his face.

"You can tell me the truth. I already know he does." Tears clogged Pierce's throat, and he choked them down. "What about Mother? D-Doesn't she want to see me at all?"

Something like sadness flickered in Mr. Waverly's eyes before he forced a smile. "I'm sure she does. Very much. But your father can't spare her right now."

"He can never spare her." He stared blindly out the window, then added in a wistful voice, "Sometimes I wish Mother and I could just go live in one of Father's other houses." Brightening, he looked back at his cousin. "Perhaps in London! You could ask her—"

"That will never happen, lad, so put that out of your mind."

Mr. Waverly's tone was quite firm. "Her place is with your father."

More than with her son?

Manton's nasty words leached into his thoughts: *I guess we both know what she saw in* him—*all that money and the chance to be a countess. She latched onto that quick enough.*

It wasn't true. Was it?

His cousin would know—he had to know something about Mother and Father, or he wouldn't have said what he did. And he had a friendly look about him. Like he could be trusted to tell the truth.

"Is . . . that is . . . did Mother marry Father for his money?"

"Who told you that?" his cousin asked sharply.

"A boy at school." When a sigh escaped Mr. Waverly, Pierce swallowed hard. "It's true, isn't it?"

Moving over to sit beside Pierce, Mr. Waverly patted him on the shoulder. "Whether it is or no, it has nothing to do with how your mother feels about *you*. In fact, she gave me this letter for you."

As he fished it out of his pocket and handed it over, the tightness in Pierce's chest eased a little. Eagerly, he broke the seal and opened it to read:

My dearest Pierce,

Your father and I think that staying at Waverly Farm will prove a grand adventure for you, and you do enjoy a grand adventure, don't you? I miss you, but I'm sure you

*will learn all sorts of fine things there. Don't forget to write
and tell me what fun you have!*

*Do be a good boy for your cousins, and keep your chin
up. I know you will make us proud.*

And always remember, I love you very, very much.

With many kisses,

Mother

Relief surged through him. She *did* love him! She did!

He read it again, this time paying closer attention, and his
heart sank a little. It had the same determined cheer as Mr.
Waverly.

And then there was the line: *I know you will make us proud.*

He sighed. She loved him, but she had still let Father send
him away. And why? *You will learn all sorts of fine things there.* Just
like Father, she wanted to see him toughen up.

Tears filled his eyes, but he ruthlessly willed them back. Very
well, then. No more crying, and no more behaving like a milksop
and a mollycoddle. He had to get big and strong, to learn to ride
and fight like the other boys.

Because clearly neither Father nor Mother would let him
come home until he did.

1

December 1826

Thirty-one-year-old Pierce Waverly, Earl of Devonmont, sat at the desk in the study of his London town house, going through the mail as he waited for his current mistress to arrive, when one letter came to the top, addressed in a familiar hand. An equally familiar pain squeezed his chest, reminding him of that other letter years ago.

What a naive fool he'd been. Even though he *had* grown bigger and stronger, even though he'd become the kind of son Father had always claimed to want, he'd never been allowed home again. He'd spent every school holiday—Christmas, Easter, and summer—at Waverly Farm.

And after Titus Waverly and his wife had died unexpectedly in a boating accident when Pierce was thirteen, Titus's father,

General Isaac Waverly, had returned from the war to take over Waverly Farm and Titus's orphaned children.

Even though Pierce hadn't received a single letter from his parents in five years, he'd still been certain that he would finally be sent home—but no. Whatever arrangement Titus had made with Pierce's parents was apparently preserved with Pierce's great-uncle, for the general had fallen right into the role of substitute parent.

Despite all that, it had taken Pierce until he was eighteen, when neither of his parents had appeared at his matriculation from Harrow, to acknowledge the truth. Not only did his father hate him, but his mother had no use for him, either. Apparently she'd endured his presence until he was old enough to pack off to school and relations, and after that she'd decided she was done with him. She was too busy enjoying Father's fortune and influence to bother with her own son.

Pain had exploded into rage for a time, until he'd reached his majority, at twenty-one, and had traveled home to confront them both . . .

No, he couldn't bear to remember *that* fiasco. The humiliation of that particular rejection still sent pain screaming through him. Eventually he would silence that, too; then perhaps he'd find some peace at last.

That is, if Mother would let him. He stared down at the letter, and his fingers tightened into fists. But she wouldn't. She'd poisoned his childhood, and now that Father was dead and Pierce had inherited everything, she thought to make it all go away.

She'd been trying ever since the funeral, two years ago. When she'd mentioned his coming "home," he'd asked her why it had taken his father's death for her to allow it. He'd expected a litany of patently false excuses, but she'd only said that the past was the past. She wanted to start anew with him.

He snorted. Of course she did. It was the only way to get her hands on more of Father's money than what had been left to her.

Well, to hell with her. She may have decided she wanted to play the role of mother again, but he no longer wanted to play her son. Years of yearning for a mother who was never there, for whom he would have fought dragons as a boy, had frozen his heart. Since his father's death, it hadn't warmed one degree.

Except that every time he saw one of her letters—

Choking back a bitter curse, he tossed the unopened letter to his secretary, Mr. Boyd. One thing he'd learned from the last letter she'd written him, when he was a boy, was that words meant nothing. Less than nothing. And the word *love* in particular was just a word. "Put that with the others," he told Boyd.

"Yes, my lord." There was no hint of condemnation, no hint of reproach in the man's voice.

Good man, Boyd. He knew better.

Yet Pierce felt the same twinge of guilt as always.

Damn it, he had done right by his mother, for all that she had never done right by *him*. Her inheritance from Father was entirely under his control. He could have deprived her if he'd wished—another man might have—but instead he'd set her up in the estate's dower house with plenty of servants and enough pin money to make her comfortable. Not enough to live extravagantly—he couldn't bring himself to give her *that*—but enough that she couldn't accuse him of neglect.

He'd even hired a companion for her, who by all accounts had proved perfect for the position. Not that he would know for himself, since he'd never seen the indomitable Mrs. Camilla Stuart in action, never seen her with his mother. He never saw Mother at all. He'd laid down the law from the first. She was free to roam Montcliff, his estate in Hertfordshire, as she pleased when he wasn't in residence, but when he was there to take care of estate affairs, she was to stay at the dower house and well away from *him*. So far she'd held to that agreement.

But the letters came anyway, one a week, as they had ever since Father's death. Two years of letters, piled in a box now overflowing. All unopened. Because why should he read hers, when she'd never answered a single one of his as a boy?

Besides, they were probably filled with wheedling requests for more money now that he held the purse strings. He wouldn't give in to those, damn it.

"My lord, Mrs. Swanton has arrived," his butler announced from the doorway.

The words jerked him from his oppressive thoughts. "You may send her in."

Boyd slid a document onto Pierce's desk, then left, passing Mrs. Swanton as he went out. The door closed behind him, leaving Pierce alone with his current mistress.

Blond and blue-eyed, Eugenia Swanton had the elegant features of a fine lady and the eloquent body of a fine whore. The combination had made her one of the most sought-after mistresses in London, despite her humble beginnings as a rag-mannered chit from Spitalfields.

When he'd snagged her three years ago it had been quite a coup, since she'd had dukes and princes vying for her favors. But the triumph had paled somewhat in recent months. Even she hadn't been able to calm his restlessness.

And now she was scanning him with a practiced eye, clearly taking note of his elaborate evening attire as her smile showed her appreciation. Slowly, sensually, she drew off her gloves in a maneuver that signaled she was eager to do whatever he wished. Last year, that would have had him bending her over his desk and taking her in a most lascivious manner.

Tonight, it merely left him cold.

"You summoned me, my lord?" she said in that smooth, cultured voice that had kept him intrigued with her longer than with his other mistresses. She had several appealing qualities, including her quick wit.

And yet . . .

Bracing himself for the theatrics sure to come, he rose and rounded the desk to press a kiss to her lightly rouged cheek. "Do sit down, Eugenia," he murmured, gesturing to a chair.

She froze, then arched one carefully manicured eyebrow. "No need. I can receive my congé just as easily standing."

He muttered a curse. "How did you—"

"I'm no fool, you know," she drawled. "I didn't get where I am by not noticing when a man has begun to lose interest."

Her expression held a hint of disappointment, but no sign of trouble brewing, which surprised him. He was used to temper tantrums from departing mistresses.

His respect for Eugenia rose a notch. "Very well." Picking up the document on the desk, he handed it to her.

She scanned it with a businesswoman's keen eye, her gaze widening at the last page. "You're very generous, my lord."

"You've served me well," he said with a shrug, now impatient to be done. "Why shouldn't I be generous?"

"Indeed." She slid the document into her reticule. "Thank you, then."

Pleased that she was taking her dismissal so well, he went to open the door for her. "It's been a pleasure doing business with you, Eugenia."

The words halted her. She stared at him with an intent gaze that made him uncomfortable. "That's the trouble with you, my lord. Our association has always been one of business. *Intimate* business, I'll grant you, but business all the same. And business doesn't keep a body warm on a cold winter's night."

"On the contrary," he said with a thin smile. "I believe I succeeded very well at keeping you warm."

"I speak of you, not myself." She glided up to him with a courtesan's practiced walk. "I like you, my lord, so let me give you some advice. You believe that our attraction has cooled because you're tired of me. But I suspect that the next occupant of your bed will be equally unable to warm you . . . unless she provides you with something more than a business arrangement."

He bristled. "Are you suggesting that I marry?"

Eugenia pulled on her gloves. "I'm suggesting that you let someone inside that empty room you call a heart. Whether you make her your wife or your mistress, a man's bed is decidedly warmer if there's a fire burning in something other than his cock."

He repressed an oath. So much for this being easy. "I never guessed you were such a romantic."

"Me? Never." She patted her reticule. "This is as romantic as I get. Which is precisely why I can offer such advice. When we met, I thought we were both the sort who live only for pleasure, with no need for emotional connections." Her voice softened. "But I was wrong about you. You're not that sort at all. You just haven't realized it yet."

Then with a smile and a swish of her skirts, she swept out the door.

He stared bitterly after her. Sadly, he *did* realize it. Leave it to a woman of the world to recognize a fraud.

Matrons might panic when he spoke to their innocent daughters, and his exploits might appear so regularly in the press that his Waverly cousins kept clippings for their own amusement, but his seemingly aimless pursuit of pleasure had never been about pleasure. It had been about using the only weapon he had—the family reputation—to embarrass the family who'd abandoned him.

Leaving his study, he strode to the drawing room, where sat his pianoforte, his private defiance of his father. He sat down and began to play a somber Bach piece, one that often allowed him to vent the darker emotions that never saw the light of day in public, where he was a gadabout and a rebel.

Or he had been until Father's death. Since then his petty rebellions had begun to seem more and more pointless. There'd been no deathbed reconciliation, but also no attempt to keep him from his rightful inheritance. And no explanation of why he'd been abandoned. None of it made sense.

The fact that he *wanted* it to make sense annoyed him. He was done with trying to understand it. The only thing that mattered was that he'd triumphed in the end. He'd gained the estate while he was still young enough to make something of it, and clearly that was the most he could hope for.

Of course, now that he was the earl, people expected him to change his life. To marry. But how could he? Once married, a man had to endure the whims of his wife and children. He'd grown up suffering beneath the whims of his parents; he wasn't about to exchange one prison for another.

He pounded the keys. So for now, everything would stay the same. He would go to the opera this evening to seek out a new mistress, and life would go on much as before. Surely his restlessness would end in time.

Leaving the pianoforte, he was walking out of the drawing room when the sight of Boyd heading toward him with a look of grim purpose arrested him.

"An express has come for you, my lord, from Montcliff."

He tensed. His estate manager, Miles Fowler, never sent expresses, so it must be something urgent.

To his surprise, the letter Boyd handed him hadn't come from Fowler but from Mother's companion. Since Mrs. Stuart hadn't written him in the entire six months she'd been working for him, the fact that she'd sent an express brought alarm crashing through him.

His heart pounded as he tore open the letter to read:

Dear Sir,

Forgive me for my impertinence, but I feel I should inform you that your mother is very ill. If you wish to see her before it is too late, you should come at once.

Sincerely,

Mrs. Camilla Stuart

The terse message chilled him. Based on Mrs. Stuart's recommendation letters and references, not to mention the glowing accolades heaped on her by Fowler, Pierce had formed a certain impression of the widow. She was practical and forthright, the sort of independent female who would rather eat glass than admit she couldn't handle any domestic situation.

She was decidedly *not* a woman given to dramatic pronouncements. So if she said his mother was very ill, then Mother was at death's door. And no matter what had passed between them, he couldn't ignore such a dire summons.

"Boyd, have my bags packed and sent on to the estate. I'm leaving for Montcliff at once."

"Is everything all right, my lord?" Boyd asked.

"I don't believe it is. Apparently my mother has fallen ill. I'll let you know more as soon as I assess the situation."

"What should I tell your uncle?"

Damn. The Waverlys were expecting him in a few days; he

still spent most holidays with them. "Tell Uncle Isaac I'll do my best to be there for Christmas, but I can't promise anything right now."

"Very good, my lord."

As far as Pierce was concerned, the Waverlys—his great-uncle Isaac and his second cousin Virginia—were his true family. Mother was merely the woman who'd brought him into the world.

He ought to abandon her in death, the way she'd abandoned him in life. But he still owed her for nurturing him in those early years, before he was old enough to be fobbed off on relatives. He still owed her for giving birth to him. So he would do his duty by her.

But no more. She'd relinquished the right to his love long ago.

2

In a cozy sitting room of the dower house on the Montcliff estate, Camilla mended a petticoat while keeping a furtive watch on her six-year-old son, Jasper. With his blue eyes wide, he sat in Lady Devonmont's lap, waiting for her to read him a story.

"What shall we read?" Lady Devonmont asked him. "*Cinderella?*"

"That one's stupid," Jasper said airily. "Princes don't marry servant girls."

Camilla bit back a smile as she pushed up her spectacles. Lady Devonmont had a fondness for German fairy tales because of her late mother being German, but Jasper had no such bias. He also didn't like girls in his fairy tales. Not surprising for a boy his age.

"Why wouldn't a prince marry a servant?" her ladyship asked.

"He has to marry a princess. That's the rule. Everybody knows that. I never saw a servant marry a prince."

Her ladyship shot Camilla a rueful glance. "Clearly he spends far too much time in the servant hall."

"Better there than at his uncle's," Camilla said softly.

After Camilla's husband, Kenneth, had died unexpectedly, leaving her and Jasper destitute, she'd had no choice but to go to work, and most employers frowned on having children around who distracted their mothers. So until she had come to work for the countess, she'd always been forced to leave her son with Kenneth's brother, a somber Scot with a dour wife and three children of his own.

But when Lady Devonmont learned of Jasper through the servants, she'd insisted on having him brought to the dower house to live. For that kindness alone, Camilla adored her ladyship.

Of course, neither the earl nor the estate manager knew about Jasper. Nor must they ever. Mr. Fowler, who'd hired her, had been adamant that she be unencumbered with children—he'd said the dictum had come straight from the earl himself. So she and Lady Devonmont had agreed that Jasper's presence had to be kept a secret.

"Read the poem about Christmas again," Jasper said. "I like that one."

The countess's American cousin had sent her a newspaper clipping of a poem that was becoming very popular in America during the season, called "A Visit from St. Nicholas." Camilla had thought it perfectly lovely the first three times she'd heard it, but its magic had begun to fade now that they were up to the fifteenth reading.

Lady Devonmont laughed. "Aren't you sick of it by now, lad?"

"I like to hear about the reindeer. Will there be reindeer at the fair in Stocking Pelham next week? I want to see one." He turned a sly glance up at the countess. "Mama says we can't go, but I really want to."

Camilla tensed. "Jasper, you mustn't—"

"Of course we can go," Lady Devonmont put in. "We have to. I'm in charge of a booth there."

"Forgive me, my lady," Camilla said, "but we can't risk Jasper being seen with us in town by Mr. Fowler."

The countess sighed. "Oh. I didn't think of that. I suppose that *would* be unwise." Her tone turned wistful. "It's a pity, though. I used to take my own boy when he was only a bit older than Jasper."

"And now he's a fine earl," Jasper said.

"Yes, a fine earl," Lady Devonmont echoed.

Camilla nearly stabbed her finger trying not to react to *that*. "Fine earls" did not abandon their mothers.

Still, she probably shouldn't have sent his lordship that misleading letter. But she'd had to do something. How could the wretch not even plan to visit his own mother for Christmas? It was unfathomable.

Besides, he would no doubt ignore the summons. Mr. Fowler might praise the earl for his handling of the estate, but that was clearly his lordship's only virtue. And it wasn't much of a virtue at that—any man who neglected his property was a fool, and apparently the earl was no fool. But according to London gossip, the man was also a selfish scoundrel who spent most of his time in an empty pursuit of pleasure. If he didn't come, it would at least prove what she'd known all along—he might have brains, but he had no heart.

Then Camilla could reveal to her ladyship what she'd done, and the woman would recognize once and for all that her son wasn't worthy of all the pining she wasted on him every day.

Of course, if he did appear . . .

She swallowed. She would cross that bridge when she came to it.

"And anyway, I don't think there will be any reindeer at the fair," Lady Devonmont said, stroking Jasper's wild, red-brown curls. "Just a lot of boring cattle and horses."

"What about St. Nicholas? Will he be there?"

"I doubt that," Camilla said with a laugh.

"Do you even know who St. Nicholas is?" her ladyship asked.

"He's a 'jolly old elf.'" Jasper slipped off her lap, impatient with being petted. "His belly shakes like a 'bowlful of jelly.' And he comes down the chimney. Do you think he'll come down *our* chimney?"

"Perhaps," the countess said. "My cousin tells me that Americans believe St. Nicholas brings gifts to children on Christmas Eve."

Jasper stared at her in wide-eyed wonder. "Will he bring *me* a gift?"

"I'm sure he will," her ladyship said, her twinkling gaze meeting Camilla's over his head. "Why should he only bring presents to American boys, after all?"

Camilla stifled a smile. The woman spoiled Jasper shamelessly and encouraged all of his wild imaginings, but Camilla didn't mind. She wanted him to have a better childhood than her own. There'd been no gifts in St. Joseph's Home for Orphans. And no fairy tales and stories of St. Nicholas to dream on, nothing but Bible readings and moral stories of children who got into trouble whenever they disobeyed. Perhaps that's why she'd developed such a perverse tendency to disobey as an adult.

Suddenly a great noise rose up beneath them, of voices calling and footmen and maids rushing about.

"Good Lord, what has happened?" Lady Devonmont said.

Mrs. Beasley, the housekeeper, rushed into the room, uncharacteristically panicked. "Begging your pardon, my lady, but his lordship has sent a man ahead to say he will arrive here in a matter of minutes!"

Lady Devonmont tensed. "I don't see how that affects *us*. I'm sure he'll be staying at Montcliff Manor as usual."

"No, my lady—here! He's coming *here,* to the dower house. He asked that we prepare the Red Room for him and everything!"

"Oh, my word!" The countess leaped to her feet. "But I'm not dressed. . . . I look a fright!" She cast Camilla a look of such joy that it cut her to the heart. "My son is coming to visit, my dear!" She hurried toward the door leading into her bedchamber. "I must change my gown at the very least. And perhaps freshen my hair." She ran into the other room, crying for her lady's maid.

Mrs. Beasley turned for the door to the hall, but Camilla

called out to stop her. "Please, madam, would you take Jasper upstairs to Maisie?"

The housekeeper blinked. "Oh, yes, of course. I forgot about the lad." She made an impatient movement with her hand. "Come, boy, come. You must spend your day with Maisie, do you hear?"

Lady Devonmont had hired a maid to look after Jasper whenever Camilla couldn't. Maisie, a sweet little Scottish girl of about seventeen, also served as a sort of lady's maid to Camilla.

Though Jasper was fond of Maisie, at the moment he was obviously more excited about the arrival of the master of the estate. "I want to see the great earl!" he protested.

Camilla knelt to catch his hands, aware of Mrs. Beasley's impatience to be off attending to her duties. "Listen, muffin, do you remember what I told you about the earl's being too important to have little boys underfoot?"

With a hard swallow, Jasper nodded. "But I just want to—"

"You can't. If you wish to continue to stay here with me and her ladyship, and not be sent back to live at your uncle's, then you must do as I say. Go with Mrs. Beasley. I'll see you tonight when I come to tuck you in, all right?"

Though he cast his eyes down, he thrust out his chin like a little man and mumbled, "Yes, Mama." Then he let Mrs. Beasley take his hand and lead him from the room.

Only after Camilla heard their footsteps dying away on the stairs did she let out a breath. It wouldn't do to have his lordship discover both her deception regarding his mother *and* Jasper's presence.

My, but he had come quickly. Since the earl never answered his mother's letters, Camilla had assumed it would take him a while to get around to reading the express. And that even then he might not care.

Clearly she'd made a disastrous assumption.

But what was she supposed to have done when she'd found the countess sobbing on the evening of her fiftieth birthday? Lady Devonmont had spent the entire day hiding her feelings about her son's absence, but once alone, she'd apparently been unable to do so.

When Camilla, in trying to comfort her, had said that she was sure he would come for Christmas, the countess had dismissed the very possibility. She admitted that she hadn't seen him at Christmas in some years. Then she'd mumbled something about having only herself to blame for that. But Camilla had scarcely heard that.

Not see his own mother at Christmas? How could he? Camilla might not have had a family growing up, but she knew how one ought to work. The parents loved and supported their children, and in return the children did the same, even as adults. What sort of man trampled over a mother's love without a thought?

Obviously, a man who needed reminding of what he owed the woman who had raised him. So Camilla had fired off her letter without considering the consequences.

Well, she was considering them now. He might very well dismiss her for her deception. Although really, it wasn't *that* much of a deception—his mother *had* been feeling poorly, and Camilla was almost certain it was all for lack of him. So it did seem—

"Who the devil are you?"

Startled, Camilla spun around to find a finely dressed gentleman standing in the sitting room doorway. Heaven save her. His lordship had come.

She curtsied deeply. "I am Mrs. Stuart, my lord. That is, I assume you are—"

"Yes, yes, of course," he said impatiently. "I'm your employer." He scanned her with a narrowed gaze as he entered the room. "And *you,* madam, are not what I was expecting."

Nor was he. His mother had spoken of an asthmatic child with a slim build and slight frame, so Camilla had imagined the earl as a fashionable coxcomb with extravagant manners and dress, a perfumed handkerchief eternally pressed to his nose.

Fashionable he might be, but this was no coxcomb. The Earl of Devonmont was an imposing fellow indeed. She'd once seen a portrait of his father in Montcliff Manor, and they were very like. Both were lean and tall, with eyes the color of mahogany and hair a shade darker, and both had the same brooding stare.

The present earl was less formally dressed, but he wore his clothes better. His exquisitely tailored frock coat of brown cashmere skimmed broad shoulders, while his buff trousers and striped waistcoat showed the rest of his figure to good effect. His snowy cravat emphasized his strong jaw, and he had a high brow somewhat altered by a frown fierce enough to frighten small children. Not to mention paid companions who had vastly overstepped their bounds.

"How's my mother?" he asked, his voice hoarse and his hands

seeming to shake as he removed his gloves and tossed them onto a writing table.

Or was she imagining his distress? Oh, Lord, she hoped so. Because if he was as upset as he seemed, then she *really* had gone too far when she'd sent that letter. Although it did mean he might care for his mother more than she'd realized.

"Well, sir," she began, nervously pushing up her spectacles. "I believe I should probably explain . . ."

"Pierce!" Lady Devonmont cried from the doorway. "It's wonderful to see you, my boy."

He couldn't have looked more shocked if a ghost had risen from the grave to speak to him. Relief seemed to flicker briefly in his eyes, but it was swiftly supplanted by anger as he realized the deception that had been played on him.

Casting Camilla a hard glance that made her shiver, he faced his mother with an unreadable expression. "You're looking well," he said civilly, though he made no move to approach her.

Her smile faltered. "So are you."

"I was told . . ." His voice cracked a little before he got control of it. "I was under the impression that you've been very ill."

The countess paled. "I've been a little under the weather, but nothing of any consequence. I told you that in my last letter."

Her mention of letters made his jaw go taut. "So you are not near to death, as I was led to believe."

Lady Devonmont lifted her chin. "I'm sure you can tell that I am not. I don't know who would lie to you about such a thing."

Camilla froze, waiting for the accusation that was sure to come.

His gaze didn't so much as flick to her. "It's of no matter. A misunderstanding, I'm sure." He jerked up his gloves, his motions oddly mechanical. "So I'll be returning to London in the morning. It's too late to set off tonight."

"Of course." With a forced smile, his mother pretended not to care.

Only Camilla noticed how her shoulders shook.

Or perhaps not only Camilla, for his lordship turned for the door quickly, as if he couldn't bear to look at his mother one moment more. "Have Mrs. Beasley send dinner to my room," he ordered. "The footmen have already put my bags in the Red Room, so I might as well remain here for the night instead of at the manor."

"Certainly, Pierce," the countess said in a voice tinged with bitterness. "Whatever you wish."

Something in her tone must have pricked his conscience, for he paused at the door. Then he stiffened and walked out without a backward glance.

Camilla could only gape after him, then turn to gape at his mother. "I can't believe it! That is the most despicable behavior I've ever witnessed!"

"Do not blame him, my dear. He has his reasons." She watched after him, her gaze thoughtful. "At least he came when he thought I was ill. That's something, isn't it?" Ignoring Camilla's lack of a response, she added, "And I got to see him for a bit, too. He's very handsome, don't you think? He grew up to be so strong and tall. He was such a sickly child that I never expected—"

"How can you ignore his abominable treatment of you?" Camilla broke in.

"On the contrary, he treats me better than I can expect, given . . ." She managed another determined smile. "You don't understand, my dear. Better to leave it alone."

"How can I? He tucks you away here in the country—"

"Because I prefer the country to town, and always have."

"That's not the point! He acts as if you don't even exist!"

"Ah, but there you're wrong. He acts very much as if I exist," she said acidly. "Or he wouldn't demand that I stay out of his way whenever he's here."

"And that's another thing. When he came this summer, I didn't know you well enough to say anything about his avoidance of you, but now—"

"Good Lord," her ladyship said, whirling on Camilla. "*You're* the one who told him I was near to death." When Camilla looked guilty, the countess scowled at her. "Are you mad? Do you realize what you've done?"

The reproach, coming from the generally mild-mannered lady, took Camilla by surprise. "I-I suppose I shouldn't have presumed, but—"

"You certainly shouldn't have. You could lose your position over it." At Camilla's stricken expression, Lady Devonmont added hastily, "Not that *I* would dismiss you, my dear. Surely you realize I can't do without you." Her ladyship began to pace. "But my son could very well send you packing."

"I know," Camilla said, letting out a relieved breath. She could deal with his lordship's temper as long as Lady Devonmont didn't hate her.

The countess rounded on Camilla with her shoulders set. "Well, I shan't let him. He has every right to be angry at me, but you're an innocent bystander, and I won't let him punish you for your ill-considered actions."

"They were *not* ill-considered! And I'll tell him so myself, if it comes down to it."

Lady Devonmont flashed her an impatient glance. "You will do nothing of the kind. You have your boy to think of." She mused a moment, a sudden look of calculation on her face. "But since Pierce didn't mention that you were the one to write him, perhaps he's not so very angry about it, after all. So we'll leave it alone, make no more mention of it." She paced before the fire. "Yes, that's how to handle it. And if he tries to dismiss you, I'll hire you myself, using my pin money. He gives me enough for that."

Guilt attacked Camilla with a vengeance. "My lady, I don't want—"

"Nonsense, that's the only thing to do." Lady Devonmont pressed her hand to her forehead. "I have a bit of a headache, so I think I shall lie down for a while before dinner."

Camilla sighed. That was one thing about Lady Devonmont; she always made it perfectly clear when she wanted to end a discussion. "Of course. I'd be happy to read to you, if you like."

"No need for that." She glanced at Camilla. "Though if you don't mind telling Mrs. Beasley about his lordship wanting a tray in his room . . ."

"Certainly." She was being sent off. Miraculously, her ladyship had overlooked her impertinence.

Unfortunately, his lordship probably wouldn't. And despite everything she'd said to Lady Devonmont, the woman was right. Camilla had risked much with her deception. She deserved to lose her position over it.

But she hadn't dreamed he would have such a visceral reaction after the way he'd been behaving, never answering his mother's letters, never coming to see her. Camilla had expected him to flit in, say a few words to his mother, pretend to be relieved that she was well, and flit out. And if seeing his mother coaxed him into staying for a bit, all the better.

Not in a million years had Camilla expected him to be alarmed at the possibility of his mother dying. And then angry that he'd been deceived.

Indeed, the more Camilla thought about that as she headed for the kitchen, the angrier *she* became. What could Lady Devonmont possibly have done to deserve such behavior? How could any man resent a woman of such grace and kindness? It was unfathomable.

Her ladyship thought she should leave it alone, but she just couldn't. If not for the countess, Camilla might be working for some condescending matron who insisted that Jasper be left at his uncle's. So as long as Lady Devonmont was on her side, she would fight for the woman, even against the earl. Her ladyship was the closest thing to a family that Camilla had ever had.

She entered the kitchen, where Mrs. Beasley was whipping the servants into a frenzy with preparations for dinner.

"Is Mr. Fowler going to be here for dinner, too?" Cook asked the housekeeper as she basted a pork loin. "He don't like pork, y'know."

"I don't think he's coming," Mrs. Beasley said. "I hope not, anyway. With his lordship here, he's sure to put on airs."

"I doubt that," Camilla interjected. "Mr. Fowler never puts on airs."

Mrs. Beasley eyed her askance. "That's only because he's sweet on you."

"Oh, please, not that again," Camilla murmured. "Mr. Fowler is nearly old enough to be my father."

"That don't mean nothing," said Cook, who saw romance blooming everywhere she looked. "And he's always asking how you're getting on with her ladyship, always wanting to know what you two are up to. He's got his eye on you—I'm sure of it."

Camilla did think he had his eye on *someone,* but not her. Of course, if her suspicions were correct and he was sweet on the countess, she could never tell the servants such a thing. They would be appalled.

It was fruitless anyway—Lady Devonmont always said she didn't mean to marry again, and in any case, the social gulf between Mr. Fowler and her was nigh unto impassable. Especially when her ladyship might not even share his feelings.

"Like most widowers," Camilla said, "Mr. Fowler is merely desperate for another woman to look after him."

"True, true." Cook cast her a considering glance as she tucked back a gray curl. "Though it would be a good situation for you, given Master Jasper and all."

Camilla sighed. *Any* marriage would solve her problem of what to do with her son as he got older. But she'd married for practical reasons once, and except for Jasper, that had proved oddly unsatisfying. If she ever remarried it would be for love, and she felt nothing like that for Mr. Fowler.

"Did his lordship *say* anything about Mr. Fowler's coming to dinner?" Mrs. Beasley asked. "It'll be a trial for Cook to do a large meal on such short notice. She's got her hands full preparing the plum pudding for Christmas so it can sit a couple of weeks."

"No trial at all," Cook retorted. "I've already got the pudding steaming, which it has to do for a few hours. So I can cook whatever dinner you want."

"Actually," Camilla said, "his lordship is only staying the night, and he doesn't intend to come down to dinner. He wants a tray sent up."

Cook gaped at her. "Well, don't that just beat all? Waltz in here with no warning and then not even have the decency to join his mother for dinner." She sniffed. "I suppose he thinks to get a better meal up there at the manor, with that foreigner cooking the food and that snooty Mrs. Perkins running the place."

"That foreigner" was his lordship's French cook, and Mrs. Perkins was the manor housekeeper. The two cooks were archrivals, as were the two housekeepers. Mr. Fowler had hired both sets of servants upon the earl's inheriting the estate and inexplicably pensioning off the old ones. Apparently Lord Devonmont had wanted to install his own, who now took on airs because they served the earl. They were fiercely loyal to him.

Meanwhile, the dower house servants were equally loyal to

her ladyship. So with the countess and her son estranged, neither group mixed with the other to any great degree.

It left poor Mr. Fowler somewhat in the middle.

"I'll put together a tray that will have his lordship tossing the 'monsieur' out on his ear," Cook said almost militantly. "The earl will be begging to stay here a week, just see if he won't. And if we could keep him here until Christmas, I've got the biggest goose picked out—"

"I wish we could," Camilla said with a sigh. "But I fear that's impossible."

Mrs. Beasley set her hands on her hips. "Now I've got to spare Sally to go bring up the tray, just when I need her."

An idea leaped into Camilla's head. "Actually, he wants *me* to bring up the tray." Why not? It would give her an excuse to have it out with him.

"You?" Mrs. Beasley exclaimed, then exchanged a veiled glance with Cook.

"Is something wrong with that?" Camilla asked, perplexed.

Cook made a clucking noise. "The master does have a reputation, m'dear."

"Wouldn't be the first time a man took a fancy to someone in his employ, if you know what I mean." Mrs. Beasley turned to fetch a tray. "And if he's asking you in particular to carry up his meal . . ."

"It's nothing like that," Camilla said hastily, wishing she'd considered how the servants would regard her claim. Her eyes went wide as something else occurred to her. "Surely you're not saying that the female servants at the manor . . . That is, there've been no complaints of—"

"No, indeed," Cook said firmly.

"Not yet, anyway," Mrs. Beasley said in her usual voice of doom. "But plenty of gentlemen do toy with their servants, and your being so young and handsome—"

Camilla burst into laughter. "I don't think you need worry about that. I'm not all that young."

And "handsome" was what people called a woman between plain and pretty. "Handsome" was merely acceptable. Not that she minded being thought of that way. If every woman was a beauty, the word would mean nothing. But "handsome" would never be good enough for the sophisticated earl. Even if he wasn't on the verge of dismissing her from her post, he would never set his lecherous sights on a short, slightly plump widow with spectacles, reddish hair, and freckles. Not when he could have any blond goddess in London.

She had nothing to fear on *that* score.

3

Pierce paced the bedchamber, badly shaken by the sight of his mother. Great God, but she'd aged. When had she gone gray? She hadn't been that way at the funeral two years ago.

Actually, back then she'd worn a hat and veil that covered her hair and her face, and he'd barely spared her a glance anyway. If he'd stayed to see her without them, would he have noticed the gray? Or the crow's-feet around her eyes and the thin lines around her lips? Because he'd noticed them today, and they'd unsettled him. She was getting older. He should have expected it, but he hadn't.

And he certainly hadn't expected her face to light up when she saw him. It brought the past sharply into his mind. All those years of nothing, no word, no hint that she cared . . . Why, he couldn't even remember the last time she'd looked on him so kindly.

How dared she do it *now*? Where had she been all those damned years at Harrow, when Manton was knocking him around? When the boys had taunted him for his asthma, before he'd grown out of it and begun standing up for himself?

How many Christmases had he lain in bed praying that this would be the one when she came sweeping in to kiss him on the forehead and make it all better? As mothers ought to do. As the other boys' mothers routinely did.

He loosened his cravat, trying to catch his breath. It wasn't a return of his asthma that plagued him but the weight of the past on his chest. The literal *smell* of the past.

The dower house had actually been his first home. Father began building the grand mansion that was now Montcliff Manor when Pierce was fourteen, so Pierce hadn't even been inside it until after his father's death. *This* was his childhood home—that's why he had put Mother here, so he would never have to stay in it himself and suffer reminders of all that he'd lost at age eight.

One of those reminders was the smell of Mother's favorite plum pudding being steamed. She'd always specified that certain spices be used, and that's why the house now reeked of cloves and lemon peel. It would choke him for certain. He should never have come.

He *wouldn't* have come if not for the impudent Mrs. Stuart. The audacity of the woman to lie to him! And to Mother, too, apparently, since Mother had looked perplexed by his assumption that she was dying. Meanwhile, her companion, the conniving baggage, had looked guilty.

But even if Mother hadn't known of Mrs. Stuart's letter to him, she somehow had to be complicit. Probably she'd spun enough tales about her son's poor treatment of her to make Mrs. Stuart take it upon herself to right the wrong. Clearly Mother had done an excellent job of hiding her true nature around Mrs. Stuart, who seemed willing to risk losing her livelihood just to make her scheming charge happy. And she *ought* to lose her livelihood—he should have her dismissed at once for her impertinence.

Yet in his mind he kept seeing the shock on her face when he'd entered. Apparently, he hadn't done a very good job of hiding his panic over the idea of Mother dying. What had the damned woman thought—that he was some monster with no soul?

Probably. After he'd announced he was leaving, she'd certainly glared at him as if he were. Insolent chit! No telling what his mother had said to secure the young widow's sympathies.

Whatever it was, it wouldn't be the truth—that once he'd turned old enough to be passed off to some relative, Mother had deliberately cut him out of her life. And now that he had inherited everything, she was suddenly eager to pay attention to the son she'd ignored for *years*.

To hell with that! He was *not* going to yield, no matter how gray Mother looked, and no matter what some officious companion with a penchant for meddling—

A knock at the door interrupted his pacing. "What?" he barked.

"I have your tray, my lord," a muted voice said from beyond the door.

He'd forgotten entirely about that. "Set it down and go away!"

A moment of silence ensued. Then the same voice said, "I can't."

"Oh, for the love of God . . ." He strode to the door and swung it open, then halted.

There before him stood the very woman who'd brought him here under false pretenses. "It's *you*," he spat.

Though she blinked at the venom in his voice, she stood her ground. "May I please come in, my lord?"

He considered slamming the door in her face, but a deeply ingrained sense of gentlemanly behavior prevented him. Besides, he wanted to hear what she had to say for herself.

With a curt nod, he stood aside to let her pass, taking the opportunity to get a good look at her. He still couldn't believe she was so young. She couldn't be more than twenty-five, far too young to be a widow *or* a paid companion.

And far too attractive, though he hated that he noticed. Despite what everyone thought of him, he did not run after every creature in petticoats. He'd gained his reputation as a rogue in the years when he was determinedly embarrassing his family, and those days were waning.

But the rogue in him wasn't dead, and it noticed that she had the sort of voluptuous figure he found attractive. She was a bit short for his taste but her evocative features and the red curls she wore scraped into a bun made up for that. Even with her spectacles on, she had the look of a fresh-faced country girl—eyes of a fathomless blue, a broad, sensual mouth, and a smattering of freckles across ivory skin. The odd mix of bluestocking and dairy-maid appealed to him.

She dressed well, too. Her gown of green Terry velvet was out of fashion and too sumptuous for her station, so since servants' clothes generally were castoffs from their employers' wardrobes, it must once have been Mother's. Given that it fit her like a glove, she was obviously good with a needle.

That would serve her well in her *next* post, he thought sourly, though he still hadn't decided if he would dismiss her.

As she set the tray down on a small table by the fire, he snapped, "I suppose you've come to beg my pardon."

She faced him with a steady gaze. "Actually, no."

"What?" he said, incredulous. "You brought me racing here from London by lying about my mother's illness—"

"I did not lie," she protested, though her cheeks grew ruddy. "Granted, she isn't ill in the conventional sense—"

"Do enlighten me about the *un*conventional way to be ill. I must have missed that lesson in school."

At his sarcasm, she tipped up her chin. "Anyone can see that she has been ill with missing you, her only family."

He let out a harsh laugh. "Has she indeed? I suppose she's been shedding crocodile tears and weaving a sad story about how I fail to do my duty by her."

Mrs. Stuart's pretty blue eyes snapped beneath her spectacles. "On the contrary, whenever we discuss you, she excuses your refusal to visit or answer her letters, not to mention your wanton disregard for—"

"Her well-being? Does she complain of how I treat her?"

The fractious female cast him a mutinous glare. "No."

That surprised him, though he wasn't about to let on. "Then

there you have it." He turned toward the writing desk, where sat a decanter of brandy and a glass.

"But I'm not blind," the woman went on, to his astonishment. "I see how your lack of attention wounds her, and I hear her crying when she thinks no one is near. As your mother, she deserves at least a modicum of attention from you, yet you leave her to pine."

"My mother doesn't know the meaning of the word *pine*." He fought to ignore the image of his mother crying all alone. "And if *she* has sent you—"

"She doesn't know I'm here. She didn't know I wrote that letter. Actually, she, too, says I should stay out of it."

Despite his determination to hold firm against his mother's tactics, that shook him. "You should listen to her."

"I can't." The plaintive words tugged at something he'd buried for countless years. "I wouldn't be doing my duty to her if I let her suffer pain, whether at the hands of a stranger or those of her own son." She strode up behind him, her voice heavy with concern. "You can't expect me to keep quiet when I should do right by her."

He whirled to fix the woman with a cold glance, but he couldn't escape her logic. Her loyalty was to his mother, and *should* be, even though he had hired her. After all, what good was hiring a companion his mother couldn't trust?

Still, that didn't mean he had to let her manipulate him. "Doing right by her doesn't include lying to her family. You said she was dying."

"No, I said you should come before it was too late." She

pushed her spectacles up. "I'm sorry if you interpreted the words as meaning she might die any moment—"

"Right," he said dryly. "How could I have made such a leap?"

"But I meant them." Concern furrowed her lightly freckled brow. "She needs you, and if you put off mending your relationship with her, you will eventually regret it."

Bloody hell, the woman was stubborn. "That isn't for you to decide, madam." Crossing his arms over his chest, he stared her down. "Whatever you expected to accomplish with this stunt hasn't come to pass, so you should quit trying while you still have a post. I can easily dismiss you for your presumption."

"I'm aware of that."

Yet she held her chin firm and her shoulders squared. He'd been right to term her "indomitable" without even having met her. She was one determined woman.

"But some things are worth risking all for," she added.

"My *mother*? A woman who didn't even care that her son was alive until two years ago, when my father died and she could no longer depend on *his* largesse?"

That seemed to shake her. "You think that this is about *money*?"

"Of course! She married Father for money, and now that it's all under *my* control, she suddenly 'needs' me desperately."

Her gaze locked with his. "If her feelings are as false as you think, why does she have a chest full of your school drawings and papers? Why does she read to me your childhood letters, pointing out your witty turns of phrase and clever observations?" She stepped nearer. "Why does she keep a miniature of you by her bed?"

Her descriptions beat at the stone wall he'd built against his mother. But he couldn't believe them. He *wouldn't* believe them. He wouldn't let Mother hurt him again.

Clearly Mother had fashioned Mrs. Stuart as a weapon to get what she wanted. The young widow might not even know she was being used, but that didn't change a damned thing.

He moved close enough to intimidate. "She's trying to enlist you as an ally in her scheme. And she knows it won't work unless she can convince you that she is slighted and put upon."

Mrs. Stuart blinked. Obviously, it was the first time she'd considered the possibility that she was being taken in. "You're wrong," she whispered, though she didn't seem quite so certain. "She's not like that."

"You've known her for six months," he ground out. "I've known her my entire life. Or at least the part of my life that she—"

He broke off before he could reveal the mortifying truth— that his parents thought so little of him they'd cut him out of their lives. It was none of her affair, no matter what she thought. He didn't have to explain himself to some paid companion, damn it!

Besides, as meddlesome as Mrs. Stuart had proven to be, she clearly had Mother's best interests at heart. He didn't want to dismiss the woman, and he saw no reason to poison her against his mother. He just wanted her to stop making trouble.

He forced some calmness into his tone. "By now you've probably gathered that matters between me and my mother aren't as clear as you think. So I will forget how far you've overstepped your bounds, if you'll agree to keep your opinions to yourself and stay out of my relationship with her in future."

Though she swallowed hard, she continued to meet his gaze. "I don't know if I can do that, my lord."

"Oh, for God's sake . . ." He dragged his hand over his face. He was tired and hungry and annoyed. The bloody woman was a plague! "What do you want from me, damn it, short of attaching my mother to my side with a tether?"

The image made her start, then give a little smile. It took him by surprise. Until that moment, she'd lived up to his impression of a self-righteous bluestocking, but a sense of humor lurked inside the indomitable Mrs. Stuart. And somehow he'd tickled it.

"You needn't go to such an extreme," she said, her eyes twinkling beneath the spectacles. Then she turned earnest again. "But if you could stay here with your mother until Christmas—"

"No." He remembered only too well his last Christmas at home. The one that he hadn't realized was to *be* his last Christmas at home. "That's impossible."

He turned away. Perhaps he *should* dismiss the woman.

But she followed him as he headed for the brandy. "You wouldn't have to spend much time with her, just have the occasional meal with her. The slightest attention from you would make her happy."

"You think so, do you?" Pouring himself a healthy portion of brandy, he downed it in one swallow. If ever a woman could drive a man to drink, it was Mrs. Stuart.

"I am sure of it. You could stay at Montcliff Manor as you always do, but even if you merely came to dinner with us every night—"

"You're not going to let this go, are you?" He set down the

glass and faced her with a scowl. "You'll keep plaguing me until I do as you ask or you force me to send you packing."

That seemed to give her pause, but only for a moment. "I would of course prefer that you *not* send me packing. But I must speak what I know to be true, sir." Her voice softened. "And now that I've met you, I believe that you have more of a heart than you let on."

He snorted. "Do you, indeed?"

Then perhaps it was time he dispelled that ridiculous notion. And in doing so, perhaps he could dissuade her from meddling and tormenting him to death, without his having to dismiss her and go to the trouble of hiring another, who might not be as reliable.

He stalked forward, deliberately crowding her space, forcing her to either back up or stand her ground. Not surprisingly, she did the latter, which put him toe to toe with her, looming over her.

"I tell you what, Mrs. Stuart," he drawled. "I'm already staying here at the dower house until tomorrow. So I'll attend dinner tonight with you and my mother and try to be civil. But in exchange, I'll expect some compensation after she retires."

Her gaze turned wary. "What sort of compensation?"

"Entertainment. The kind I would normally receive in London." He let his gaze trail leisurely down her body in a way that should illustrate exactly what he was pretending to demand of her. "And I will expect *you* to provide it."

4

Camilla's cheeks heated as she gaped at the earl. What a despicable, wicked—

Then her brain caught up with her moral outrage. The earl wore a calculating expression, as if he knew exactly what her reaction would be.

That devil was making this up as he went along. He wanted her so insulted by his proposition that she would stop bothering him about his mother. That made far more sense than believing he actually meant it. She wasn't the sort of woman whom notorious rakehells tried to seduce.

She made herself look bewildered. "I'm afraid I don't understand, my lord. How could I possibly entertain a worldly man like you?"

His sudden black frown strengthened her supposition that his bargain was a humbug. "You know perfectly well how. After dinner is over, you and I will have our own party. Here. In my bedchamber, where you can slip in and out without being noticed. If I must spend dinner with her, then you must spend the night with *me*."

"Entertaining you," she said primly, buying time to figure out what answer would best gain her what she wanted. "Yes, I understand that part. I'm just not sure what kind of entertainment you want."

He gritted his teeth. "Oh, for the love of God, you know precisely what kind of entertainment a 'worldly man' like me wants."

Now that she had caught on to his game, it was all she could do not to laugh at him. He was so transparent. What was wrong with all those women in London, that they didn't see right through him?

"On the contrary," she said blithely. "I don't know you well enough to know what you enjoy. Perhaps you would prefer me to sing for you or dance or read you a good play. I understand there is quite an extensive library at Montcliff Manor. Your mother says you bought most of the books yourself. I'm sure there is some volume of—"

"I'm not talking about your reading to me!" he practically shouted.

When she merely gazed at him with a feigned expression of innocence, he changed his demeanor. His eyes turned sultry, and a sensual smile crossed his lips. "I mean the kind of entertainment most widows prefer."

My, my, no wonder London ladies were rumored to jump into his bed. When he looked that way at a woman and spoke in that decidedly seductive voice, the average female probably melted into a puddle at his feet.

It was a good thing she was *not* an average female. In her other posts, she'd seen plenty of rakehells seducing their way through halls and balls. So even though they'd never tried their skills on her, she had a good idea how to handle such scoundrels.

This was a trickier situation, however. If she was not an average female, he was definitely not an average scoundrel.

She pretended to muse a moment. "Entertainment that widows prefer . . . Works of charity? Taking care of their families? No, those are not actually entertaining, though they do pass the time." She cocked her head. "I confess, my lord, that you have me at a complete loss."

Uh-oh, that was probably doing it up too brown, for understanding suddenly shone in his face. "Ah, I see you are deliberately provoking me. Well, then, let me spell it out for you. You'll spend the night in my bed. Is that clear enough?"

He said it in such a peeved manner that she couldn't help but laugh. "Clear indeed, though preposterous."

His gaze narrowed on her. "How so?"

Time to let him know she had caught on to his game. "I'm aware of your reputation, sir. I'm not the sort of woman you take to bed."

Something that looked remarkably like admiration glinted in his eyes. "I thought you said you didn't know me all that well," he drawled.

"I know what kind of women you are most often seen with. By all accounts, they are tall, blowsy blondes with porcelain skin and clever hands."

He looked startled. "You *do* know my reputation."

She shrugged. "I read the papers. And your mother insists upon hearing all the stories of you, even the salacious ones."

Mention of his mother made his gaze harden. "Then you should know that men like me aren't that discriminating."

"Oh, but I'm sure you're discriminating enough not to wish to bed a short, mousy, freckled servant when there are any number of beautiful, blond actresses and opera singers awaiting you in London," she said coolly.

Crossing his arms over his chest, he dragged his gaze down her again, then circled her in a slow, careful assessment that made her nervous. A pity he wasn't a perfumed dandy; she could have handled one of those easily enough. But this sharp-witted, secretive rakehell was unpredictable.

Camilla had never liked the unpredictable.

"And what if I say that I really *am* that indiscriminate? Would you then share my bed in exchange for my dining with my mother tonight?"

She swallowed. Why did he persist in bamming her when he knew she'd caught on to him?

Well, two could play his game. "Why not? You *are* rumored to be quite good at that sort of thing, and I *have* been married." She couldn't keep the edge from her voice. "Besides, the likelihood of my ever again having the chance to be seduced by such a notorious fellow as yourself is slim."

Her frank statement made him halt, then shake his head. "Great God, Mrs. Stuart, remind me never to play cards with you. I daresay you're a terror at the gaming tables."

She bit back a smile. "I've won a hand or two at piquet in my life."

"More than a hand or two, I'd wager." He let out a long breath. "All right, then, let me propose a bargain that we could both actually adhere to. I'll do as you wish—I'll dine with you and Mother. Afterward, you will come here to join me in one of your more innocuous entertainments."

She let out a breath. She'd won! "I am happy to attempt to entertain you, my lord, if you will just give your mother a little time with you. That's all I ask."

"I'm not finished." He gazed steadily at her. "In exchange for my doing so, you must agree never again to try forcing my hand in the matter of my mother."

When she drew a breath as if to speak, he added more firmly, "One night of watching me and Mother together should demonstrate to you why you have no business involving yourself in our relationship. But even if it doesn't, tomorrow must mark the end of your meddling on that point. Or I *will* dismiss you, without a qualm. Am I understood?"

She hesitated, but really, what choice did she have? "Yes, my lord." The dratted devil was tying her hands. She'd have only one night to attempt some repair to his relationship with his mother. But it was better than she'd had before.

A heavy sigh escaped him. "I must be out of my mind to be letting you off so easily, after what you did."

"Easily?" she said tartly. "Did you forget that I will have to entertain you this evening?"

"Ah, yes, such a trial," he said with heavy sarcasm. "And I'll expect rousing entertainment, too. At the very least, you must show me your reputed ability at piquet, so I can trounce you." He stared her down. "Now that you've brought me here to endure this house, it's only fair that you join me in my suffering."

The bitter remark gave her pause. Hadn't Lady Devonmont said that this was the original manor house on the estate? The one where he'd grown up?

As if realizing he'd revealed more than he'd meant to, he flashed her a bland smile. "It won't be that difficult. I can be charming when I want to."

"No doubt," she said dryly.

"Then we're agreed. I'll see you here this evening after Mother has retired."

And after Camilla had put Jasper to bed, though she couldn't say that.

"But you *will* come down to dinner first, sir?"

His face turned rigid. "That's the bargain, isn't it?"

She let out a breath. "I was just making sure."

"Whatever else you may think of me," he said sharply, "I do honor my promises."

"Of course, my lord."

She turned for the door, relief overwhelming her. She'd braved the lion's den and survived. She'd even won a small concession. It wasn't much, but it might be enough to soothe the countess's hurt feelings. Spending a night "entertaining" his lordship would be no sacrifice at all, compared to that.

"One more thing, Mrs. Stuart," he said as she reached the door.

She paused to look back at him.

"You were right when you said I'm discriminating in my choice of bed partners. But you aren't remotely mousy." His gaze scoured her with a heat that didn't seem the least bit feigned.

Could he really mean it?

Oh, she hoped not. Because the last thing she needed in her life right now was a lover—not with Jasper to take care of.

Only when he had her thoroughly agitated did he lower his voice to a husky drawl. "Fortunately for you, I'm not in the habit of abusing the trust of those in my employ, whether chaste maidens or experienced widows. So as long as you want me to play the respectable gentleman, I will do so."

He fixed her with a smoldering look. "But let this be a warning to you. Give me an inch, and I will take two miles. If you offer more, I will be only too happy to take you into my bed."

"Then I shall have to take care not to offer more, shan't I?" And with that, she slipped from the room.

But as she made her way down the hall, her knees shaking and her hands clammy, she had to acknowledge that this bargain might not be quite so easy to keep. Because insane as it might be, she found the idea of being in the earl's bed rather intriguing.

Oh, what was wrong with her? He didn't mean a thing he said—clearly he'd issued his dire "warning" just to vex her. Why, the man was seen every week with some fine beauty at the opera or the theater or balls where he scandalized everyone with his flirtations.

Yes, exactly! He was an awful man with a terrible reputation. Being attracted to such a fellow was utterly unlike her. Even if he *was* so very handsome. And more clever than she'd expected. And full of secrets that intrigued her.

She scowled. They did *not* intrigue her. They all centered around his clear lack of concern for his mother's feelings.

Well, perhaps not entirely clear.

She married Father for money, and now that it's all under my *control, she suddenly "needs" me desperately.*

Camilla shook off a chill. Pausing only to tell a passing maid that his lordship's plans had changed again, she headed for the countess's bedchamber. He was utterly wrong about his mother. She was almost sure of it, and she knew her ladyship better than anyone. Didn't she?

A woman who didn't even care that her son was alive until two years ago, when my father died and she could no longer depend on his largesse?

Why would he say that? Though come to think of it, the countess only spoke of her son as a boy and as a grown man. She said nothing about his school years.

Then again, he would have been away during his school years. But he would have come home for holidays. He would have gotten into scrapes and adventures; even a sickly boy would have done *that*.

And why did the countess never speak of the previous earl? Camilla assumed that their marriage had been a formal one, since the woman rarely mentioned him, but now she had to wonder . . . Could Lady Devonmont really have married the man just for his money?

If only some of the old servants were still employed who could say what the countess's husband had been like and if he'd played a part in the estrangement between mother and son.

Since Camilla had secrets of her own, she had a firm rule against prying into her employers' private affairs. But she was sorely tempted to break her rule in this case. Dealing with the prickly earl would be much easier if she knew more about him and his mother.

She found the countess already up from her rest. "I have some good news, my lady. His lordship has decided to join us for dinner this evening."

Lady Devonmont faced her warily. "I don't understand."

Camilla forced a cheery smile to her lips. "He's had a change of heart. You see? He *does* care."

As joy lit the countess's face, she seized Camilla's hand. "You did this. I know you did. But how? What did you say to convince him?"

"Nothing of importance. I merely appealed to his sense of decency." Not for anything would she tell the countess of the bargain she'd made. The woman would leap to the wrong conclusion, and that could only worsen matters.

Unless the countess had *wanted* Camilla to do something to keep him here?

She's trying to enlist you as an ally in her scheme. And she knows it won't work unless she can convince you that she is slighted and put upon.

Ridiculous.

He was right about one thing, though—there was more to the situation than met the eye. And given his mother's words earlier, she knew his lordship wasn't the only one who didn't wish to discuss the past.

Very well. She'd have to be more creative in uncovering this tangle. Lady Devonmont had made Camilla and Jasper part of her family, and families helped each other. So the least Camilla could do was try to restore the rest of the countess's family to her. No matter what it took.

5

Dinner was pure misery.

Not that Pierce was surprised. How could it be anything else? He was sitting in the very chair his father had always used, staring at the lofty portrait of a grandfather he'd never known, and listening to the achingly familiar voice of his mother prattling on about nothing while Mrs. Stuart shot him furtive glances.

The damned woman didn't understand—he couldn't act as if the past twenty-three years hadn't happened. Mrs. Stuart expected him to make witty conversation with his *mother*. Might as well ask him to give a sermon in hell.

Especially with bitter memories resurrecting themselves every moment he sat here. As a boy, he'd taken his meals in the nursery, but he'd been allowed to join his parents for dinner at Christmas and special occasions. Those nights invariably deteriorated as Father berated him for being weak and sickly, until he retorted with some bit of insolence that got him banished from the table. The memory made his stomach churn.

He forced a spoonful of soup between his lips and swallowed, barely tasting it. Mother had always tried to mediate but had rarely been successful. It was as if Father *wanted* to drive Pierce off, so he could have Mother all to himself.

Well, if that had been Father's aim, he'd gotten exactly what he wanted, hadn't he? And Mother hadn't protested it.

Glancing over at her, he looked for signs of the heartless creature he knew her to be. But aside from her ornate gown and fine jewelry, which reminded him that what she really wanted was more of Father's fortune, he could see nothing other than the mother he'd adored as a boy.

Except a far older one. He couldn't get over how much she'd aged. Seeing it made something in his chest twist.

When that became too painful to endure, he turned his gaze to Mrs. Stuart. Instantly, the aching turned to annoyance. The woman was a bloody meddler, presumptuous and self-righteous, and so blindly loyal to his mother that it made him want to . . . to . . .

To respect her. He sighed. That was mad. Blind loyalty shouldn't be an admirable quality. But somehow, in Mrs. Stuart it was. Perhaps because she was loyal for the most naive reasons. She considered it the right thing, the caring thing, to champion his mother.

It was the caring part that stymied him. How could she care

about a woman who'd abandoned her own son? Of course, the young widow didn't seem to know that, and he wasn't ready to tell her. Not until he had a better sense of what the situation was.

"Do you not agree, my lord?" Mrs. Stuart's pleasant voice intruded.

Damn, his long stares had made her think he had an opinion on whatever nonsense she and Mother were discussing. "I suppose," he said noncommittally.

"You didn't hear a word, did you?" Mrs. Stuart said.

The woman certainly liked to speak her mind. "Listening appeared unnecessary. Once the conversation turned to decorations for Christmas, I knew any points I made would be ignored."

"Not at all," she protested. "Why would you think so?"

Feeling Mother's gaze on him, he shrugged. "I'm a man, and we're generally thought incompetent to advise in that area."

"That doesn't mean you are," his mother said earnestly. "Mr. Fowler says you've made many improvements on the estate— better roofs for the tenant cottages, a new fishery, modern additions to the dairy—"

"Those are my purview. Decorations for Christmas are not."

"They could be." A hopeful look crossed her face. "Perhaps this year you could even join us for the season."

A hard knot formed in his chest. "Impossible. I'm expected at the Waverlys'." He cast her a meaningful glance. "As usual." When his mother flinched, it soured his temper further, which made him glare at the pretty young widow who'd brought this about in the first place. "I wouldn't even be here, if not for the interference of certain individuals."

She calmly continued to eat her soup, though her cheeks reddened considerably. "As I recall, I apologized for misleading you about your mother's health, sir."

Since Mother didn't look shocked by her comment, Mrs. Stuart must have confessed all to her. That was a surprise. "Apparently I missed your apology during all the chiding and lecturing."

"You just now admitted to a certain laxness in listening," Mrs. Stuart said pertly. "Perhaps your attention wandered during my apology, too."

Perversely, that made him want to smile. The widow's impudent streak caught him unawares sometimes. "Then I'll have to pay better attention in future," he said, struggling to sound stern.

It was hard to be stern with her. He wasn't sure why. She just had this way of bringing him out of himself when he least expected it.

Suddenly he felt his mother's gaze on him. He looked over to see her eyes dart from him to Mrs. Stuart and back, and his bad mood returned. Best not to give her any ideas, or she'd be priming Mrs. Stuart to be even more of an ally.

He frowned at them both. "So what do you want my opinion on, anyway?"

"We have to decide whether to have a Christmas tree like those that your mother had in her youth," Mrs. Stuart said gamely.

"And in Pierce's youth, too." Mother cut her roast beef. "I always made sure we had at least a small one, hung round with candles and toys and such, though Pierce's father thought it a foolish waste of good timber."

He tensed. Mother was still following that peculiar German

custom? Great God. In his childhood, the scent of cut fir had permeated the house every Christmas. Even now, whenever he smelled firs he thought of that strange little tree with its sparkling baubles and little bags of nuts . . . and he ached with the bitter-sweet memory of his last Christmas at home.

Oblivious to his reaction, Mrs. Stuart generously buttered a slice of bread. "We'll have to find one ourselves, with your supervision, my lady. The servants won't know what sort of tree to choose. And once they cut it down and bring it in, you'll have to show us how to decorate it and affix candles to it."

"Excellent," he grumbled. "Might as well show you how to set fire to the whole damned house, while you're at it."

When they turned startled looks on him, he forced the frown from his face. Not for the world would he let them know how their talk of Christmas trees stabbed him through with sharp memories. "Candles on a tree are dangerous."

"Not if the tree is green," his mother put in. "And it will only stay up for a day or two." She busied herself with sopping up gravy with her bread. "No point in keeping it up until Twelfth Night if you're not even going to be here for Christmas."

If she thought her unsubtle hints that he should stay would work on *him,* she was mad. "True," he said firmly. "Then it will be fine for so short a period."

"Good," his mother said with a hint of belligerence. "Because I think a tree would make the holiday truly lovely."

Casting him a shuttered glance, Mrs. Stuart sipped some wine. "I agree. It sounds like a perfectly charming custom."

"And an expensive one, given its short duration." Which was

probably the point. He faced his mother. "How much will this cost me, anyway? You'll need baubles and candles for your precious tree, not to mention—"

"Don't be ridiculous, Pierce. I have all that already. The baubles, as you call them, are the same ones I store in the attic every year."

That caught him entirely off guard. He'd expected her to disguise a request for funds by saying it was for her precious tree. "You want *nothing* purchased for this tree?" he persisted, ignoring Mrs. Stuart's smug smile.

"Certainly not. The point is to perpetuate the traditions of one's family. My glass ornaments come from your grandmother, and the other decorations are fruit and nuts, all of which can be found here on the estate, even the candles." She brightened. "Oh, and paper cutouts! We must do those. Don't you remember, Pierce? We used to cut tiny little angels—"

"I remember," he said bitterly. "Trust me, I remember only too well." When the two women lapsed into an awkward silence, he added, "But in case you haven't noticed, Mother, I've grown too big for angels. Devils are more my style."

"Ah, but I don't think devils are a good idea for a Christmas tree," Mrs. Stuart put in, as if to draw his fire.

He turned toward her with a challenging glance. "And why is that?"

She didn't waver. "Well, for one thing, pitchforks are exceedingly difficult to cut out."

He blinked, then gave a rueful laugh. Damn the woman, but she made it hard to stay annoyed. And when she stared at him with a silent plea in her eyes, he relented for the moment.

Relaxing back against his chair, he took a sip of wine. "You'd feel differently if you'd ever tried cutting out a tiny halo, Mrs. Stuart. Or stars, for that matter. Mine always ended up round, which goes against every rule of star artistry." He leaned close to say in a confiding tone, "Apparently, they're expected to have points."

"Are they?" she said brightly. "Then clearly I shall have to stick to moons. Those are allowed to be round."

"Ah, but would you put a moon on a Christmas tree?" he asked. "The three wise men following the moon doesn't have quite the same effect."

"And it's not in the Bible besides," she said, clearly struggling not to smile.

"I wouldn't know," he drawled. "That's not a book I'm terribly familiar with."

"A fact that you regularly demonstrate to the world," his mother said archly.

He stiffened. He'd almost managed to forget she was there. "Yes. I do." He stared her down. "Every chance I get."

He was on the verge of pointing out that if she'd wanted some say in his behavior, she should have stayed to see him grow up, when Mrs. Stuart broke in. "In any case, since his lordship won't be here to join us in decorating the tree, I will be eager to assist you, my lady."

"That would be lovely," Mother said.

"And then perhaps his lordship could come back for a day or two to see it when it's all done," Mrs. Stuart said in that managing voice females sometimes used. The one that didn't work on him.

"As I said before, that's impossible."

His mother looked crestfallen. "You used to enjoy the season."

It was on the tip of his tongue to point out that she'd put an end to all that by making holidays synonymous with being unwanted. But he wouldn't give her the satisfaction.

"Do whatever you wish with your tree," he muttered, now thoroughly annoyed again. He drenched a chunk of beef in gravy and devoured it. "Just leave me out of it. My days of relishing such mundane pleasures are long past."

"That's a pity," Mother said. "Mundane pleasures are about the only kind we have here in the country."

With a meaningful glance at Mrs. Stuart, he waited for his mother to ask for some new toy to keep them amused, or perhaps a costly trip to Italy, where she could indulge her love of expensive things to her heart's content.

Then she went on, "But we do enjoy them." She smiled at Mrs. Stuart. "We sing and play and act charades and have our own sort of fun. Camilla is very good at reading aloud—very dramatic."

He was still stunned by his mother's prosaic idea of "fun" when the door opened and a footman came in bearing some confection.

"And we have an excellent cook," Mrs. Stuart said cheerily as her portion was placed before her. "There's nothing mundane about *that* pleasure." She took a bite and her face lit up. "Her almond blancmange is sheer heaven."

He arched one eyebrow. "I take it that you share Mother's love of sweets."

"I do, indeed," Mrs. Stuart said, dabbing a bit of custard from the corner of her mouth. "Dessert was rare at the orphanage, I'm afraid, and now that I can have it whenever I please, I never seem to tire of it."

He'd forgotten that she was raised an orphan. For a moment, he flashed on a little girl coveting every pastry she saw in the London bakeries, and his chest tightened inexplicably at the thought of her having something so simple routinely denied to her.

"Don't you like sweets yourself, my lord?" she asked, jerking him from his dark thoughts.

"He never did," Mother answered. "Pierce was a most unusual child—he would rather have fruit and cheese for dessert." She cast Pierce a tentative smile. "That's why I had Cook prepare some of that, too."

And with a little flourish, the footman placed a plate of apple slices and a selection of cheeses before him.

Mrs. Stuart's earlier words clamored in his brain: *If her feelings are as false as you think, why does she have a chest full of your school drawings and papers? Why does she read to me your childhood letters, pointing out your witty turns of phrase and clever observations? Why does she keep a miniature of you by her bed?*

He could feel himself weakening, feel the barricades crumbling a little, and it sparked his temper. Damn it, she could not just whisk away years of neglect with a plate of fruit and cheese and a few remarks about his childhood! He'd had as much of this as he could stand.

He forced a nonchalant smile to his lips. "I've grown up now, Mother. What I like best for dessert these days is a good cigar."

He rose. "And since that's the case, I'll step outside to indulge in one now that the meal is done." He bowed stiffly in her direction. "Good night."

Then he leveled a hard gaze on Mrs. Stuart. "Au revoir, madam."

She blushed at his oblique reminder that her evening with him wasn't yet at an end, but she managed a smile. "Au revoir, my lord."

He strode out of the dining room, relieved that he was done. Mrs. Stuart had made better use of his bargain with her than he'd expected. She and his mother had obviously decided to plague him at dinner with talk of Christmas trees and prettied-up tales of his childhood until he turned to putty in their hands.

Well, he wasn't without defenses of his own. If Mrs. Stuart insisted on making him uncomfortable at dinner, then he would damned well return the favor. Since he couldn't seduce her, he'd have to consider other possibilities. Cards wouldn't serve his purpose, and so far she'd proved herself adept at parrying his barbs in conversation. As for reading to him . . .

His eyes narrowed. She had a penchant for reading aloud dramatically, didn't she? Good. Then he would give her something damned interesting to read.

6

Though his lordship had used a flimsy excuse to absent himself from the meal, Camilla couldn't fault him for it. Dinner had been far tenser than she'd expected, and not just on his side, either. Lady Devonmont had seemed determined to provoke him. Perhaps this hadn't been such a good idea after all.

But as the dessert plates were carried away, Lady Devonmont smiled broadly at her. "Thank you."

"For what?"

"For making him join us for dinner."

"You don't know your son very well if you think anyone could *make* him do anything he doesn't want to," Camilla said dryly.

"I know him better than you think," the countess said enigmatically. "You must have said *something* to convince him to dine with us. He would never have done so just to please me."

"You're wrong," she lied. "He may be gruff, but I'm sure he loves you in his own way."

What else could she tell the woman without breaking her heart? She would walk through fire before she would see her ladyship hurt.

The countess sighed. "Perhaps." She seemed to brood a moment, then shook it off and rose from the table. "Shall we go say good night to our boy?"

"Certainly." It had become a nightly ritual for them to tuck Jasper in before they settled down with needlework or books or whatever their choice of amusement was for the evening.

Her mind wandered as they headed up the stairs. What had his lordship meant, he'd be spending his Christmas at the Waverlys' "as usual"? Camilla knew he had cousins near London, but why would he prefer to spend Christmas with them over his mother? She was tempted to ask the countess, but she hated to spoil her ladyship's happiness at having him here, however briefly.

Camilla and Jasper's room was on the third floor, next to what used to be the nursery. The earl's tutor had originally occupied their room, but it had been years since anyone had lived in it, so her ladyship had suggested it would be perfect for Camilla. Once Jasper had come to live here, too, the countess had ordered the tutor's bed changed out for a trundle bed so mother and son could be together.

It was the perfect arrangement to keep Jasper safe from discovery. Mr. Fowler was often in the servants' quarters, but he

would find it highly inappropriate to invade the floor where sup-
posedly only Camilla lived. And the room was still close enough
to her ladyship's for Camilla's purposes.

As they entered, Maisie was trying futilely to get Jasper to
settle down. He practically bounced in his trundle bed. "Mrs.
Beasley said his lordship is very big and scary," he pronounced.
"Is that true?"

"Only with young boys who don't do what they're told," Camilla said. It was a bit of a falsehood, but she couldn't take any
chance that the earl would see Jasper and banish him from Montcliff. It would break her heart. "So behave yourself."

Her ladyship sat down on the bed and chucked Jasper under
the chin. "But he'll be gone tomorrow. Just stay with Maisie, all
right? And if the earl should happen to see you and ask who you
are, tell him your mother is a servant. Don't say her name."

"But Mama *isn't* a servant," he protested.

"Actually—" Camilla began.

"Your mother is a special kind of servant very important to
me," Lady Devonmont said. "And you're important to me, too.
So if you'll be a good boy and stay out of his lordship's sight until
he leaves tomorrow, I'll let you keep one of those tin soldiers that
you like to play with so much."

As Jasper's face lit up, Camilla's heart caught in her throat.
The countess was always doing such lovely things for Jasper. Her
ladyship had rapidly become the closest thing to a grandmother
that he would ever have.

But her ladyship didn't have to buy Jasper's love—she had
it already, whether or not she realized it. "You needn't give him

anything," Camilla murmured. "I know he'll be good just for your sake."

"Even so, he deserves a prize for it. And there are a hundred in the set—one won't be missed. Let me spoil the lad a bit." Her tone grew wistful. "I didn't get to spoil my own boy near enough."

Camilla burned with curiosity to ask why not, but now wasn't the time.

Lady Devonmont kissed Jasper on the forehead, then headed for the door. "I believe I shall retire early this evening. This has been a very long day."

"Would you like me to read to you?"

She shook her head. "I suspect I'll fall asleep as soon as my head hits the pillow. In any case, you deserve an evening to yourself once in a while."

"Thank you." That would certainly make it easier for her to see his lordship alone later.

How Camilla wished she could ask her ladyship more about the stormy relationship with her son. But her ladyship had refused time and again to speak about her son's neglect. That wasn't liable to change just because he'd had dinner with her. Besides, it might be easier to startle the truth out of *him,* given how readily he got provoked when the subject involved his mother.

Camilla crooned Jasper's favorite lullaby until he fell asleep, then motioned to Maisie to join her outside the door. She considered lying to the girl, but she needed one person to know the true situation. And she trusted Maisie, who adored Jasper as if he were her own.

Quickly she explained the bargain made between her and his

lordship, making it very clear that their assignation was *not* of the intimate kind. "I would prefer, however, that you not mention this to *anyone*, even the other servants, and especially not to her ladyship. Her feelings would be hurt if she learned of it."

"I'll be silent as the grave, I swear," Maisie murmured.

The girl probably would, too. She had immediately taken to Camilla because of Camilla's Scottish surname, even knowing that it only came from her late husband. No, she would never reveal Camilla's secrets, at least not to all the English running about the estate.

"I won't be in his chambers too late, I promise," Camilla said, "but with the way her ladyship has been pining for him, I just couldn't refuse to meet his terms."

"I understand, truly I do. I know you wouldn't do anything unseemly."

"If Jasper should happen to wake and need me . . ."

"I'll take care of it. We don't want his lordship guessing that he's here, and we don't want those gossips in the kitchen thinking the wrong thing, either, do we?"

Camilla beamed at the girl. "Exactly." She glanced at the case clock in the hall. It was already later than she'd have liked. "I have to go."

Maisie caught her arm. "Be careful. With a man like that—"

"I'll be on my guard, don't you worry." Then she hurried down to the second floor, where the family rooms were.

As she approached his bedchamber, her hands grew clammy. She honestly didn't know what to make of him.

After their earlier encounter, when he'd railed at her and tried to cow her, she'd expected him to be officious and cold to her at dinner. He was an earl, for pity's sake. Her previous two employers, of far lower rank, had never treated her with anything but condescension. But although he'd been stiff with his mother, there'd been that moment when he'd joked with Camilla about the angel cutouts. . . .

She shook her head at her softening toward him. It hardly made up for the fact that he was denying his mother his presence for the Christmas season. No matter how attractive he was, with his London sophistication and his dry wit, he was still behaving quite heartlessly to the countess.

And her ladyship deserved better. That was one thing Camilla meant to do this evening—make sure that he knew it.

She reached his bedchamber and tapped on the door, and when he swung it open, her heart practically failed her. Despite the chill in the room, he was dressed only in shirtsleeves and trousers, with nary a waistcoat, coat, or cravat to be seen. The sight of him so casually attired threw her off balance and stirred feelings she'd thought long dead.

She had a hard time not noticing the impressive chest well-displayed by his thin lawn shirt. And the broad shoulders. Not to mention the muscular forearms laid bare, since his shirtsleeves were rolled up to the elbows.

Oh, how could she pay attention to such things? Why did she care that his shirt was open at the throat? Why couldn't she tear her gaze from the patch of skin so tantalizingly revealed?

Because it had been a long time since she'd spent time with a man so informally dressed. That's all.

With some effort, she forced her gaze up to his face. He held a glass of brandy, which he sipped from before stepping back just enough to let her enter. "I began to wonder if you forgot our bargain," he groused.

She slid past him, acutely aware of how his eyes followed her and how his body loomed over hers. He smelled of spirits and smoke. She wasn't used to that, for Kenneth had neither smoked nor drank strong liquor. It should have repulsed her.

But it was so . . . indescribably male. And for a woman who'd spent most of her time in the last few months with an older woman, a young maid, and a small child, it was a rather refreshing change. A little *too* refreshing for her sanity.

She moved to put some distance between them. "Perhaps *you* forgot I have other duties in the evening. Surely you didn't want me to tell your mother that I had to leave her in order to come to your bedchamber."

"Of course not." He strode over to stoke the fire. "She keeps you up this late every night?"

"It's barely ten o'clock. We often stay up later than this. And I enjoy keeping your mother company, no matter how late." She cast him an arch glance, determined to provoke him into revealing more about his estrangement from the countess. "Just because you find your mother irksome doesn't mean that *I* do."

"It's not that I find Mother irksome," he snapped. "It's—" He caught himself. "Never mind. It's of no matter."

Stifling a sigh, she tried another tack. "At dinner, I couldn't help but notice that she confounded your expectations about her need for money."

"No doubt you warned her of my suspicions."

"As a matter of fact, I did not," she said stiffly. "Though I do think you ought to give her the chance to—"

"Let us be clear on one thing." He bore down on her with a fierce scowl. "Talking about my mother is not entertaining. So if you intend to spend the evening trying to soften me toward her, you'd better readjust your plans. I will not discuss her with you."

"But—"

"Not one word. Not if you want to keep working here. Understood?"

She huffed out a frustrated breath. The man was maddening! How was she supposed to find out anything when he and his mother were so bent on being stubborn? Clearly, she would have to be more subtle.

When she didn't answer, he glowered at her. "Do we understand each other, Mrs. Stuart?"

"I'm not hard of hearing," she grumbled. "Nor am I lacking in comprehension."

His glower faded, and he cast her a thin smile. "We'll see about that."

"I'm sure we will, my lord."

"No need to be so formal when we're alone," he drawled, dropping into one of two well-upholstered chairs by the fire and taking another sip of his brandy. "You could call me Devonmont, as my friends do. Or 'darling.'"

She rolled her eyes. "We've already settled that we're not to have that sort of . . . friendship, sir."

"Yes." He let his gaze trail down her with an exaggerated heat clearly meant to provoke. "What a pity."

"Tell me, do women generally respond to your transparent attempts to get beneath their skirts?"

"Probably about as often as gentlemen flee your transparent attempts to reform them."

A smile tugged at her lips. She'd never tried reforming an employer before. Something in him must bring out the devil in her. "*You* don't flee."

"No need—I'm not the reforming type, so you don't frighten me." He lifted his glass in a pantomime of a toast. "And *you* aren't responding to my attempts to get beneath your skirts. So that makes us even."

Only because he wasn't *seriously* trying to get beneath her skirts. And thank heaven, too. If he ever did, she might have trouble resisting him.

She glanced about the room, which had been closed up until today. As with many such rooms in country houses, "Red Room" was a misnomer—there wasn't anything red in it. Probably it had been red a hundred years ago, and the name had stuck long after it was refurbished. Now the curtains and linens were an azure print, and the walls were painted a similar blue.

It was furnished with an imposing canopy bed and the two armchairs by the fire, separated by a little table. The only other piece of furniture was a bookcase of walnut that sat against the wall, next to a surprisingly large window that looked out over the lawn.

"Was this your room when you lived here?" If so, he'd left it utterly barren of anything that might have been his as a schoolboy—no globes or telescopes or even old racing journals. Only a few books were there, which was odd, given his rumored obsession with increasing Montcliff Manor's library.

"No," he said tersely. "The nursery was my room."

"Well, of course, until you were older, but after you went off to school, you must have had—"

"I've decided what entertainment I wish for tonight," he said bluntly.

Shrugging off his lack of interest in discussing his room, she walked toward him. "All right. And what might that be?"

With a sudden, suspect gleam in his eye, he reached for a book on the table next to him. "Since Mother said you were an excellent reader, I thought you might read aloud to me."

His manner reminded her of Jasper when he thought to play some trick on her.

Warily, she sat down in the chair opposite him and took the volume he offered. Then she pushed up her spectacles so she could better view the cover. *Fanny Hill: Memoirs of a Woman of Pleasure.*

A woman of pleasure? Oh, dear.

She felt the earl's gaze on her, felt him waiting for her to make some expression of horrified dismay. The desire to thwart his expectation was too overwhelming to resist.

Opening the book, she read the title aloud in a resounding voice that surprised her almost as much as it seemed to surprise him. Then she turned the page and began to read the text:

Madam,

I sit down to give you an undeniable proof of my

considering your desires as indispensable orders.
Ungracious then as the task may be, I shall recall to view
those scandalous stages of my life—

"You're actually going to read it," he interrupted.

Biting back a smile, she lifted her gaze. "That *is* what you asked of me, isn't it?"

His gaze hardened. "Of course. Do go on."

So she did. It was the account of a country girl who set off to make her fortune in the city, only to be taken in by a suspiciously friendly older woman. Camilla instantly recognized the older character as a bawd in disguise. Not for nothing had she helped her vicar husband with his work in Spitalfields. She knew how easily naive girls were deceived.

But the narrator, relating the beginnings of her own downfall, didn't seem overly bothered by it. Indeed, she had no sense of shame at all.

Camilla found that fascinating. She was becoming quite intrigued by the book when his lordship said, "You can stop now if you wish."

She glanced up to find him looking nervous. "Don't be ridiculous. I've only read ten pages."

"But I doubt you'll like where it goes from here."

He seemed so uncomfortable with the idea of her going on that she couldn't resist provoking him. "Nonsense. This happens to be a book I read often," she lied blithely. "I'm enjoying revisiting it."

Perhaps she had done it up a bit too brown, for he eyed her

with rank skepticism. "Are you indeed?" He leaned back in his chair. "What's your favorite part?"

She gauged the length of the book and took a guess. "Page ninety-six."

He lifted an eyebrow. "Then by all means, do read that aloud."

"All right." So far there hadn't been anything terribly shocking, so she thumbed through to it without a qualm.

But page 96 did not contain text. Instead, there was only a crudely drawn illustration so appalling it took her breath away.

A woman lay on a bed, naked from the waist down, with her legs parted as she prepared to receive a man whose overly large appendage, also quite naked and rendered in some detail, jutted out from his breeches. The female actually had her hand on it, as if to . . . to assess its dimensions.

Nothing in Camilla's experience had prepared her for such a blatant display of carnality.

"Well, read on," the earl taunted when she hesitated.

A blush rose on her cheeks. "I can't." She lifted her stunned gaze to his. "There are no words. Just a . . . picture."

The color drained from his face. Reaching over, he snatched the book from her and stared at it, then shot her a horrified look. "Oh, holy hell. It has pictures."

7

If Camilla hadn't been so mortified, she would have laughed. "Surely you knew that."

"Not exactly." When she eyed him skeptically, he shut the book and set it down. "I recently acquired this edition as part of a lot of fifty books I won at auction. I hadn't looked at it since I bought it. My other edition, in London, is not . . . er . . . illustrated."

"You have *two* editions of that?"

His eyes narrowed. "You shouldn't be surprised. You read it 'often,' remember?"

The jig was clearly up. "You know perfectly well I've never read that book." She stared him down. "And if that's what the illustrations are like, I shudder to think what's in the text."

"You have no idea." He released an exasperated breath. "You, madam, are the most stubborn female I've ever met. If not for that picture, I wonder how far you'd have read before throwing the book at my head."

"I'd never throw it at your head, sir." She tilted up her chin. "Just into the fire."

"I would have *your* head if you did. It's damned difficult to obtain a copy of it. There are only a few hundred."

"Yes, I can see why," she said dryly. "The illustrations are very poorly rendered."

He laughed full out. "They are indeed. Perhaps we should choose some other book." His eyes gleamed at her. "One with art of a higher quality."

"Or *writing* of a higher quality," she countered. "Poetry, for example." When he groaned, she added, "Lord Byron's *Don Juan* ought to be just your cup of tea. Or perhaps some of Lord Rochester's poems. I believe he used a great many naughty words."

"I believe he did." He picked up his glass to down some brandy. "But alas, there are no pictures."

She forced a stern expression onto her face. "You, sir, are nothing more than an overgrown child."

"Indeed I am," he said without a trace of remorse. "That's what happens when a man has no real childhood to speak of. He has to make up for it later."

Even as she caught her breath to hear him reveal something about his past, he realized what he'd said and added, "But how the devil does a sheltered female like you know of *Don Juan*? Or Lord Rochester's poems?"

"I'm not so sheltered as all that. As you well know, I was raised in a London orphanage."

"Where they fed you on risqué poetry?" he quipped.

"Well, no. I found out about Lord Byron's scandalous *Don Juan* from the newspaper."

"Ah. So you haven't actually read the poem."

"I don't believe I've had the pleasure, no," she said primly.

He lifted one eyebrow. "Trust me, you'd know if you had."

"I suppose *you've* read it."

"I have my own copy. But I don't have Lord Rochester's poems. So how did *you* get them?"

Heat rose in her cheeks. "I didn't. Not exactly. When I served as paid companion to an elderly lady with a bachelor grandson, he gave me free access to his library, which contained a few . . . questionable books of verse."

"That you decided to read?"

She scowled at him. "I didn't *know* they were questionable until I read them, now, did I? And I happen to like verse. I'd read some of Lord Rochester's more respectable poems, and I never guessed—"

"That he was such a naughty boy?"

"Exactly." Her tone turned arch. "Apparently you're not the only lord out there who's a naughty boy."

"We do get around." He took another sip of brandy, then eyed her seriously over the rim of his glass. "And speaking of that—did this bachelor with the vulgar library ever behave as a naughty boy to *you?*"

"No more than you have."

"I've been a perfect gentleman to you. For me, anyway."

"Trying to blackmail me into your bed and then asking me to read naughty literature to you is not gentlemanly."

"But it's certainly entertaining," he pointed out.

She rolled her eyes. "To answer your question, the bachelor grandson never laid a hand on me. For one thing, he lived in terror that his grandmother, my employer, would cut him off. For another, he had no time for me. He spent it all courting women with large fortunes."

"Ah. Why did you leave?"

"His grandmother died." Camilla had been torn between dismay and relief. She hadn't wanted to look for a new post, but neither had she wanted to continue with the miserly and highly critical Lady Stirling. "He wasn't nearly as bad as the man who employed me next, as companion to his widowed sister. *He* wanted her to marry a rich marquess twice her age in order to gain him an entrée into White's and further his political career."

"And did he succeed?"

She smirked at him. "She ran off with his best friend. And he couldn't blame *me* for it, since he was the one who'd thrown them together." Her smile faded. "Unfortunately, he also no longer had any need for my services, which is how I ended up here."

He drank more brandy. "I keep forgetting this isn't your first post. Indeed, that's why I was so surprised to see how young you are."

"I'm not all *that* young. I'm nearly twenty-eight."

"A greatly advanced age indeed," he said sarcastically.

"Only three years younger than you," she pointed out.

One corner of his mouth quirked up. "True. But it's different for a man. We see more of the world in thirty-one years than a woman sees in a lifetime."

"Trust me, I've seen plenty enough of the world at my age."

He fell silent, his brow pursed in thought. "Twenty-seven. And you had two posts before this. You must have married very young."

That observation put her on her guard. "I was old enough."

"How old?"

"Why do you care?"

"You work for me. I have a right to know more about your circumstances." When she bristled, he softened his tone a fraction. "Besides, why should your age at marrying be such a secret? Were you ten and sold off from the orphanage to a ninety-year-old fellow with gout?"

"Don't be ridiculous. I was nineteen. And the orphanage was perfectly respectable. Indeed, I stayed there to work until I married."

"Ah. So you met your husband there."

"Yes," she said warily, not sure she wanted to talk about Kenneth with *him*. "He used to perform religious services for the children, and I would help him."

"And he fell in love." His voice was almost snide. When she hesitated a bit too long in answering, he added, "Or not."

Uncomfortable with his probing, she rose and went to the bookcase. "Perhaps you'd like me to read another book."

Setting down his glass, he rose, too. "You don't wish to talk about your marriage. I wonder why."

She faced him with a frown. "Probably for the same reason you don't wish to talk about your relationship with your mother. Because it's private."

He ignored that. "Did your husband mistreat you?" he asked in a hard voice. "Is that why you don't wish to discuss him?"

"Certainly not!" she said, appalled at the very thought. "You always assume the worst of people, don't you? He was a vicar, for pity's sake."

"That means nothing," he said evenly. "Men who mistreat women exist in every corner of society, trust me."

"Well, my husband didn't mistreat anyone. He was a crusader for the poor and the sick."

"Yet not in love with you?" Before she could answer, he added, "Let me guess. He saw you at the orphanage and determined that you would be the perfect helpmeet for him in his work."

She shot him a startled glance. "How did you know?"

He shrugged. "The average crusader tends to see women only as an extension of his mission."

"That's a most astute comment for an overgrown child."

He walked over to lean against a bedpost. "Children often pay better attention to their surroundings than adults give them credit for."

"Another astute observation," she said.

"I have my moments." He crossed his arms over his chest. "So how did you end up married to this crusading vicar? You seem the kind of woman who would marry only for love." His eyes glittered obsidian in the candlelight. "Did he tell you that he didn't love you? Or did he pretend to be enamored of you until after he got you leg-shackled for life?"

"You're very nosy, aren't you?"

"If you have nothing to hide, why should you care?"

Since she preferred to keep her most important secrets from him, she should probably fob him off with inconsequential ones. "If you must know, he never pretended anything. We'd been friends a few years when he made his proposal. He pointed out that he needed a woman of my skills, and I could use a home and a family. So he suggested—" She caught herself with a scowl. "I don't know why I should tell you this. I haven't even told your mother. Then again, she was never so rude as to pry."

"No, Mother isn't much interested in anyone's situation but her own."

She glared at him. "That's not true! She's kind and thoughtful and—"

"Don't change the subject," he bit out. "You were saying that your vicar gave you a most practical proposal. Go on. Didn't he spout *any* romantic drivel to get you to accept him?"

A pox on him. He was going to push her until he knew it all, wasn't he? And if she refused to tell him, she risked having him delve deeper into her past, which she couldn't afford.

"Kenneth wasn't the romantic sort," she said tersely. "If he felt anything deeper than friendly affection for me, he didn't say. For him, our marriage was more of a fair trade in services."

"That sounds cold-blooded even to me, and I'm definitely not the 'romantic sort.'"

"What a surprise," she muttered.

"So, was it? A fair trade, I mean."

She pushed up her spectacles. "Fair enough . . . until his heart failed him three years after we married, and he left me a widow."

"Ah, now I understand. You married him because he was older, more mature—"

"I married him because he offered," she said blandly, annoyed that he presumed to know so much when he knew so little. "And he was only a few years older than you. The doctor told me that it happens like that sometimes, even to young men in good health. One day Kenneth was well; the next he was gone." Leaving her alone with an infant, very little money, and her grief.

Some of her distress must have showed on her face, for he said, "You loved him."

The earl had misunderstood entirely, but she wasn't about to explain how complicated even a loveless marriage became when there was a child involved. She'd sought to build a family; instead she'd gained a dissatisfying union with a man she barely knew. Turning on her heel, she headed for the bookcase again. "If we're to do any more reading tonight, then you'll have to choose another bo—"

"You were in love with your husband," he persisted, pushing away from the bedpost to follow her. "It might have been a marriage of convenience for your vicar, but it wasn't for you, was it?"

Determined to ignore him, she ran her fingers over the books in the case. "There's a novel by Henry Fielding here that I understand is very good," she said firmly.

"Admit it!" He caught her arm and pulled her around to face him. "You loved your husband."

"No, I did not!" She wrenched her arm free as he stood there gaping at her. "I grieved him, yes. But I did not love him." That was the most embarrassing thing of all to admit. "I wanted to love him. I thought that once we were married, I would feel something, but I never . . . I couldn't . . ."

His gaze on her was intent, penetrating. "Don't blame yourself for that. Romantic love isn't for everyone."

For some reason that sparked her temper even more. "You mean a woman like me is incapable of love."

He scowled. "I didn't say that."

"You think that a woman with no resources is *always* on the hunt for a man with money," she went on hotly.

He looked as if she'd punched him. "I don't think any such thing!"

"Don't you? I married to escape the orphanage and a future as a spinster." To gain a family, though to say so would make her sound even more pitiful. "You said your mother married your father for money. Neither of us married for love. So I'm not much different from her."

"That's not true," he gritted out. "You didn't marry a man of means and rank whom you *knew* could aim higher. You came to a mutual agreement with a fellow who didn't profess to love you—"

"How do you know that she didn't do the same?" When he merely glowered at her, she thrust her face up in his. "You don't know *what* she did, do you? You don't even know the full circumstances of her situation, yet you pass judgment on her."

She must have hit a nerve, for his face closed up. "I won't talk about my mother."

"Of course not. You might learn that you don't know her as well as you think. That you might be wrong about—"

"Quiet!" he growled. "I won't discuss her with *you*!"

"You're ready to defend *me*, whom you barely know," she persisted, heedless of how reckless she was being to provoke him, "yet you refuse to defend your own mother, who bore you and raised you."

"She did not—" He caught himself. "You don't know anything about it, damn you!"

"No, I don't! So *tell* me! How else can I learn if you don't?"

"If you don't stop talking about her, I'll—"

"What?" she pressed him. "You'll dismiss me? Run back to London, where it's safe? Except that it isn't safe, is it? Because even I, a complete stranger, can see the noose that is choking you more and more with every day that you—"

"Damn you!" He grabbed her by the shoulders as if he meant to shake her. "Damn you to hell!"

She stared him down, daring him to do his worst.

Then he kissed her. Hard. Fiercely. On the lips.

It startled her so much that she jerked back to gape at him. "What in creation was that for?"

"To shut you up," he said, eyes ablaze. Then his gaze dropped to her mouth, and the blaze became smoldering coals. He removed her spectacles and tossed them onto the nearby bed. "But this one, my dear, is for me."

His second kiss was a revelation. The fact that he was kissing her at *all* was a revelation. Men just didn't kiss her.

Of course Kenneth had done so whenever he'd come to her bed, but his kisses had always been brisk and no-nonsense, as if he was trying to get right to the point.

There was nothing brisk and no-nonsense about the *earl's* kiss. It invaded and persuaded, inflamed and invigorated. His brandied breath intoxicated her, made her want to drink him up even as he was fogging her good sense. She could hardly think, with his hands sliding into her hair and his mouth possessing hers.

And when he deepened the kiss, delving between her lips with his tongue, she couldn't prevent the moan that rose in her throat. She'd forgotten how good it felt to be held by a man, kissed by a man, even one who didn't love her. But this was so much more even than that. It was heady, thrilling . . . magical.

She caught herself. Of course it was magical. Rogues built their reputations on magical kisses. Magical *seductions*.

The thought made her tear her mouth from his. "You probably shouldn't . . ."

"Damned right I shouldn't." He clasped her head in his hands, his eyes dark and fathomless as he gazed into hers. "Even I know better. But it doesn't stop me from wanting to. Or you from wanting me to."

How had he guessed?

Probably because she'd just let him repeatedly thrust his tongue inside her mouth. And her hands now gripped his waist like those of a woman drowning.

She forced her hands to release him. "My lord—"

"Don't call me that." He bent his head, stopping his lips a breath away from hers. "In this room, we're Pierce and Camilla, understood?"

For no reason she could explain, she nodded, and that was all the invitation he required. With a sharp intake of breath, he took her mouth again.

8

Pierce knew what he was doing was unwise. He might be a scoundrel and a thousand other vile things, but he didn't attack women in his employ. He didn't pinch the maids or sneak a fondle from the housekeeper. And he did *not* kiss his mother's paid companion.

Except that he *was*. And he couldn't seem to stop.

It didn't help that she was kissing him back. It didn't help that he knew she was a widow, that he knew she hadn't loved her husband, that he found her enticing and clever and all those things that made him desire a woman.

He certainly desired this one. Her fierce soul made him ache to lay her down on the bed and take her with slow, hot intent until she cried out her pleasure beneath him. She smelled of honey water and tasted of cinnamon, and he'd have liked nothing more than to eat her up.

She broke the kiss again to stare up at him with that clear-eyed gaze that seemed to see deeper than she let on. "Is this how you always silence a woman?"

He brushed kisses over her cheek. "Never needed to before," he murmured in her ear.

"So I'm the only woman who plagues you?" she asked skeptically, then gasped when he nipped her earlobe.

She was certainly the only one who'd ever plagued him about Mother. But then, he'd never let anyone else close enough to even know he *had* a mother.

"The only one I couldn't silence with a few words," he murmured as he kissed her neck. "Or with a threat to cut off their tidy allowances."

Her breath came in staccato bursts against his brow. "Then you must know some . . . very weak-willed women."

"Or very avaricious ones," he said dryly. Then he kissed her again to prevent her from pointing out the obvious—that perhaps he had different rules for women when it came to money. The first time she'd pointed it out had made him angry enough.

Besides, he wanted to keep kissing her. She kissed like a woman who didn't know her own sensual power. Most women did—even the virginal ones. The fact that she didn't made him want to show it to her.

Graphically. Thoroughly. Over and over, until she realized what he'd known from the moment she first stood up to him—

that she was one of those rare women who understood how the game was played . . . and then played it by her own rules.

He just wanted to break all the rules, even his own. With her. Now. In his bed.

So he covered her breast with his hand and kneaded it, exulting to feel her nipple harden through the fabric. For a brief, hot moment, she leaned into his caress, making him want to tear her gown off so he could tongue the sweet, ample softness of her breasts until she gasped her enjoyment.

But when he tugged at the fastenings of her gown in back, she froze and shoved him away. "Don't." Devoid of their spectacles, her eyes glittered a perfect cobalt blue in the firelight. Her lips were swollen and flushed from his kisses, and her chest rose and fell with her quickened breath. "That is not . . . part of our agreement."

No, it wasn't, and he knew it. He just couldn't make himself care. "It could be," he rasped, his body hard with need, and his blood running molten through his veins.

Her expression grew wary as she moved to the bed to snatch up her spectacles and don them once more. "I won't let you seduce me just to prove that you can."

The words sparked his temper. "Is that what you think this is?"

"You want a woman, and I am near to hand."

"Not near enough to hand," he said testily, and reached for her once more. But this time she darted across the room and put a chair between them.

Oh, for the love of God . . . He'd be damned before he took

to chasing a woman about the furniture. Bad enough that he'd put her on her guard just by kissing her and giving her one little caress.

One delicious, intoxicating little caress that made him want more, made him want—

Devil take it all. He mustn't do this.

As he stood there, breathing hard, fighting for control, he began to come to his senses. What was he thinking? She was in his employ. He did *not* attempt to seduce servants. She wasn't even his preferred type! He liked his women tall and blond and self-involved so they didn't peer too deeply into his secrets.

She was none of that, yet he couldn't remember the last time he'd wanted a woman so much. Even now, looking at her lush mouth and even lusher body made him ache. . . .

Bloody hell, what was wrong with him?

He was bored and alone and randy. That's all. And he wasn't about to let his uncharacteristic desire for some plague of a female make him do anything he'd regret.

Leaning back against the bookcase, he crossed his arms over his chest and forced his breathing to slow. Then he donned his rakehell facade. Because that was the safest one. The only one that felt comfortable.

"Fine," he drawled. "We'll do it your way." He skimmed his gaze down her with deliberate heat. "Though I can't say I'm happy about it."

"It wouldn't be wise for us to—"

"I'm aware of that." He cast her a humorless smile. "I merely got caught up in the moment. It won't happen again."

Her wide, beautiful eyes looked uncertain. "You said that if I gave you an inch, you would take two miles. At the time, I didn't think you meant it, but—"

"I believe we just established that I meant it." Pushing away from the bedpost, he noted how she tensed as if to flee, and he halted. "But I'm in full control of my urges now, I assure you."

She gave him a tight nod. "Then I suppose I should choose another book to read to you."

"No, you may go," he said in a dismissive tone. At her look of surprise, he added, "I traveled long and hard today, and even a wicked fellow like me gets tired occasionally."

But that wasn't why he was ending their evening. Nor was it because he couldn't have her in his bed. The truth was, the longer she stared at him with that deeply probing gaze, the more uncomfortable he grew.

If she guessed it, she didn't show it. Relief was the only emotion on her face. "Thank you, Pierce. I'm rather tired myself."

Her use of his Christian name unsettled his insides. No one except his family called him Pierce. Even his mistresses had always called him Devonmont or "my lord." He almost wished he hadn't asked her to go against that long-standing rule; it made him feel oddly vulnerable. But he wasn't about to take it back and have her guess why.

"You're welcome," he said tightly. When she headed for the door, seemingly eager to flee his presence, he added, "Tomorrow evening we'll play piquet."

Damn it, why had he said that?

She faced him with a wary gaze. "I thought you were returning to London in the morning."

He'd planned to. Until she'd looked so bloody glad to leave
him, so bloody scared that he might toss her into his bed and
ravish her. Which was only marginally worse than her looking at
him as if she understood things she couldn't possibly understand.

*You'll dismiss me? Run back to London, where it's safe? Except
that it isn't safe, is it? Because even I, a complete stranger, can see the
noose that is choking you more and more with every day . . .*

She could see no such thing, devil take her! He'd fought hard
to bring himself to the point where he didn't care one whit *what*
Mother did. But if he left for London now, Camilla would think
he did care, and that galled him.

"I need to consult with Fowler before I go, and that always
ends up taking longer than I expect. Since I'll be on the estate
anyway . . ." He shrugged.

Tipping up her chin, she stared at him with those penetrating
blue eyes. "Does that mean you'll dine with me and your mother
again, too?"

Damn. She'd misunderstood him. She thought he wanted to
repeat tonight's bargain.

At his silence, she blushed and went on hastily, "Because otherwise I don't think it would be appropriate for you and me to—"

"Same bargain as before," he heard himself say as if through a
fog. "I dine with the two of you, and you come here afterward."

Idiot. Yet he could hardly compel her to show up in his bedchamber again, unless he wanted to be one of those loathsome
employers who forced their servants into their beds. And what

would one more dinner with Mother matter, anyway? He knew her game. He could remain immune to it. Indeed, he would show Mrs. I Can See Your Darkest Secrets Stuart that he wasn't letting any damned "noose" choke him.

Camilla's gaze softened, making him regret he'd even suggested staying another night. "All right. Same bargain as before. Though I think we should avoid the naughty books."

"Indeed." Just the thought of her reading more of *Fanny Hill* aloud to him in her sultry voice made his cock harden again. "No naughty books."

"And no more kisses," she said firmly.

It rubbed him raw that she thought him incapable of controlling himself. He was known for his control. "Of course." When she looked skeptical, he managed a bored expression. "Don't worry, Camilla. As I said this afternoon, I don't make a practice of abusing the trust of those in my employ. We'll merely play piquet. Or rather, I'll trounce you at piquet."

"If you can," she said lightly.

He snorted. "I've spent a good portion of my life in gaming hells. I think I can beat a woman whose only experience at the game is with little old ladies and orphans."

"I take it you don't remember the name of that little old lady I served as companion to." When he frowned, trying to recall the contents of her reference letters, she added, "Lady Stirling. And she taught me everything she knew about piquet."

Which was plenty. The late viscountess had been one of the best piquet players in England. "Then it's a good thing I beat her twice during my salad days."

Her face fell. "You're bamming me."

"You'll find out tomorrow night, won't you?"

"I suppose so," she said with a nod, and swept out the door.

A pity he would have to run the gauntlet of dinner with Mother again before he got a few hours with Camilla, who still had no idea what her meddling had wrought.

So tell *me! How else can I learn if you don't?*

He scowled. He ought to do just that—tell her everything and let her see just how heartless was the woman she apparently adored.

But she wouldn't believe him. Mother had spent the last six months persuading Camilla that everything was *his* fault. He wasn't going to overturn that just by giving her a few facts. And that rankled. Because Camilla seemed to be a sensible woman who ought not to be taken in by such machinations. It bothered him that she was. That he might be missing something in all this.

Missing something? Not bloody likely.

No, Camilla was naive, that's all. Charming and pretty, but a babe in the woods when it came to the sort of manipulative woman Mother was. Given a bit more time seeing him and Mother together, she would recognize the truth. That she'd been wrong about him and Mother and his blame in all this.

Then there would be no more reckless letters summoning him to Montcliff.

In the hall, Camilla leaned against the wall to catch her breath and steady her racing pulse. He was staying for another day, another dinner with her and the countess. Earlier, she would have exulted at a second chance to convince him that his mother deserved his attention.

Now she wasn't so sure. Because the way he'd kissed her . . .

Oh, heavens, the man knew exactly how to kiss. There was no hesitation or awkwardness. He just seized a woman and ravished her mouth like a marauding Viking. Thoroughly. Repeatedly. With great enthusiasm.

But he'd promised not to do it again. Could she trust that? She'd never had a man desire her so intently before. And his attraction to her had *not* been feigned. She'd felt his arousal when he'd held her.

Sadly, she shared the attraction. She wasn't sure why. Yes, he had an interesting face and brooding eyes and a mouth that could turn any woman wanton, but he was also childish and arrogant. Such men generally annoyed her.

It was just that he seemed so very . . . lost. Tonight, his nonchalant mask had slipped long enough to reveal the bravado beneath. He was like the orphan boys who told everyone they didn't *need* parents, so they could hide how very desperately they did.

But *he* had a mother who loved him. Somehow Camilla had to make him see how precious that was. For the good of everyone.

Right. Selfless altruism is your only motive.

She pushed away from the wall. All right, so there was more to it than that. She wanted not to be at odds with him. She wanted another chance at feeling that warm mouth on hers and those knowing hands kneading her flesh . . .

Sweet heaven, she must be losing her mind! The last thing she needed was to make a lover out of her employer. Once an affair with him ended—and it always did with men like him—she'd lose both a lover *and* a good position. She couldn't afford that.

Especially when she and Jasper had finally found a family for the first time in their lives. Kenneth had been exactly as Pierce described him. He'd spent all his time in Spitalfields helping the poor, sick, and wicked. She'd run herself ragged to help him with his work and make a home for him and Jasper and rarely received thanks for her trouble. Their home together had been mostly a prison for her. Whereas here . . .

She sighed. Montcliff was a haven. Here she got not only thanks but warmth and kindness and the closest thing she'd ever had to a mother. Here Jasper was flourishing. And she wouldn't ruin that.

Thoughts of her son made her quicken her steps. She paused outside his room to check her reflection in the glass of the case clock and groaned. She looked disheveled and unsettled. Wanton. She couldn't let Maisie see her like this.

Swiftly, she repaired her hair and straightened her bodice, hoping she didn't look as if she'd just been thoroughly kissed by her employer. Her handsome, incredibly virile employer, who'd asked her to read a naughty book and then been horrified to realize it had pictures.

The thought made her smile, then curse herself for being so charmed by it.

Heading resolutely to her room, she entered to find Jasper sound asleep with Maisie dozing beside him. The girl roused as soon as Camilla neared the bed.

"Oh! You're back, are you?" Maisie rubbed sleep from her eyes and rose to help Camilla undress. If she noticed anything untoward, she didn't mention it.

But Camilla couldn't relax until the girl had left for the maids' rooms, upstairs. Even then it took her a while to get to sleep. She kept remembering his lordship's husky voice: *Even I know better. But it doesn't stop me from wanting to. Or you from wanting me to.*

That was the worst of it—she really *had* wanted him to kiss her. To keep kissing her. And to do even more.

She'd never been kissed with such passion. How alarming to discover that she would very much like it to happen again. Like delicious desserts, kisses provoked cravings for more at odd hours. And she'd never been good at resisting dessert . . .

Oh, she'd have to watch herself around him until she and the countess settled back into their normal life.

But that wasn't what Camilla wanted, either. Clearly, her ladyship and Pierce were both miserable in their present state. If she could just figure out what had torn them apart, then perhaps she could . . . could . . .

What? Knit them back together? She sighed. She hadn't even been able to turn her marriage of convenience into something solid. Why on earth did she think she could mend this very broken relationship?

Especially when she had only one more night in which to do it.

9

To Camilla's shock, it turned out to be more than one night, and for the most unlikely of reasons. His lordship's whim.

The night she'd gone to play piquet with him, he had indeed trounced her. Then he'd stated offhandedly that he had more work to do concerning the estate, so he was staying another day. He might as well have dinner with her and his mother again. If Camilla would agree—again—to come to his bedchamber to "entertain" him afterward.

So she had. And he'd stayed another day.

Then another. And another. Then three more. Each time, he'd claimed that some matter of estate business kept him at Montcliff.

She would have believed him, except that it wasn't estate business that had him staying at the dower house instead of the manor. Or dining with her and the countess every evening. Or demanding that she come to his room afterward. She didn't know what to make of it.

She didn't know what to make of *him*. As far as she could tell, nothing had changed between him and his mother. Their dinners were still awkward. The earl was largely quiet during dinner, unless Camilla drew him into a conversation that interested him. She found herself making a game of figuring out what would engage him enough to keep him from bolting his dinner and running off to have his cigar.

Meanwhile, the countess seemed grateful for every halfway polite word he bestowed on her. It made Camilla want to slap him. And given how congenial he could be when her ladyship wasn't around, his behavior was perplexing, too.

Especially since his mother refused to talk about him, no matter how much Camilla hinted and cajoled and finally asked outright for answers. It sometimes astonished her that neither saw how much alike they were—both of them maddeningly obstinate.

Most disturbing was how he changed when Camilla was alone with him in the evenings. He turned into the clever, entertaining, and utterly false creature whom she'd begun to call Devil May Care Devonmont. Oh, she didn't think he lied to her, but that was only because he didn't discuss anything worth lying about. He hid his true opinions, his real self, beneath layers of wit.

They played chess and cards, they read books, and last night she'd told him amusing stories about her years as a lady's companion. But it was all very superficial. And he hadn't once tried to kiss her. Of course, that was a relief—or so she told herself every time she saw Jasper.

But sometimes, in those moments at the end of the evenings with him, while she was holding her breath and wondering if this would be the last time she saw him, she found herself wanting so fiercely for him to kiss her that she had to crush the urge to throw herself at him. Because it maddened her that he hid himself from her. It made her want to force him out of his facade.

And she was *still* no closer to finding out why he and his mother were at odds, *still* no closer to mending the breach between them. It was enough to make a sane woman run mad through the estate.

Now, as she sat in the drawing room with the countess and Jasper, she wondered yet again how to convince the countess to confide in her. Camilla could sense his lordship's growing impatience to be away, feel his building irritation with the situation. She might not have much more time to uncover the truth.

Unfortunately, today wasn't ideal for raising the subject. Since Pierce was at Montcliff Manor handling estate affairs and wouldn't return until dinner, she and Lady Devonmont were spending the afternoon with Jasper. And Jasper's presence made it awfully difficult to have a deep discussion with the countess.

Lady Devonmont glanced up from the stocking she was embroidering. "That looks lovely. The net bags were an excellent idea."

Camilla wrapped another circle of net about a few walnuts, then tied it with a ribbon so it could be hung on the tree. "How many do you think we should make?"

"Lots and lots!" Jasper said from his seat at the table. "Then my soldiers can have some nuts to eat, too."

After Pierce had begun extending his stay, her ladyship had told Jasper that he would get a tin soldier for every day he stayed out of his lordship's way. He was up to six now, and for the past twenty minutes he'd been keeping the little fellows engaged in a lively battle. That was ten minutes longer than he could usually keep his mind on one thing.

"What makes you think these nuts are for *you,* muffin?" Camilla teased.

He shot her an alarmed frown. "Won't I get any of them?"

"Of course you will," Lady Devonmont said soothingly. "We'll give you some now if you like."

"Not before dinner," Camilla cautioned.

"Oh, a few won't hurt him." The countess put aside her embroidery to crack open several nuts and hand the meats to Jasper. "There, my boy."

"What do you say?" Camilla asked.

"Thank you, my lady." He downed them in a flash, then asked, "Can I have the shells, too?"

Looking perplexed, the countess handed them over. Jasper turned them into pieces of the battle landscape and continued with his explosions and attacks as Camilla and her ladyship laughed.

After a while, however, he grew bored with that and glanced over to where the countess was embroidering. "Is that a stocking like in the poem? The ones that are 'hung by the chimney with care'?"

"That's the idea," Lady Devonmont said. "We're hoping to

start a new tradition in Stocking Pelham. Given the name of our town, why not? We could make Stocking Pelham famous for stockings. And at the same time make some money for the church by selling them at the fair."

"So everyone can hang them by their chimneys 'in hopes that St. Nicholas soon will be there.'"

Camilla eyed him in surprise. "You remember that."

He nodded. "I know the whole poem by heart."

She and her ladyship exchanged a skeptical glance.

"I do! I really do. After the part about the stockings, it says, 'The children were nestled all snug in their beds, / While visions of sugarplums danced in their heads.'"

"Very good," the countess said.

"I *like* sugarplums," Jasper announced slyly.

"So do I," said her ladyship with a grin. "We'll have to get some."

Camilla rolled her eyes. Either the countess was oblivious to how deft Jasper was at extracting treats from her, or she didn't care. Camilla suspected it was the latter.

"Then the next part says:

And Mama in her 'kerchief, and I in my cap,
Had just settled down for a long winter's nap.

When out on the lawn there arose such a clatter
I sprang from my bed to see what was the matter . . ."

He cast Camilla a knowing glance. "It was St. Nicholas, you see."

"Aren't you getting ahead of the story?" the countess asked with a soft smile.

But Jasper had apparently given up on a word-for-word recitation and had settled for paraphrasing. "He's on the sleigh with the tiny reindeer and—" He halted. "What's a sleigh?"

"It's like a sled, only big," Camilla said.

"Or like a carriage for driving on snow," her ladyship said.

"And for flying, right?"

Lady Devonmont glanced at Camilla, amusement in her gaze. "Well, I've never seen one that flies."

"But St. Nicholas has one. That's how he gets up to the roof to come down the chimney."

"The reindeer pull him up there," her ladyship reminded him.

"Right." He ticked them off on his fingers. "Dasher and Dancer and Prancer and Vixen and Comet and Cupid and Dunder and Blixem."

"You know all their names?" Camilla said, rather surprised. He really did have the poem memorized. Or mostly, anyway.

He held up his toy soldiers. "That's what I named the fellows. Well, six of them. I don't have Dunder and Blixem yet."

Camilla swallowed. Her ladyship would have to invent a reason to give him Dunder and Blixem if his lordship didn't stay.

"What will you do when you have all eight?" the countess asked him.

"Why, make them pull a sleigh, of course. They're soldiers, so they're very strong." He frowned. "That's why I need to know what a sleigh is. So I can get them one."

"Ah," her ladyship said.

"Do you think they might have one at the fair that I could look at?"

Camilla sighed. No matter what she told him, he couldn't give up the idea of attending the fair. "I told you before, dearest, we can't go."

He looked crestfallen. "I could pretend to be your groom."

"Aside from the fact that you're too young, everyone in town knows that I don't ride," Camilla said gently.

She'd never learned. Indeed, she'd hoped when she took this post that she might get to do so, for she could imagine nothing more enticing than racing along a road on horseback.

But alas, her ladyship had a bad hip that made riding painful, so the possibility never arose. "And since her ladyship doesn't, either, no one would believe that you're our groom."

"You know what?" the countess put in. "I think there just might be a picture of a sleigh over there in one of the books on the bookcase. It's the one about travels in America and Canada. Do you think you could find it?"

"Yes, my lady!" He grabbed up his soldiers and carried them off to the bookcase.

"That's all he's been talking about for the past week," Camilla said in an undertone. "Going to the fair."

The countess cast her a rueful smile. "Earlier he told me he wanted to go so he could buy you a present. When I asked him how he would pay for it, he thought a bit, then said he would sell the soldiers I'd given him."

"Oh, dear." Camilla's throat tightened. How sweet that was.

"You're so lucky," Lady Devonmont said wistfully as she watched him hunt through the books. "To have a son who would do anything for you, even sell his own toys."

Camilla caught her breath. Now was her chance to bring up the subject of her ladyship's relationship with Pierce. "Yes. I'm lucky to have a son who doesn't begrudge me a few 'baubles.'"

The countess stiffened, then leveled a dark gaze on her. "What do you mean by that?"

Camilla chose her words carefully. "Didn't you hear his lordship at dinner his first night? Haven't you noticed how he keeps attempting to provoke you into asking for money?"

Lady Devonmont frowned. "Well, yes, but I just figured he's like most men—worried about finances."

"Actually . . ." She debated, but decided it would be better for the countess to hear it from her than from the earl one night when he was in a black mood. "The earl thinks that you . . . He seems to be laboring under a misapprehension that . . . well . . you want him here so you can ask him for more funds."

Any fears she might have had that his lordship was right were instantly put to rest by his mother's astonished expression. "The devil you say!"

"He thinks you married his father only for his money, and now that your husband is gone . . ."

"Ah." Lady Devonmont visibly withdrew. "I see that my son has ignored what I said in my letters, preferring to listen to old gossip."

"Which is clearly lies," Camilla said.

The countess forced a smile. "I'm afraid not. I mean, the idea that I want more money from Pierce is absurd, but . . ."

When she paused, Camilla drew in a ragged breath. "But?"

"I did marry Pierce's father for his fortune." Her gaze grew distant. "My late husband made sure of that."

Camilla frowned. "What do you mean?"

Just then Maisie burst into the drawing room. "His lordship is coming up the front steps!"

"So soon?" Camilla jumped up.

"He must have finished his business early," her ladyship murmured. "He probably won't come in here, but just in case—"

Camilla was already rushing over to Jasper. "You must go with Maisie now, dear. The earl is coming."

"But I just found the book!" he complained.

"Take it with you, and Maisie will show you the picture." Swiftly Camilla grabbed the tin soldiers sitting on the top of the case and thrust them into his hand.

They heard boot steps in the hall as Lady Devonmont scanned the room, looking for anything else that might give Jasper away. Grabbing up Jasper and the book, Maisie darted to the servants' door.

She slipped through it right before the boot steps paused outside the drawing room. Camilla hurriedly took a seat at the table, as did the countess, although it was highly unlikely Pierce would come in. He avoided them except at dinner, and he already knew that they spent most of their afternoons in the drawing room.

So she was quite surprised when the door opened and he stepped inside.

Trying to quell her pounding heart, she looked up and forced a smile. "Good afternoon, my lord."

"Good afternoon, ladies." He glanced about the room and then frowned. "I could have sworn I heard a child's voice coming from in here."

Camilla swallowed hard. What on earth was she to say to *that*?

10

Pierce was surprised that Camilla looked panicked by his appearance.

"A child?" his mother said with a brittle laugh. "You must have heard us talking, that's all."

"Probably." His remark had merely been an excuse for entering the drawing room. He knew this old house well; sounds could travel and change within it. He didn't really care what he'd heard. He'd just seized on a chance to talk to Camilla.

He was tiring of seeing her only during their stiff dinners with his mother and their slightly less stiff encounters after. He wanted to see her during the day, to catch her unawares in her natural environment, when she wasn't on her guard against him—as she was in his bedchamber, thanks to his unwise kisses that first night. She showed her carefree side only to his mother, never to *him*.

That was one reason he was still here after a week. At first he'd stayed to prove to her—and himself—that he was in complete control of his emotions when it came to Mother. That he was no longer bound to the pain of the past. But that soon changed into a determination to figure out why a woman as astute as Camilla continued to champion a woman like his mother.

He couldn't understand her, and it nagged at him. So he had come in here, hoping that Mother might be upstairs napping and he could chat alone with Camilla in a place where she didn't feel threatened.

No such luck.

He chided himself for the keen disappointment that shot through him. Apparently this idiotic behavior was what happened when he denied himself a woman he desired, something that had never occurred before. That would explain why he was reacting like some besotted arse.

Yet he couldn't bring himself to leave the room.

Something was going on. He could feel it. Camilla's hands shook as she fiddled with some piece of fabric. And for the first time since his arrival a week ago, Mother wasn't pretending to be happy to see him. Her mouth was set in a thin line, and she was stabbing her needle with sharp strokes into her embroidery.

"You're back early, aren't you, my lord?" Camilla said.

He focused on her. "It started to snow, so I came back in case it got too deep for riding."

"It's snowing?" Camilla said. "Oh, dear, I hope that doesn't ruin things for the day after tomorrow."

"What's happening then?" he asked.

"The fair that's held in Stocking Pelham twice a year," Camilla explained. "I suppose you haven't been to one in a while."

"A long while." Pierce shot his mother a veiled glance, wondering if she remembered. "I was about eight the last time. In fact, I believe it was the same one—right before Christmas."

Mother had the good grace to color. "Yes, that was the one."

When silence stretched out between them, Camilla sought to smooth over the awkwardness. "Your mother and I are running a booth to raise money for repairs to the church's organ. It's in bad need of refurbishment."

"Ah."

Feeling like an intruder, he scanned the room he'd avoided heretofore. He'd forgotten how cozy it was, with its large hearth, its faded but thick carpet, and the pianoforte his fingers itched to play.

Odd that Mother had done nothing to make the room more fashionable. It had the same peeling red wallpaper with a large pomegranate design, the same mahogany Pembroke table with its matching chairs upholstered in red velvet, and the same marble pedestal displaying a bronze bust of the first Earl of Devonmont. It even had the same cold draft coming from the window.

It all felt terribly familiar. He'd spent many an hour here as a boy, playing at Mother's feet or sitting beside her on the bench as he learned to play the pianoforte.

Shoving that disquieting memory from his mind, he wandered over to the table and noted the walnuts, net, and festive ribbon. "What's all this? Something for the booth?"

"Bags of nuts for our Christmas tree," Camilla said.

That damned tree again. "You're eating as many as you bag, apparently," he quipped as he swept some shells to the side. Beneath the pile, he found a tin soldier.

He froze, recognizing it as one of his. He'd played with an entire set of them as a boy. His father had given them to him, no doubt to encourage him in warlike pursuits, but he'd pretended the tiny figures were all explorers and had sent them off on great adventures.

He'd wanted to take them with him to Harrow, but the rules hadn't allowed it. Little had he known that it would be the last time he would see them.

"Are you planning to hang tin soldiers on the tree as well?" he asked hoarsely, unable to look at his mother as he turned the toy round in his hand.

"Why not?" Mother said with an edge in her voice. "There are plenty of them. They'd make an original 'bauble,' don't you think?"

He lifted a bitter gaze to her. "They certainly make an inexpensive one. I'm surprised you don't want something more costly, though."

"I can't imagine why you're surprised by that," his mother said sharply. "I've never cared about it before."

"My lord, perhaps you would like—" Camilla began.

"Oh, don't pretend with me, Mother," Pierce snapped. He

was tired of waiting for Mother to show her true self. It was time to force her into it. "We both know that you care a great deal about money. For once in your life, be honest and admit that this entire farce is about your wanting to get your hands on Father's fortune."

She paled. "Camilla, dear, if you would leave me and Pierce alone to have a private word . . ."

When Camilla rose, Pierce stayed her with a glance. "What my mother doesn't want you to know is that my maternal grandfather, the baron, liked to live a bit too well for his income. Mother grew up in luxury, but by the time she was old enough to marry, Grandfather Gilchrist had been forced to economize, which I gather he wasn't very good at. That's why Mother cast her net for Father, so she could return to the wealth and prestige of her girlhood."

He smiled coolly at his mother. Let her deny it to his face, damn her.

But her gaze on him was steady and unabashed. "Since you seem determined to air our family affairs before Camilla, pray do not mince words. As you know perfectly well, my papa wasn't ruined by high living but by gambling. He amassed so many debts that he was in danger of going to debtors' prison."

That took Pierce completely aback.

Mother shifted her gaze to Camilla. "Pierce's father bought up all of Papa's vowels and offered to forgive them entirely in exchange for my hand in marriage. So yes, I married him. It seemed the best course of action at the time." She rose abruptly, her color high. "Now, if you'll excuse me, I'll get someone to bring us some tea."

Pierce stared, thunderstruck, as his mother swept from the room. What the hell was she talking about?

"You didn't know," Camilla said in a hushed tone.

He glared at her. "She's lying."

"Why would she? That would mean telling the sort of secret about her family that no woman could want known. And telling it before me, who isn't part of your family."

Her logic beat at his defenses. "Then why is this the first time I'm hearing it?" Shoving the tin soldier into his coat pocket, he paced beside the table. "My cousins told me she married Father for his fortune. And it took a great deal of wheedling for me to find out the little I know—that Grandfather was practically penniless when Mother married Father. There was no mention of gambling debts."

Abruptly he realized why. Who would have told him? Father's last solicitor had been hired well into the marriage. The Waverlys were from Father's side of the family; they would know only what they'd been told. And Father would have been too proud to let it be known how he'd acquired his wife.

Consumed by a need to hear it all, Pierce strode out the door, with Camilla following. They both stopped short when they found the countess standing there, breathing hard, clearly trying to regain her composure.

"Father *bought* you?" he demanded.

Setting her shoulders, Mother faced him. "Don't be so dramatic. He courted me like any other gentleman. He just made sure that his suit would be received more favorably than most. I could have refused him. No one forced me to accept, not even your grandfather." She tipped up her chin. "I made my own choice."

He stared at her. Perhaps. But somehow it didn't seem quite as mercenary as before. "I didn't know," he rasped. "I never knew any of this."

She looked perplexed. "But I explained it in my letters."

Pierce felt the familiar guilt like a punch to his gut.

She must have read it in his face, for she paled. "You didn't read them." When he let out a low curse and turned away, she murmured, "I thought you just . . . couldn't forgive me for . . . I understood that, considering. But you didn't . . . you haven't even . . ."

Releasing a low moan, she turned for the stairs. "Pray excuse me. I feel a sudden headache coming on."

Camilla watched as his mother fled, then whirled on him with eyes flashing. "You didn't read them? *Any* of them? I thought you might just have been ignoring what they said, but not to read them at all . . ."

The outrage in her voice roused his own temper. "Don't condemn me without knowing the entirety of the case." He nodded jerkily toward the stairs. "Didn't you hear her speak of my not being able to forgive her? Don't you wonder what it is I can't forgive her for?"

"Oh, I'm sure you blame her for all sorts of silly things."

"Silly thi—" He choked out a laugh. "Ask her about my matriculation from Harrow, about every school holiday." He scowled at her. "Ask her what happened when I came into my majority. I daresay she won't answer you. And until she does, you have no right to judge me."

"Why not tell me yourself?" she demanded.

"You're not going to believe any of it unless you hear it from her. That has become perfectly clear."

Besides, before he destroyed Camilla's faith in his mother, he needed to know more of the truth. He was obviously missing a few pieces.

Wheeling around, he walked away and headed toward his father's old study, the one place where he might find answers. But when he reached it, he halted at the door. He couldn't bring himself to go in there—not after the last time.

In any case, if Father had left documentation, it would be at Montcliff Manor, not here, since he and Mother moved into the manor when Pierce was twenty-two. And after Pierce inherited, he went through every inch of the place, looked over all his father's papers for some indication of the truth. He found nothing.

Perhaps you should have read her letters.

Mother's expression when she realized he hadn't swam into his mind. She'd looked wounded. Shocked. Betrayed.

The eight-year-old inside him wanted to shout, "Good! Now you know what it's like to be ignored and abandoned!"

But the mature man felt shame—then anger at himself for even feeling shame. Why was he letting her affect him? For all he knew, she was inventing this to suit her needs. Had she given any proof in her letters? Referred him to anyone who might confirm her tale?

Damn it, he should have read them, if only to be prepared for whatever she threw at him. That would have put him ahead of the game when he came here. Now he had to muddle through this as best he could.

Had she really written to him about Grandfather's gambling? She must have—she'd assumed he'd read the letters, so there'd be no point now in her lying about *that*. What else might she have told him? Something to explain her complete lack of interest in him until two years ago?

No, at Father's funeral, she'd refused outright to give him answers. There was no reason to think she had put them in a letter, especially given her reticence to talk about the past since he'd been here. But the fact that he'd so thoroughly misunderstood the nature of his parents' marriage made him wonder what else he'd misunderstood.

He threaded his fingers through his hair. If Grandfather had sold her to Father, if it really hadn't been a love match, then perhaps Father had been behind her refusal to see her son. Might he have threatened her with something to keep her by his side and away from Pierce?

That made no sense. Why would Father essentially abandon his only heir? Why would he demand that she do the same? Besides, that day when he'd come here at twenty-one, she had been just as cruel as, if not more so than, Father when—

He spat an oath. It made far more sense to believe that Mother had thrown in her lot with the man who could give her everything, and Pierce had been an inconvenience. When he was in school, he always read of Lord and Lady Devonmont flitting to this dinner or that ball in Bath or York or London. They'd seemed to be going incessantly to house parties with the loftiest members of society.

At the same time, it was getting harder and harder to see Mother as some . . . frivolous, money-grubbing female who'd snagged an earl to move up in society.

His throat tightened. This was why he hadn't wanted to come here, damn it! There were no answers here, just more questions, more opening of wounds he thought he'd sewn shut with steel thread.

Damn her! *And* her meddling companion.

That thought swirled in his brain the rest of the afternoon, fortifying him for dinner. He would demand to know what was in the letters. Then he would demand to know what exactly she wanted from him after so many years of neglect. And if she wouldn't tell him, he would lay out for Camilla why he'd been estranged from his parents.

Yes, that's what he would do.

But when he came down to dinner, fully prepared for a confrontation, no one was there. On his plate was a folded sheet of paper addressed to "Lord Devonmont" in what must be Camilla's hand, since it certainly wasn't his mother's.

He gritted his teeth. God, but he was sick of missives. Letters were what people resorted to when they didn't want to lie to your face. When they wanted to pretend they weren't ripping your heart out.

With an oath, he opened it to read:

Your Lordship,

Your mother has a fierce headache and will not be coming down to dinner. With your permission, I shall stay with her this evening.

Sincerely,

Mrs. Stuart

Balling it up, he tossed it into the fire. With his permission—right. As if he had any say in the matter.

He could read between the lines. No dinner with Mother, so no evening with Camilla. He was being punished—for speaking the truth, for not reading Mother's letters. Punished for not opening Camilla's eyes to what his mother really was.

Except he wasn't sure anymore what his mother really was. *Who* she was. He couldn't even be sure anymore what he meant to her.

And that was driving him insane.

11

Camilla paced the countess's sitting room, praying that she would emerge soon. The lady's maid insisted that her ladyship had asked not to be disturbed because of her headache.

Camilla sighed. More likely, the woman's heart had been cleaved in two by her unfeeling son.

Ask her what happened when I came into my majority. I daresay she won't answer you. And until she does, you have no right to judge me.

All right, so perhaps he wasn't so much unfeeling as wounded. But why? And how? As a paid companion, she'd seen plenty of families torn apart over foolish nonsense—a father embarrassing his son in public, a daughter who turned down a marriage proposal. Families were difficult to fathom.

But she began to think it wasn't something small that had torn this family apart. The rift seemed deeper and wider than she'd assumed.

Perhaps Pierce was right. Perhaps she should *not* have meddled. Certainly she'd brought more pain to Lady Devonmont in the process. Still, how could he not have read his own mother's letters? It didn't seem worthy of him.

Then again, she didn't really know him, despite having spent a week of evenings with him. He was entertaining—witty, clever, and even charming when he wanted to be. She'd poked at his mask, lifted it a bit, tried to peek beneath it, but whenever she got a good glimpse of his real self, he jerked the mask back into place.

It was maddening.

The door to the bedroom opened, and the countess walked out. At once Camilla's heart dropped into her stomach. Her ladyship's eyes and nose were red, her features drawn.

She looked startled to see Camilla. "I thought you'd be at dinner."

"I'm not about to abandon you when you're upset."

The countess forced a smile. "I'm not upset. I'm just a bit . . ." Her face began to crumple, and she turned away to hide it.

"You *are* upset, and you have every right to be so." Camilla hurried over to put her arm about the woman's shoulders. "It was cruel of him to ignore your letters."

"He had his reasons," she choked out.

"You keep saying that. But what could they possibly be?" When the countess just shook her head and pulled free to walk back toward her bedchamber, Camilla steadied her nerve and added, "He told me to ask you about his holidays from school."

Lady Devonmont froze.

"He didn't tell me why I should ask, and he wouldn't tell me why he mentioned it. He left that to you. Why? What happened during his holidays?"

The countess stood there a long moment, as if debating something. Then she sighed. "Nothing happened. That's the trouble."

"If nothing happened, then why—"

"I wasn't around for his holidays. *That's* what he wants you to know."

Camilla blinked, sure that she had misunderstood. No feeling mother was absent for her child's holidays from school. "None of them? No Christmases, no Easters?"

"Not a one," she whispered.

Shock coursed through her. Even when she'd been forced to leave Jasper with her husband's family, she'd always made an effort to be with him for important occasions. She couldn't imagine not seeing Jasper for Christmas, for pity's sake.

The rest of Pierce's words leaped into her mind. "And his matriculation ceremony? He said I should ask about that, too. Don't tell me you weren't there for that, either."

The countess faced her with a shattered expression. "He spent every school holiday from the time he was eight with his cousins at Waverly Farm. They were the ones, along with his great-uncle, to attend his matriculation ceremony. I couldn't go. I wasn't allowed."

"What do you mean?"

Lady Devonmont's eyes, the same warm brown as Pierce's,

darkened, and she released a long, tortured breath. "Pierce's father wouldn't allow it."

"The earl?"

"Yes, of course the earl," she snapped. "Who else?"

"Right, sorry," Camilla mumbled. Her mind reeled at the very idea of Pierce being left to relations when he had two perfectly good parents. "I don't understand."

"Of course you don't. Neither does Pierce."

No, how could he? It must have driven a stake through his heart to essentially lose his parents so young. He'd been only two years older than Jasper!

Her ladyship began to pace. "That's why I've never told him that his father was the reason for my absence. Because it would only raise more questions that I can't answer."

"So you don't know why the earl kept you from your son?" she said incredulously.

"I do know why." The countess's face closed up. "But I shan't discuss it. I can't. Some things must remain private."

"Private? The reason your son was abandoned is something you consider *private*?" Camilla cried. "I daresay he deserves to know why."

"He does, but I can't . . ." Her voice broke. "I won't speak of it. I begged his forgiveness in my letters for not being a mother to him all those years, and I understand if he can't forgive me. But as I told him, I had good reasons for agreeing to let others raise him. I did what I had to. He will simply have to accept it."

Camilla gaped at her. "Don't you see why he can't, not without knowing why?"

The countess shot her a warning glance. "Stay out of this, my dear."

"How can I, when I see how it pains you both?"

"Curse it, why can't you both just leave the past be? Why can't we just start anew and forget—"

"Because you can't! Not if you want to repair your relationship with your son."

Her ladyship let out a low moan but wouldn't say more.

"Why wouldn't the earl let you see him?"

The countess just shook her head.

Drat it, the woman was as stubborn as Pierce! And what did she mean, some things were private?

Oh. Camilla could think of only one reason the countess might feel a need for privacy in such a situation. And it would explain why her ladyship had snapped at Camilla for unwittingly implying that Pierce wasn't the earl's son.

Perhaps Pierce really *wasn't* the earl's son.

It would explain so much—why the countess didn't want to talk about it, why Pierce didn't want to talk about it. If he were another man's son . . .

The thought brought her up short. She'd seen a portrait of the late earl. Pierce was the very image of his father. Anyone with eyes could tell *that*.

Besides which, he'd been born well on the right side of the blanket, for the countess often said she'd had him ten months after her marriage at eighteen. And while Camilla could almost imagine the countess giving herself to one man, and then being forced to marry another after she found herself with a babe in her belly, Camilla had trouble imagining her ladyship as an adulteress. Especially married to a man as rigid as the earl.

Nor did Pierce seem to think such a thing. Surely he would have hinted at it if he'd known. But perhaps he didn't know. *If* there was even anything to know, which she began to doubt. He *did* look amazingly like his father.

Which meant something else was at work here.

Remembering other things Pierce said, Camilla added, "At least tell me what happened when he reached his majority. He said you would never say."

The color drained from Lady Devonmont's face. "He's right."

"But why?"

"Because . . . because you would hate me if I told you." Her throat moved convulsively. "And I just can't . . . bear to have you hating me, too."

Camilla couldn't imagine anything her ladyship could have done that would be as awful as all that. "I would never hate you, my lady. If you'd only explain—"

"Enough, curse it!" The countess drew into herself, putting on her own mask—a cold, uncaring one that didn't hide a thing, for her eyes blazed bright within it.

Then she turned on her heel and headed for her bedchamber. "I'm retiring for the evening. We will not speak of this again."

"But, my lady—"

"No!" She halted just short of the door, her shoulders trembling as if she fought to contain tears. Then she seemed to steady herself. "I never asked you to interfere in this, Camilla, and if you continue . . ." She left the words hanging, but the implication was clear.

Camilla choked down the sudden raw pain in her throat. Her ladyship would never dismiss her. Would she? No, Camilla couldn't believe it. But the fact that she would even threaten such a thing showed how desperate she was.

It also showed that Camilla had gone as far as she dared. It was one thing to defy the earl. But defying the woman who'd been good enough to bring Jasper here would be madness. She couldn't afford to behave irrationally; she had her son to think of.

"As you wish," Camilla said quietly. "We won't speak of it again."

But that didn't mean she would stop trying to learn more another way.

As soon as the countess gave a tight nod and disappeared into her bedchamber, Camilla turned on her heel and headed for the earl's room. She was tired of seeing two people she'd begun to care about hitting their heads against the brick wall of the past.

Part of her understood. There were things about her own past that she'd rather not have revealed. But this was carrying "privacy" too far. At least when *she* had briefly given her son over to relatives to be raised, she'd told him why. He'd never doubted that his mother loved him.

Clearly Pierce doubted that very deeply. Something inside her chest twisted at the thought. She hadn't known her own parents, which was why she realized how precious it was to have ones you could trust and believe in.

She knocked on the door. His voice bade her enter. Drumming up her courage, she opened the door, only to find the room completely dark. The fire had burned out, and there were no candles lit except the one in her hand.

Sweet heaven, he must already have retired for the night.

"I beg your pardon," she mumbled, and began to ease the door shut.

"Don't go," he said, his voice low but commanding. It certainly wasn't the voice of someone just roused from sleep.

She hesitated. "I think I must."

"I'm not in bed. I'm just sitting here in the dark." A hint of sarcasm laced his tone. "I'm fully dressed, and I promise not to pounce." When she still stood uncertain, he said, more softly, "Please come in and keep me company awhile."

Please. It was a word he rarely used—a word that men of his rank had no need to use. But something in the tenor of his voice, in the way he asked for her company so humbly, made tears start in her eyes. No doubt he'd asked for his mother's company many times in his childhood and never got it.

She slipped inside, shutting the door behind her. As her eyes adjusted to the dim room, she saw him in his favorite armchair, which he'd apparently dragged over to face the window. "Do you often sit in the dark?" she asked as she headed toward him.

"Only when there's a full moon and snow on the ground." He gestured before him. "Look at that."

She had to blow out the candle to be able to see beyond her reflection in the glass, but when she did, she was treated to a rapturous view. Spread out below them was the snow-draped lawn, turned magical by moonlight. The bushes were like frosted cakes served up on a blanket of marzipan, and footsteps in the snow looked like almonds dotting the pastry of a tart. Only the black, leafless beeches skirting the edge of the gardens struck a somber note.

"I used to love this view." His voice was a rumble in the dark. "During the day, you can see the dairy, the trout stream, even a few tenants' cottages. When I sat here as a boy, I imagined what it would be like once I inherited. I had grand plans for the estate. I was going to be the benevolent ruler of all from this very room, even though it wasn't the master bedchamber."

A choked laugh escaped him. "Of course, Father, in his infinite idiocy, decided to build a bigger, grander palace next door. He never liked this house. He said it was too dilapidated to be worthy of an earl. So now when I come to Hertfordshire, I spend my days in a soulless mausoleum that doesn't have one tenth of the charm and beauty of this old place."

He shook his head. "Meanwhile, Mother lives in the place I love. And all because I thought to punish her. I assumed she hated it as much as Father did. That she must have been the one to press him into building Montcliff Manor." His voice turned distant. "Instead, she settled in here and made it her own, as cozy and warm as I remember from my childhood. I thought my fond memories of that time were an illusion. Now I just don't know."

Her heart leaped into her throat. So that was why he'd said this was his favorite room. And why he'd said that first day that it wasn't *his*. If the countess were to be believed, he'd never had a room in this house, except the nursery.

But he'd mentioned something that had happened when he

reached his majority. Had he lived here briefly? She had to find out.

"I asked your mother those questions you told me to," she ventured.

When she heard his sharp intake of breath, she wondered if she should have left the subject alone. But he had started this, and surely he had expected a report once she'd done as he commanded.

A long moment passed before he rasped, "Did she answer you?"

"Somewhat. From what she said, I gather that you left home to go to school at eight and weren't brought back here for years. You spent holidays with your cousins?"

He gave a terse nod.

"Did anyone ever say why?"

"The Waverlys gave different reasons each time." His voice grew taut, thick. "They told me my parents were in Brighton or they'd gone to a house party in York. Or they were in London for the season." He fisted his hands in his lap. "There was always some excuse. But it all came down to one thing—Mother and Father were flitting about the country to anywhere that *I* wasn't."

"Oh, Pierce," she murmured, trying to imagine what that must have been like. It seemed almost worse to have parents who willfully abandoned you than to have no parents at all.

She wanted to tell him what his mother had said about not being *allowed* to see him, but he seemed willing to speak of the past here in the dark. She was loath to say anything that might stop the flow of words—*genuine* words—about himself and his childhood.

"At first I wrote to Mother," he went on. "Once a week, faithfully. But she didn't write back, and after a couple of years I stopped. By then the Waverlys had also stopped making excuses for why my parents—" He muttered a curse under his breath, then went on in a harder tone. "Why they didn't want to see me anymore. My cousins simply adopted me into their family."

"That was very laudable." She might not like Kenneth's brother very much, but he'd been kind to add Jasper to his responsibilities.

She considered telling Pierce about Jasper. It had begun to feel wrong somehow to hide her son from him, but she simply couldn't risk it without being sure how he would react. "Anyone who takes in someone else's child to raise has a core of good in them."

"Yes. They're good people, the Waverlys." He gazed out the window. "They did their best to hide the painful truth from me, but when my parents didn't even bother to show up for my matriculation, I figured out that Mother and Father really didn't want anything to do with me. That they never intended to bring me home."

His voice had grown more choked by the moment, and it made her heart lurch in her chest. "It sounds awful," she whispered.

With a shrug that looked forced, he shot her a quick glance. "Not as awful as growing up in an orphanage, I'd imagine."

"It's not the same, but no less awful. I never knew my parents, so I didn't feel I'd had them snatched from me, the way you must have. The orphanage was all I ever knew."

"Your parents must have died very young then," he said.

They hadn't spoken of her parents before. She'd managed to avoid the subject whenever their conversation headed in that direction. But she couldn't avoid it now.

So she searched for a way not to lie to him. "I went to the orphanage as an infant." That was the truth. But she'd left out so much. "Fortunately, it was a good place—not one of those dreadful ones where they mistreat the children."

He gave a self-deprecating laugh. "You must think me spoiled, to be complaining about not having my parents around when I had so many more advantages than you. I went to Harrow and spent my holidays with fine people like the Waverlys. I even had a sort of parent. My great-uncle Isaac was—still is—like a father to me."

His attempt to put a good face on things made her heart break for him even more. "Not spoiled in the least," she said softly. "It must have been very painful, not knowing why your parents didn't . . ."

"Want me?" he clipped out. "Yes, that was the hardest part. I was always a difficult child, but if they would have told me what I'd done to deserve such banishment—"

"You did nothing to deserve it!" she said hotly. "No child deserves that."

"Then why did they do it?"

She sighed. "Your mother said that your father wouldn't allow her to see you."

He dragged in a heavy breath. "And do you believe her?"

"I do. She was very upset over it." She stared down at his dark head, wishing she dared to stroke his silky hair, to soothe him somehow. "Would your father have done such a thing? She never speaks of him, and none of the servants seem to know what kind of man he was."

"He was an arse most of the time. He never liked having me around. So yes, it's possible."

"Even though you were his heir?"

"That never seemed to matter to him. I honestly don't know what did." After a moment's hesitation, his tone turned speculative. "Although now that I think of it, he was always very possessive of Mother. If he cared about anything, it was her." He glanced up at Camilla. "Did Mother happen to say *why* he kept her from me? Or is that something she put in those letters I didn't read?"

"No." She debated telling him the rest of it, but it might hurt him more to hear that his mother knew the truth and still wouldn't tell him. "I . . . I . . . we did not talk long. She said she would prefer that I . . . stayed out of the matter."

He uttered a harsh laugh. "Clearly she doesn't know you very well."

"I'm sorry," she whispered. "I had no idea when I summoned you here—"

"I realize that you meant well," he said coolly.

"Honestly, I didn't expect all of this." When he said nothing, she realized that she still hadn't gotten answers to some of her questions. And as long as he was in a talkative mood . . . "So you were away from home for ten years? You didn't see them in all that time?"

"More like thirteen years. Until I reached my majority." He

glanced up at her again, the moonlight glinting off his dark eyes. "Did she tell you about that, too?"

"No. That was one question she refused to answer. She said I'd hate her if she did, and she couldn't bear to have us both hating her." Camilla hesitated, then laid her hand on his shoulder. "So you will have to be the one to tell me what happened."

He stiffened. Then, to her disappointment, he shrugged off her hand and rose to pad across the room on stocking feet to the hearth. He bent to start the fire.

When he still didn't say anything, she imagined all sorts of awful scenarios. "Your father didn't . . . I mean, he wasn't the sort of man to knock you around or anything, was he?"

"No, nothing like that," he ground out.

Thank heaven. If his father had abused him somehow, Pierce and his mother might both be reluctant to speak of it. And she supposed that even at twenty-one, Pierce could still have been thrashed by his father.

Or even by— "And . . . what about your mother? She didn't . . . I mean, I can't imagine that she would, but—"

"Neither of them ever laid a hand on me," he assured her. He continued to feed kindling into the burgeoning flame. Then he let out a ragged breath. "But she's right, you know. If you heard the whole story, you might very well hate her. You might even tender your resignation. And I can't have that."

"Why not?"

He rose to face her, his eyes glittering in the firelight. "Because I don't want you to leave."

Her heart thumped madly in her chest. The very air changed,

sparking with meaning. His gaze locked with hers—intense, fathomless . . . hungry.

Then his usual mask shuttered his face, and he shrugged. "After all, I can't afford to lose a good companion for my mother. She needs *someone* to keep her occupied so she won't meddle in estate business. And you seem to do that admirably."

She stood there, stunned, as he strode for the brandy decanter. Once more, Devil May Care Devonmont had reappeared, and it hurt. His words, so casually spoken, hurt.

Then her common sense reasserted itself. Sweet heaven, she had quite the imagination. Had she thought that he might actually care about her? That he might even miss her if she left?

She was losing all sense of proportion. They'd had a handful of kisses one night, which probably meant nothing to a rogue like him. He may have confided in her, but that was only because she was handy. And no matter how many evenings they spent together, he was still an earl, and she still had no connections. Earls did not develop deep feelings for penniless vicars' widows of no consequence. If he wanted her here at all, it was for his mother.

Shoving up her spectacles, she said with determined cheer, "If you are to have any entertainment from me tonight, I suppose we ought to begin. What are you in the mood for?"

He concentrated on pouring brandy and didn't look at her. "Since I didn't dine with Mother, you don't need to stay."

His dismissive tone made it clear that he preferred to be alone. "Of course." She fought to keep the disappointment out of her voice. She'd begun to look forward to their evenings together, but she would die before she let him know it. No doubt he was already growing bored with them.

"Besides," he added, his voice softening, "you haven't had any dinner, I expect. Bad enough that you're having to play the arbiter between me and my mother. Our nonsense shouldn't be the cause of your wasting away."

"I hardly think I'm going to waste away from missing one dinner," she said dryly. "But I do appreciate your concern. And I am a bit hungry, now that you mention it."

Feeling only slightly less disappointed, she headed for the door.

"Camilla," he called out as she reached it.

"Yes?" She turned to look at him.

"Thank you for asking her those questions." He stared down into his glass. "And thank you for giving me the benefit of the doubt when you first found out I hadn't read her letters. I suppose I should have, but—"

"I understand. You were justifiably angry. Sometimes anger provokes a person to do things they might not otherwise. If it makes you feel any better, I don't think she revealed anything of consequence in them."

"What makes you say that?"

"If she won't talk to you about it, and she won't say anything to me, I can't imagine she would put it in a letter." She measured her words, not wanting to wound him more. "Besides, she acted as if she . . . er . . . wasn't ready to talk about it."

He sipped his brandy. "All the same, I'd like to read them, find out what's in them."

"That's probably a good idea."

"And just so you won't think me a complete arse, in the past I did demand answers of her. At Father's funeral, I asked her why the two of them sent me away. She wouldn't say. She just told me she wanted to keep the past in the past."

"She said much the same to me tonight. I told her that it wouldn't work—that she couldn't leave you wondering like that." She shook her head. "She ordered me to stay out of it, so I'm afraid I didn't do much good."

"You did enough," he said enigmatically. He gulped the rest of his brandy, and when he spoke again, he was back to being Devil May Care Devonmont. "Now go have your dinner, before I drag out some naughty books for you to read."

She wanted to ask if he meant to stay, but she had *some* pride, after all. So she left, wishing she hadn't learned so much about him tonight. Before that, she'd been able to keep from caring too deeply for him by reminding herself of how awful he'd been to his mother.

But now, with everything a muddle and her ladyship's hands seeming dirtier by the moment, she was finding it far more difficult to protect her heart.

12

After Camilla left, Pierce poured another glass of brandy. He didn't know what to think. He could see Father wanting to keep Mother to himself, but why had Mother gone along with it? She'd always stood up to Father before. What had changed when Pierce turned eight?

Perhaps she really had just been waiting until he was old enough to be packed off to school. But if she hadn't wanted to send him away, why not write to him? Why not try to see him? By that point, Mother's parents had long been dead, so what hold could Father have possibly had over her that would keep her from a son she truly loved?

Unless she didn't truly love you, came the insidious voice that had plagued him ever since that day at Harrow. *Unless she's just working on you another way, for her own ends.*

He gulped down some brandy, wishing it could wash away his suspicions. But too much had happened between him and Mother; too many questions were left unanswered. Father was dead—she had no reason to keep his secrets anymore. So why was she?

Damn it all!

He threw the glass into the fireplace, feeling only a cursory satisfaction from the sound of it shattering and the sight of the brandy flaring as it caught fire. This madness of incessant questions and uncertainties was precisely what he'd been trying to avoid. He had been better off in London, believing that Mother hated him, believing she merely wanted more of Father's money.

But then you wouldn't have met Camilla.

He stared blindly into the fire. Ah, yes. That was the rub.

Though why he cared about meeting some widow with a warm smile and a generous heart was beyond him.

She understands your pain.

She did. She saw right to the bone of it. Perhaps because she was an orphan, she knew what it was like to yearn for parents. That must be what drew him to her, along with her stubbornness and her loyalty to her charge and the way she made him want and want and . . .

Damn it all to hell! This was mad. He was imagining some intimate connection that simply didn't exist.

Imagination isn't what made you practically beg her not to leave.

Even as he'd said the words, he'd known they were unwise.

She would assume they meant something, when he'd only been clutching at the sympathy she offered.

Right, that's all. And that's why you've never told any other woman the things you told her tonight. That's why you're letting her get under your skin. Because she offers you sympathy.

He swore under his breath. All right, so perhaps there was a bit more to it than that, but only because of this situation with Mother. And all the talk of Christmas. And his painful memories of that day in the study—

No, damn it—he wasn't going to let this affect him! He certainly wasn't going to let *Camilla* affect him. Just because she turned that soulful gaze of hers on him didn't mean he had to spill out all his hurts.

It was time he put her out of his mind. He was a rogue, damn it! He didn't care about anything or anyone. He would go back to London tomorrow.

Taking up another glass, he filled it to the brim with brandy. Tonight he was going to get drunk and forget he'd ever come to this cursed place, forget he'd ever met the meddling Camilla. Then tomorrow morning, he'd be able to see everything with clearer eyes.

So he began to drink. And drink. And drink some more. He carried out his plan with such ruthless determination that by the time he went to bed, he was well and thoroughly sloshed.

Unfortunately, when he awoke midmorning, he was not only incapable of seeing everything with clearer eyes, he was incapable of seeing much of anything without wanting to retch.

Clearly his plan had gone awry. Especially since he belatedly remembered that he'd promised to meet with Fowler this morning to discuss the servant gifts for Boxing Day. The man would await his leisure, of course, but Pierce never liked to keep his people waiting. Father had always done that, and though people said Pierce looked like his father, he didn't want to resemble him in character, not if he could help it.

So Pierce rang for the footman acting as his valet at the dower house and then dragged himself out of bed to call for coffee. It took three cups to still the churning in his belly so he could be dressed. It took another three to steady him for the ride over to Montcliff Manor.

By the time he arrived there, it was nearly noon. So he wasn't surprised to find Fowler hard at work in the study where Pierce did most of the estate business.

When Pierce entered, the man jumped up. "I hope you don't mind, my lord, but I went ahead and started making a list. I thought if I laid everything—"

"It's fine," Pierce gritted out, wishing the man didn't have to speak *quite* so loudly. "I meant to be here sooner."

"No doubt it's hard to sleep comfortably at the dower house," Fowler said politely.

That was an understatement. "You know how it is—an unfamiliar bed and such. Takes some getting used to." As did being around his mother, although being around Camilla took no getting used to at all. He'd never met a woman so easy to converse with.

No, he wasn't going to think about her anymore, remember?

Frowning at his unruly tendency to let her invade his thoughts,

Pierce took his seat behind the desk. Fowler moved around to the front and sat down.

Nearly fifty, Miles Fowler was an interesting fellow. Born a bricklayer's son, he'd won a spot as a poor scholar at Harrow. He'd excelled in all his subjects and had so impressed his school chum the Viscount Rathmoor that the man had hired him as his estate manager.

But then Rathmoor died some years ago, leaving his son, Pierce's schoolboy nemesis George Manton, to inherit everything. Typical of the arse, Manton apparently alienated so many of his servants that several sought other positions, including Fowler.

Pierce never regretted stealing the man out from under Manton's nose. Fowler was a damned good estate manager. Nothing got by him, and he had an impenetrable code of honor.

Unfortunately, he was also very diligent, and today Pierce wasn't in the mood for diligence. His brain still felt like mush as he stared down at the documents and tried to focus.

"I do hope your lordship is finding the rest of the dower house comfortable," Fowler ventured when Pierce remained silent a long while.

It would be infinitely more comfortable if there were no people in it, he wanted to say. Except that wasn't true. He liked having Camilla there.

Damn it, there he went again, thinking about her. "It's fine."

"Good. Because there's something of great importance regarding your stay there that I wish to discuss."

The strain in Fowler's voice came through clearly, forcing

Pierce to pay attention. He sat back in his chair to stare at the older man. "Go on."

"I was shocked to receive a letter from Boyd this morning expressing his concern for her ladyship and wanting more particulars about her condition. Imagine my surprise to hear that you came here last week because of a message from Mrs. Stuart informing you that the countess is deathly ill."

Uh-oh. He should have sent a note of reassurance off to Boyd at once, but in the midst of everything, he'd forgotten that he'd told anyone about Mother's supposed illness. And he hadn't intended to stay here so long.

Fowler was watching him with consternation. "Since you haven't mentioned it and the servants here have heard nothing of it, I can only assume that either your mother never *was* deathly ill or she had a miraculous recovery between the time you left London and the time you arrived here. The servants at the dower house can be very closemouthed about her ladyship, but I doubt that even they would keep such a situation quiet for long."

"You're right," Pierce said smoothly. "My mother is fine." If that term could *ever* be used in connection with her. "It was merely a misunderstanding."

Sadly, Fowler was too sharp a fellow to let Pierce slide that one past. "If you don't mind my asking, sir, what exactly was the nature of the misunderstanding? I thought when I hired Mrs. Stuart that she was a forthright woman. I can't imagine why she would alarm your lordship by inventing some tale about her ladyship being deathly ill."

Inwardly cursing Fowler for being so perceptive, Pierce debated what to tell the man that wouldn't have him marching over to chastise Camilla.

"Because if I'd dreamed that the woman had any propensity to lie," Fowler went on, "I would never—"

"It wasn't Mrs. Stuart's fault," Pierce said firmly. "It was Mother's. She actually had been ill, and she gave Mrs. Stuart to understand that she was more ill than she was."

That was sort of true; Mother had claimed to be pining for him. And if Camilla was to be believed, she really had been.

Fowler's face cleared. "Ah. I see. So Mrs. Stuart was overly hasty in informing you?"

"Exactly. You know the sort of careful woman she is. And once I realized that matters weren't as bad as I'd feared, I was so relieved that I decided to stay on a few days." When Fowler looked perplexed by that, he added, "In case Mother has another bout of illness, you see."

The man nodded, though it was clear that he still found the situation odd and was simply too discreet to say so.

Although Fowler knew that Pierce and his mother were estranged, he didn't know the reasons for it. Pierce hadn't wanted his own feelings to be reflected in how Fowler treated the residents of the dower house.

"But you *are* pleased with Mrs. Stuart," Fowler persisted. "She hasn't done anything to . . . concern you?"

Clearly the man was worried about how Camilla's behavior might reflect on him, as the one who'd hired her.

"Of course I'm pleased with her. Mother seems to like her a great deal."

Relief spread over Fowler's hawkish features. "That's good. Very good." Fowler glanced away. "I thought her ladyship might enjoy having someone young and lively about her. Mrs. Stuart has such a cheery nature that it would be hard *not* to like her."

The man had written similar things about Camilla before, but hearing him speak them gave Pierce pause. "And the lady is quite pretty, too," he ventured as he kept a keen eye on Fowler's face, "which is always an added advantage."

Fowler's startled gaze swung back to Pierce. "Is she? I hadn't noticed."

That was a feigned response if Pierce had ever seen one. "I noticed at once," he said, then added dryly, "but then, I'm considered quite the rogue, and we rogues always notice such things."

An uneasy laugh escaped Fowler. "You'd be wise not to let her ladyship see you 'notice' Mrs. Stuart. Your mother wouldn't approve."

Interesting. "Why not?"

"Lady Devonmont thinks the world of the young widow. She's very protective of her and would be most upset if she thought that you . . . that is, that anyone might try to take advantage of the lady." He added hastily, "Not that you would do such a thing, of course, but your mother might . . . interpret any friendliness toward Mrs. Stuart in that way."

Pierce gave the man a hard stare. Was Fowler trying to warn him off Camilla? And how did he know so much about the relationship between Mother and Camilla anyway?

"You sound as if you spend a great deal of time with my mother and Mrs. Stuart."

"Not a great deal, no." He tugged nervously at his cravat. "But when they invite me to dinner, I generally accept."

"Do they invite you often?"

"Once every couple of weeks. They're amiable ladies, and I sometimes crave a bit of female companionship."

As did every man. But a widower might crave it more than most. And Fowler wasn't too old or ugly to attract a woman, either. Indeed, most women would probably consider him well-favored. His position as estate manager to a wealthy earl would also open the door of many a female heart.

Camilla's? Would she be attracted to Fowler?

A ridiculous thought. Why, the man must be twenty years her senior!

Father was nearly twenty years Mother's senior, and it didn't stop him . . . or her.

"Female companionship can be useful," Pierce said blandly, determined to ferret out the truth.

"It certainly can." Fowler sighed. "With Mrs. Stuart's past experience working at an orphanage, she is always full of sound advice about how to deal with the various servants at the two houses. She has this way of getting right to the heart of the problem—"

"I know exactly what you mean. She's very astute."

"And eager to help and sensible without being overly pushy, as some women are. Between her and her ladyship—" He broke off, coloring a bit, as if realizing how he was gushing about Camilla. "Well, anyway, they are both very informative."

"I see." Oh, yes, he saw a great deal. Fowler had his eye on Camilla. And why wouldn't he? She had an open heart, a sweet manner, and a great deal of common sense. And all of that came in a body that was most appealing. Any man with eyes would want to bed her.

Or court her.

He scowled. Yes, Fowler would aim for that, wouldn't he? He was a respectable widower, probably eager for a second wife. He had no children, so he would want a son.

But did Camilla welcome his attentions? She'd never mentioned the man, but then, she wouldn't. Most employers didn't approve of their servants courting each other.

Was it possible she'd nurtured some secret tendre for Fowler all this time? That Fowler nurtured some secret tendre for her?

There was a very easy way to find out. "Well, then, you should come to dinner this evening," he said, priding himself on the fact that he sounded nonchalant.

Never mind that he'd sworn to return to London today. He didn't feel much like traveling right now anyway, not with this devil of a headache. Besides, it was past noon already, not the best time to start a trip. And what difference would one more night make?

"Come to dinner," he repeated. "It's the least I can do to make up for interrupting a long-standing tradition."

"Oh, no, it hasn't been anything so settled as that, my lord," Fowler said hastily, his cheeks now scarlet. "I wouldn't dream of intruding on your time with your mother."

"Nonsense. It will be nice to have an ally at the table," he said tightly. "The two ladies are wearing me out with all their talk of Christmas preparations."

Fowler relaxed a fraction. "Ah, I can well imagine that."

"If it makes you feel any better, we can discuss business. You have no idea how much that would please me."

That garnered a chuckle from the man. "Believe me, my lord, I'm well aware of how women can go on about such matters."

"So you'll come save me?"

"When you put it that way, how can I refuse?"

"Excellent," Pierce said. "You won't get the fine French fare you'd receive from my table here, but as you've probably noticed, the cook at the dower house is surprisingly good. I'll send word to Mrs. Beasley that you're coming."

Tonight he would watch Fowler and Camilla to figure out just how intimate their connection was. After all, he couldn't have his servants sneaking around behind his back, having assignations, and—

Hypocrite.

He could practically hear Camilla say it. And she'd be right, too. He'd never before cared a fig if any of his servants were courting. What they did in their free time was their own business. As long as it didn't interfere with their work, they were free to hang from the trees like monkeys, as far as he was concerned.

Yet the thought of Camilla keeping secrets from him . . . Damn it, he had to know. He couldn't stand being left in the dark.

And if she *did* fancy Fowler?

Pierce snorted. It wasn't as if he had a claim on her. Just because she had a way of spreading balm over the pain that continually crushed his chest didn't mean anything. Nor did the fact that she looked up at him with those soft, understanding eyes that made him feel as if someone *did* care if he lived or died. And just because she soothed his temper and—

What an idiot he was.

It might be better for him if she *did* have a tendre for Fowler. Because then he could put his obsession with the pretty widow to rest once and for all, before he made a complete bloody fool of himself.

13

Camilla generally didn't mind having Mr. Fowler join them for dinner, but tonight she wished he hadn't come. Especially since his lordship hadn't returned to London. It was silly of her, she knew, but after she and Pierce had talked so intensely last night, she'd hoped . . .

Oh, she didn't know *what* she'd hoped. That they might continue their intimate discussions this evening? That she could play mediator between him and his mother this time, and it might actually work?

That was foolish. Her ladyship hadn't said one word today about last night's events. Meanwhile, the servants said his lordship had slept until noon, and there'd been whispers about how he'd drunk himself into a stupor last night. Clearly neither he nor his mother was ready to be honest with each other.

It was driving Camilla mad. And Mr. Fowler's presence merely confused the matter. Perhaps that was why Pierce had invited the man—to escape discussion about anything weightier than the weather. Avoiding things did seem to be his favorite way of handling them.

She cast him a furtive glance from beneath her spectacles. Tonight he was playing Devil May Care Devonmont. He'd dressed more formally, in a tailcoat of black superfine, a waistcoat of white figured velvet, and silk breeches, looking fiendishly handsome as always. No sign of the conflicts that must have been raging within him showed in his faintly bored expression.

Her ladyship thrust her fork into a stewed cockle. "How lovely it is to have you here with us again, Mr. Fowler. It's been a couple of weeks, hasn't it?"

Mr. Fowler was finely dressed as well, though he looked nervous. That was understandable, given that he was dining with an earl and a dowager countess. "Yes, my lady, I believe so."

"And how are things at the manor house?" Camilla asked, to put him more at ease. "Did Mrs. Perkins get over her nasty cold?"

"She did indeed." He shot the countess a quick glance. "And she said she would send some of the maids to help the two of you with the booth at the fair tomorrow, if you need them."

"That's very kind of her," Lady Devonmont said, then added, under her breath, "and rather unexpected."

"Why unexpected?" Pierce asked in that low rumble of a voice that never failed to strum Camilla's senses.

Lady Devonmont stiffened but doggedly kept eating her cockles.

Since this wasn't the time or place to explain that the estrangement between her ladyship and his lordship was effectively carried on between the servants of the two houses, Camilla said hastily, "Because they're so much busier over there than we are here. The manor house is quite a bit larger, after all." She smiled at Mr. Fowler. "That's why it's so lovely of Mrs. Perkins to offer her help for the booth."

Mr. Fowler served himself some ham. "I confess that until she said it, I didn't even know that you ladies were having a booth. But I suppose I shouldn't be surprised. The fair has become quite a big undertaking this year. All the females in town are quite aflutter over it. Apparently some woman read a poem by an American fellow about hanging up stockings by the chimney for St. Nicholas. Now the ladies have all got it into their heads to make ornamental stockings for sale there."

Camilla blinked at him. Did he not realize the "woman" was his employer's mother? Oh, dear.

"This woman has got them convinced that hanging Christmas stockings will become all the rage," he went on in a faintly condescending tone. "An absurd notion that will never catch on."

Her ladyship's eyes narrowed on him. "How can you be so sure?"

"Because it's silly." Mr. Fowler cut his ham. "If people start hanging stockings, what will we have next—handkerchiefs hung by the staircase? Caps hung by the windows?"

"Mr. Fowler—" Camilla began.

Her ladyship cut her off. "It's no more silly than hanging dead tree branches in a hall, or dangling mistletoe from a ribbon and expecting people to kiss each other when they pass under it."

The oblivious Mr. Fowler lifted an eyebrow. "On the contrary, my lady, those are all time-honored ways to celebrate the season. But hanging a stocking is just doing laundry. Hardly festive, I should think."

Lady Devonmont blinked, then gave a rueful laugh. "You do have a point, Mr. Fowler. Though in truth, if you read the poem yourself, you might understand what a charming idea it is." Her eyes gleamed at him. "And why the woman in question is producing such stockings to raise money for refurbishing the church's organ."

"Wait, I thought that's what your booth—" Though he paled a little as the truth dawned on him, he fixed her with a steady gaze. "Forgive me, my lady. I see that I have inadvertently insulted you."

Her ladyship flushed at his gentlemanly apology. "On the contrary, sir. I confess to having a bit of fun at your expense, and it was very wrong of me." She flashed him a tentative smile. "But truly, I should read the poem for you later. You might find the custom of hanging stockings not quite so silly after hearing it described properly."

Beneath the warmth of her smile, he relaxed. "While that sounds enticing, I should much rather hear you play the pianoforte. You do it so well."

This time when the countess flushed, it was with pleasure.

Camilla narrowed her gaze on Mr. Fowler. He'd asked her lady-ship to play the last time he'd been here, too. And the time before. Her suspicions about how the man felt toward the countess grew stronger by the minute.

"I'm not the only one who plays the pianoforte," the countess pointed out.

"My playing is wretched and you know it," Camilla put in.

"Actually, I was speaking of Pierce. He used to play as a boy."

Pierce stiffened. "That was a long time ago, Mother. I'm sure we would all rather hear *you* play."

Lady Devonmont gazed softly at him. "You used to enjoy hearing the Sussex Waltz."

"I'd forgotten about that." Pierce sipped some wine. "And as I recall, you played a livelier version of it than most."

"Your mother plays a livelier version of everything," Mr. Fowler put in. "She likes lively music. As do I."

"Is that why you always request that she play?" Camilla asked.

After a furtive glance at her ladyship, Mr. Fowler met Ca-milla's question with a smile. "I request that she play because then I know I will get to hear *you* sing, Mrs. Stuart."

"Oh, yes," Lady Devonmont chimed in. "You must sing, my dear."

"You must indeed." Mr. Fowler turned to Pierce. "You may not have discovered this yet, my lord, but Mrs. Stuart has the voice of a nightingale."

Pierce pinned her with his dark gaze. "I had no idea. Then we should definitely have a performance later."

Camilla stared at him, perplexed by the edge in his voice. "I'm always happy to entertain you, my lord. And Mr. Fowler, too, of course."

"Of course," Pierce echoed, his eyes boring into her. "I'm merely surprised I hadn't heard of this talent of yours before. But perhaps you save it for special guests, like Mr. Fowler."

What was *that* supposed to mean? "I save it for when I have accompaniment. You're always in such a hurry to leave us for your cigars in the evening that I never have the chance to offer."

"Well, then, I'll have to put off my cigar smoking tonight," he said tersely. "I don't want to miss hearing you sing."

"Oh, and Mr. Fowler, you must sing, too!" the countess exclaimed. She cast Pierce a bright smile. "Your estate manager is quite the fine tenor."

"Is he, indeed?" Pierce said, shooting Camilla another of those shuttered glances he kept throwing her way.

"He certainly is," his mother went on blithely. "When he and Camilla do duets, you'd think you were listening to paid opera singers in London."

"You would certainly know, Mother," Pierce snapped. "You went to opera houses plenty enough when I was in school. I was always reading about it in the papers."

As the countess paled, Camilla tensed, wondering if he was going to drag poor Mr. Fowler into his fight with his mother now. Then Pierce forced a smile and added, "My parents used to be such gadabouts, Mr. Fowler. I never knew when their escapades would turn up in the *Times*."

"I didn't have to worry about that with my parents,"

Mr. Fowler said amiably. "My mother was best known for her figgy pudding. It's hardly something to make the papers."

"Depends on what she did with her figgy pudding," Pierce said dryly. "If she shot it out of a cannon, I can guarantee it would make the papers."

They all laughed, breaking the tension. From there, the conversation drifted to a discussion of what was worthy of being mentioned in the papers.

With a relieved sigh, Camilla turned her attention to her dinner, hoping there would be no more crises. It was hard enough playing arbiter of the dispute between the countess and Pierce. She didn't think she could handle it if the estate manager jumped in, too.

Once again, Pierce felt like an intruder. Clearly Camilla, Mother, and Fowler had spent plenty of time in one another's company. They shared jokes he didn't understand, told tales about the servants that he'd never heard, and seemed quite at ease together. In the midst of so much camaraderie, how was he supposed to tell exactly how Camilla felt for Fowler?

She'd certainly dressed sumptuously for the man. Her dinner gown of rose satin was bedecked with puffy things around the skirt, and it had smaller puffy things at the bodice that drew attention to her ample bosom. So did the necklace of paste gems nestled between her lightly freckled breasts. She'd never worn that before. Or the gown, for that matter. Had she been saving it for Fowler?

If so, she'd made a good choice. Pierce couldn't stop looking at her, wondering what it would be like to lick his way down the smooth hollow between her breasts to find one taut nipple with his mouth—

Bloody hell. This was maddening.

He cast a furtive glance at Fowler, but the man was too polite to stare at Camilla's bosom. Fowler did glance at her a great deal, but he glanced at Mother a great deal, too. That proved nothing except that he was enjoying their "female companionship."

As for Camilla, Pierce could tell that she liked Fowler. She'd obviously tried to head the man off when he was blundering into insulting Mother. But was that just the act of a kind woman? Or a woman taking the side of a man she hoped to marry one day? She didn't seem to smile at Fowler with any particular regard, but could he trust that?

After all, Camilla was good at hiding her feelings. She had never once let on to Mother that she and Pierce were spending time together in secret every night.

So Camilla might be madly in love with Fowler and just being discreet. Though it was odd that she would choose discretion for something like that when she was never discreet about other things. Like her championing of Mother.

"What do you think, my lord?" Fowler asked, breaking into his tangled thoughts. "Shall we forget about our brandy and cigars for one night, and go right to the music?"

"Certainly," Pierce said.

He rose to help Camilla from her chair, but Fowler beat him there, damn his eyes. Pierce watched her face—she didn't blush as

Fowler offered her his arm, but she did flash the man a soft glance as she clasped it. Something very disquieting settled in Pierce's chest.

Then belatedly he realized that he'd been left to accompany Mother into the drawing room. Bloody hell.

With a tightness in his throat, he offered her his arm. Only after she took it did he remember the last time he'd done so—at Father's funeral. With so many eyes on him, he'd been unable to avoid it. He'd been angry about it, since the last thing he'd wanted was to escort the woman who'd abandoned him.

But now that his heart had thawed a little toward her, he realized how hard it must have been for her to lose her husband of nearly thirty years. Had she cried at the funeral? He didn't know. He hadn't been able to see beneath her veil.

She'd trembled, though. He remembered that. And she was trembling now, too, her small hand gripping his arm as if she never wanted to let go.

Trying to ignore the childhood memories that her touch roused, he stared ahead to Fowler and Camilla, who was laughing at something Fowler said, her pretty face animated as she stared up at him.

Pierce scowled. "Is Mrs. Stuart sweet on Fowler?" he asked Mother in a low voice, unable to help himself. She was the only person who might know.

"Not to my knowledge," Mother said. "Why?"

He swiftly invented a reason. "Because if she marries him, he'll expect her to bear him a passel of children, which means she won't be around to keep you company anymore."

"I don't care about that," she surprised him by saying. "I want her to be happy. I'd be thrilled to see her find a man who loves her and wants to marry her. She deserves better than to be sitting around playing cards with a middle-aged woman."

She did; he just didn't want it to be Fowler. Because then he would have to see her on the man's arm at social affairs and be forced to endure them cooing at each other.

He snorted. Since he came here only when necessary, he would never see Fowler at social affairs. And somehow he couldn't imagine either of them "cooing." Though that didn't make the thought of Fowler with her any less disturbing.

Mother narrowed her eyes on the pair as they walked into the drawing room ahead of them. "But I think Mr. Fowler would be wrong for her."

So did Pierce, though he doubted his reasons would match Mother's. "Why? Because he's too old?"

She eyed him askance. "He's not too old—he's younger than I am."

Not by much. No, he'd better not say that.

"He's too cautious," she continued. "Not that Camilla is reckless, mind you, but she doesn't always follow society's dictates."

That was certainly an understatement.

She went on. "Mr. Fowler would hate that. He's always so circumspect."

"Not always," Pierce pointed out. "You certainly had him going there for a while tonight."

To his surprise, Mother looked ashamed. "I know. It was

very bad of me. I just get annoyed when men are so firm in their opinions."

"I remember," he said softly, thinking of the fierce arguments between her and his father.

Her gaze darted to him, then returned to Camilla and Fowler. "But Mr. Fowler deserves better from me. He's generally a nice man." Mother's voice grew curiously taut. "Even if he is overly aware of what's appropriate for his station."

They'd reached the drawing room. It was only after Mother left Pierce's side to go to the pianoforte that he realized he'd just had a fairly normal conversation with her without Camilla acting as a guide and buffer.

How had that happened?

"All right," Mother said to Fowler as she sat down before the instrument and took out a piece of music. "I know how you scoff at it, sir, but the two of you *must* sing 'The Gallant Hussar.' Otherwise, I shall be very disappointed."

Camilla laughed, then released Fowler's arm to begin hunting through the music atop the pianoforte. "You'll have your wish, madam, but only if I get mine. We must sing a few Christmas carols." She smiled at Pierce. "That way his lordship can join in."

"Not me." Pierce dropped into a chair. "I make a better audience than I do performer."

"Come now, my lord." Camilla shoved up her spectacles. "It doesn't matter how well you sing. It's all in good fun."

Fowler shot Pierce a quick, apologetic glance. "I think his lordship isn't fond of Christmas carols."

"Oh," Camilla said, awareness dawning on her face. Obviously she was remembering that he'd spent all his holidays without his parents. "Well, then, in that case—"

"It's fine," Pierce ground out, chafing at being the object of her pity. "I enjoy hearing a carol as well as the next person. I just don't want to sing any." He glanced at Mother. "Besides, it's been a while since I heard Mother play, and I can't enjoy it if I'm up there caterwauling."

Surprisingly, he really was looking forward to it. Now that he knew he'd misread so much of his parents' relationship, he was finding a sort of pleasurable pain in reliving the past and trying to make out what he might have misunderstood. And part of that past had included Mother playing carols on the pianoforte.

Once the music started, however, it wasn't Mother's playing that he noticed but Camilla's singing. Fowler had been wrong. She wasn't a nightingale at all, a comparison often used for those preening sopranos at the opera house. No, Camilla was a siren . . . with a contralto so rich and sultry that it made those sopranos' voices sound like screeching.

And expressive! She swept him up in the tale of a woman who begs her soldier love to let her go off to war with him. Fowler took the part of the Hussar and Camilla took the part of Jane, the maiden, and for the length of the song, Pierce could easily believe they were lovers.

Too easily. When Fowler gazed down into Camilla's face as he sang of "her beautiful features," Pierce wanted to throttle him. Nor did the song end tragically, as so many of the broadside ballads did—this one had Jane and her gallant Hussar heading off to the war "united forever."

It was churlish, but he wished Jane and her Hussar to the devil, especially when Camilla and Fowler blended their voices so splendidly for the final verse that anyone, even a man as jaded as himself, would want to weep from the beauty of it. Despite Mother's opinion, it appeared to him that Fowler and Camilla made a perfect pair, damn them.

As the last notes died, he forced himself to applaud. They deserved it, even if he resented the fact that Fowler had gained so much enjoyment from joining his voice to hers.

Then Camilla smiled warmly at Pierce in response, and somehow that calmed his agitation. For the moment, anyway.

"So tell me, Fowler," Pierce said, "why does my mother say you scoff at this particular song?"

"I don't scoff at it," Fowler protested. "I just think any soldier who contemplates taking his true love off to war with him is a fool. Don't you agree?"

Pierce shrugged. "Depends on which war. If they're just going to be marching up and down some Belgian town, he might do well having a woman to cook and clean for him."

As Fowler laughed, Camilla frowned at Pierce. "Is that the only thing you think a woman is good for—cooking and cleaning?"

"And providing entertainment," he drawled, thinking ahead to when she would come to his room later. *If* she would come, with Fowler hanging about. When she blushed, he added, in a tone of pure innocence, "As you're doing here . . . with the singing."

Camilla eyed him askance. "And where does love come in? Can't the Hussar just want Jane with him because he loves her?"

Pierce snorted. "Love is for children and fools. No grown man with an ounce of sense makes monumental decisions based on some half-baked sentiment he read on a St. Valentine's Day card." He certainly didn't give up everything for it.

"*I'm* a grown man," Fowler put in solemnly. "And I spent many happy years in love with my wife." He cast a furtive glance over to where Camilla stood beside Mother. "That's why I would do almost anything for another chance at love."

The bottom dropped out of Pierce's stomach. At least now he had his answer from Fowler. "What about you, Mrs. Stuart?" he asked, fighting to ignore his visceral reaction. "You were married. Do *you* want another chance at love?"

Though she flinched at his veiled reference to her loveless marriage, she answered with great gravity. "Of course, my lord. A life without love is like a voice without a tune to sing. No grown *woman* with an ounce of sense wants to go on without love. Not if she can help it . . . not if she can catch that elusive tune. Sadly, not everyone can."

Silence fell on the room as every eye turned to Pierce. But for once, he was at a loss for a snappy rejoinder.

To his surprise, it was Mother who jumped in to save him. "Are we going to sing Christmas carols, or not? I believe we should start with 'The Cherry Tree Carol.' Don't you agree, Pierce?"

He demurred but didn't hear the rest of the discussion, his mind whirling around Camilla's words. A life without love. He'd had that, and he'd once thought himself fortunate to escape the emotional dramatics that plagued a life *with* love.

Now he wasn't so sure. And the fact that she made him doubt it irked him.

So did the possibility that she hoped to find love with Fowler. She didn't belong with Fowler. It would be a mistake. And it was high time he made her see that.

14

Her ladyship had retired at last, so Camilla went up to kiss the sleeping Jasper before heading for Pierce's room. It was later than usual, so she wasn't even sure that Pierce would want her there this evening. But she had to make sure, in case their bargain from the previous nights held firm.

She snorted. Right. Their bargain was why she couldn't wait to see him alone, why she couldn't breathe for the thought of being with him. What a fool she was. But she couldn't help it. He'd looked so unsure of himself when they'd spoken of love; it broke her heart.

She quickened her steps, but as she reached the floor where the bedchambers were she heard a faint sound wafting up from the drawing room. It was the pianoforte.

Had the countess roused again in the brief time Camilla had darted up to kiss Jasper? Was she unable to sleep? If so, Camilla dared not go to Pierce. She couldn't take the chance of her ladyship wanting her and not being able to find her.

She hurried down to the drawing room to investigate, then halted abruptly as she entered. The earl himself was playing the instrument. And doing it extremely well, too.

"I assume that Mother has gone to bed," Pierce said without looking up from the music.

"Yes." She closed the door. "Aren't you worried she'll hear you?"

"Not likely. This house is sturdy, and the master bedchambers are at the other end. When I was a boy, Mother used to play sometimes while Father was sleeping. He never heard."

"Is that when you learned to play? While your father slept?"

His jaw went taut. "Occasionally."

When he kept on playing, she edged behind the pianoforte so she could watch his fingering. "You're very good."

He shrugged. "It's what I do to relax. I have an excellent instrument in my London town house."

"Does this mean you're planning to provide tonight's entertainment?" she said lightly. "Or are we going upstairs?"

"Neither." He stopped playing to stare up at her intently. "I want you to sing for me."

That startled her. "Your mother will surely hear *that*."

"If she does, she'll figure that you're playing and singing for yourself."

"Or she'll come to see why I'm still up and find us here together."

"And what if she does?" A faint smile touched his lips. "Surely we can be allowed to entertain ourselves in the drawing room after she's in bed."

"Is there some reason you suddenly don't mind if she finds us alone together?"

He stared steadily at her. "Is there some reason you suddenly *do* mind singing for me?"

"No. Why would there be?"

A shadow crossed his face, and his voice turned bitter. "Perhaps it's something you only save for when Fowler is around."

She blinked. He'd made a similar remark at dinner. At the time, she hadn't thought much of it, but now . . . "Don't be absurd. Why would I do that?"

"I don't know." Pushing the bench out, he rose to stand near her, his expression stormy. "Why did you never once offer to sing to me for our evenings together?"

"For obvious reasons." She gazed up into his glittering eyes. "If I sang to you upstairs, your mother would definitely hear. Her room is near enough to yours for that."

Her logic seemed to catch him off guard. Then he leaned against the pianoforte with a scowl. "Perhaps, but why didn't you ever even mention that you could sing? That you could do it so well?"

Pleasure that he liked her singing warred with confusion over this peculiar conversation. "It never came up. Why didn't *you* ever mention that you play the pianoforte?"

He crossed his arms over his chest. "It's not the sort of thing a man admits. It's not the sort of thing a man *does*."

"Nonsense. Men play instruments all the time." When he glanced away, a muscle ticking in his jaw, she added, "Ah, but not earls, I suppose. Not often, anyway."

His gaze shot back to her. "No, not often. Not when their fathers think it's *dandyish*."

Her heart caught in her throat. "I'm beginning to hate your father."

"You wouldn't be the only one." Narrowing his gaze on her, he added, "So your refusal to sing for me has nothing to do with Fowler." He bent close and lowered his voice to a hiss. "Nothing to do with how he looks at you. How he speaks of you."

Confused by the anger in his voice, she stared up into his finely etched features. "How *does* he look at me?"

"As if you're the answer to all his loneliness."

And that's when it hit her. "You think Mr. Fowler . . . and I . . ." She laughed. "You're quite mad, you know. He's twenty years older than I, at least."

Apparently he didn't share her amusement, for all he did was glare at her. "Some women like older men. And I can see why the attentions of a man like him would be appealing to—"

"A mere lady's companion?" Her temper flared. "An orphan?"

"A widow from a loveless marriage who wants to, as you put it, 'catch that elusive tune.' He practically said he's in search of love, so I can see how you might fancy yourself in love with him, too."

"Oh, you can, can you?" she said tartly.

"But it would be wrong, the two of you."

She stared at him, not sure what to make of his new concern that she might "fancy" herself "in love" with Mr. Fowler. She could think of only two reasons he might feel that way—one was insulting, the other intriguing. She was almost afraid to find out which.

But she had to know. "Are you worried that I might leave your employ to marry Mr. Fowler, forcing you to find another companion for her ladyship?"

"No!" he said, the look of outrage on his face relieving her. "I'm speaking to you as a friend, that's all."

"A friend," she echoed. "Are we friends?"

That took him aback. "I thought we were."

"I see. So you, as my *friend*, think me and Mr. Fowler wrong for each other."

"Exactly."

"Do you have any particular reason for feeling so? Since you think his age isn't a problem?"

Glancing away, he threaded his fingers through his hair. "I didn't say it wasn't a problem—just that you might not consider it so yourself."

"If I'm not bothered by it, then I don't see why it should concern *you*."

"It's not just his age," he grumbled. "The two of you wouldn't suit. He's too straitlaced. And you're too . . . too . . ."

"Wild?" she said archly.

"Of course not," he snapped. "But you have life and vitality. He would crush it in his attempt to make you respectable."

"How odd—I thought I was already respectable," she said, beginning to enjoy his discomfiture.

He let out a low oath. "I didn't mean it like that. I meant—"

"That I shouldn't have a life beyond being companion to your mother."

"Damn it, no!" When she couldn't resist a laugh, he frowned at her. "You're enjoying this."

"I certainly am. So far you haven't given one sensible reason that I should *not* marry Mr. Fowler."

His frown deepened to a glower. "You're considering it?"

"You seem to think I am."

"Tell me the truth—do you and Mr. Fowler have an understanding?"

"If we do, why do you care?" she countered. If her suspicions were correct and he was actually jealous of the man, she wanted to hear him admit it. And without this nonsense about his concern for her "as a friend."

But she could tell from the sudden chill in his expression that he was withdrawing. "I wouldn't want to see you make a mistake."

"Because you're so selfless."

He flinched. "Because he's wrong for you."

"So you say." She turned for the door. "I suppose that means I shouldn't invite you to the wedding."

He caught her by the arm and tugged her back around to face him. "Don't marry Fowler, damn it!"

She thrust her face up to his. "Give me one good reason—one *genuine* reason—why I shouldn't."

Something dark and feral flickered in his gaze. Then he said, in a low, guttural voice, "Because I don't want you to."

And while she was still reeling from that incredible admission, he brought his mouth down on hers.

Her heart soared as he kissed her in a fever of need that mirrored her own. Even though she knew how mad it was to let this go so far, she couldn't help but respond. They'd spent the last week dancing around their attraction to each other, trying to shove it into a closet. But it kept creeping out when they least expected it, and she was tired of it.

She wanted him. Some part of him clearly wanted her. And for once, she was going to let herself enjoy being desired by a man.

His kisses were so hot, so deep . . . so lovely that she let them carry her where they would. He took her mouth with what felt like possessiveness, even though she knew he wasn't the possessive sort. But apparently he could be jealous, which astonished her. She hadn't thought he cared even that much.

After several long, mesmerizing kisses, he tore his mouth free to growl, "Promise me you won't marry Fowler."

She drew back to stare at him, amazed. He was serious. Even after the way she'd let him kiss her, he still thought . . . He really was so oblivious sometimes. She wanted to laugh, but the part of her that ached for him settled for teasing him.

"Convince me not to," she said.

He dragged in a harsh breath. Then without warning, he grabbed her by the waist and lifted her atop the pianoforte so forcefully that her spectacles fell off. Music skittered to the floor but she didn't even notice, for he was kissing her again, pressing his body into hers, parting her legs until he was plastered so close against her she could feel his arousal.

A thrill shot through her. She slid her hands inside his coat, wanting to be closer to him, and when the silk of his waistcoat thwarted her, she slipped her hands up beneath it. Feeling his muscles flex and tighten through his shirt, she explored them shamelessly. His mouth grew almost savage.

He kissed gloriously . . . ravenously, as if he couldn't sate his need. He covered her breasts through her gown, kneading, rubbing, teasing her mercilessly. It wasn't nearly enough, so when he brought one hand behind her to loosen her gown, she didn't protest.

He tore his lips free to rake kisses down the arch of her throat. She knew where he was headed. And she couldn't wait for him to get there.

Just as her gown came free, she lifted her bosom to him. With a groan that showed he knew what she wanted, he dragged the fabric down so he could get to her corset cups and chemise and pull them below her breasts.

"Pierce . . ." she whispered. "Sweet heaven, Pierce . . ."

"I've wanted to do this all night," he murmured as he drank in the sight of her bosom bared to him. His dark eyes were alight, hungry. "Every time you drew breath to sing, I wanted to put my mouth right here." He pressed his lips to the top of one breast. "And here." He kissed his way down the slope. "And here."

At last, he closed his mouth over her nipple and sucked.

It was wonderful. *Wonderful.* She clasped his head close,

burying her fingers in his silky hair as he tongued her nipples, first one, then the other, playing with them so deliciously that she thought she might lose her mind. Kenneth had never spent time on her breasts. She'd had no idea they could provide such a feast of sensation.

Drawing back to stare at her, he murmured, "Have I convinced you now?"

"Perhaps a little," she teased.

A storm spread over his brow as he caught her at the waist and pulled her against him. "If you think I shall stand by and watch while Fowler—"

She began to laugh. She couldn't help it. "He doesn't . . . he doesn't even *want* me . . . you fool," she managed to gasp between laughs.

"You're wrong. You may not want him, but he definitely wants you. It was you he wanted to hear sing. It was you he was looking down at when he spoke so feelingly of love."

"Think, Pierce," she said as she stroked his hair. "Who was sitting right next to me on that bench?"

He blinked. "Mother?" Shock filled his face. "Oh, God."

"He's nearly her age. He always asks her to play when he comes here, and he always worries about her. *She's* the one he's sweet on."

With his hands still on her waist, Pierce glanced away, a frown knitting his brow. "But he's an estate manager and she's—"

"A countess, yes. Why do you think he keeps his feelings so close to his chest? I don't even know if she returns them. But I suspect that won't stop him from wanting her."

"Wait a minute." Pierce swung his narrowing gaze to her. "You knew all along he felt that way."

She caught her breath. Uh-oh. She'd been found out. "I might have . . . guessed, yes."

"Yet you let me go on and on about his wanting to marry you." He scowled. "I never took you for a coquette."

"That's because I've never been one before." She felt giddy. Who could have dreamed it would be so delightful to tease a man? "I never took you for the jealous sort."

"I'm not." At her raised eyebrow, he admitted sullenly, "Or at least I haven't been until now."

She eyed him skeptically. "Never?"

"Never. There was no need." He drew himself up. "I'm considered something of a catch."

"I am well aware of that," she said dryly. "You forget that I've read all about you in the papers."

That seemed to bring him up short. "I'm not as bad as they make me out to be."

"Says the man who already has me half naked in a drawing room."

His gaze drifted down to her breasts and grew heated once more. "Do you mind?" He reached for her hem with both hands and began dragging her gown up her legs.

Her silly pulse jumped. "No." She shivered as his fingers passed her garters to brush naked flesh. "I should. But I don't."

"I did warn you that if you gave me an inch . . ."

"Yes, you did," she rasped, looping her arms about his neck. "So now you may take a mile or two if you like."

That was all the encouragement he seemed to need to slide his hands up her thighs until he found the damp, aching center of her. He rubbed her there, his thumb working magic on the very sensitive spot Kenneth had always ignored.

But when he slipped two fingers inside her, she gasped, taken by surprise.

"God, dearling," he choked out, "you're so warm and tight."

"It's been a long time," she admitted.

Her eyes slid closed as he fondled her with a fervor she'd never known from her late husband. Oh, what an amazing feeling . . . She'd had no idea.

Pierce bent to whisper hoarsely in her ear, "I want to see you come. I want to see you break apart in my hands, right here in this drawing room. And then I want to take you upstairs to my bed and have my wicked way with you."

"What if I . . . don't wish to go?" she asked, though she did. Rather fervently.

"Then I'll have to convince you, won't I?" he said, his breath coming heavier now.

So was hers. She couldn't find it, couldn't catch it. A slow heat was building between her legs that made her squirm and ache, made her press herself harder against his hand.

He responded by increasing the pressure of his caresses, quickening the rhythm until she was writhing atop the pianoforte, shamelessly riding his hand. It began like ripples on water, sensation building on sensation until suddenly it erupted like the hot springs at Bath. She gripped him to her with a little cry that he silenced with his mouth.

It was like nothing she'd ever known. Was that what he'd meant by wanting to see her "break apart"? Because if so, he'd gotten his wish. She felt broken open, exposed to him in the most intimate way a woman could be.

His mouth on hers was intense, eager, even as her own desire ebbed a little. He tore his lips free to murmur, "Come to my bed, Camilla. I can't bear it anymore. And I want privacy for all the things I want to do to you. With you."

"All right," she whispered, still insensible of anything but how perfect it felt to be in his arms.

He tugged her off the pianoforte and began to help her repair her clothes. She couldn't believe she was doing this, preparing to go to his bed, but she was tired of fighting her own urges, tired of being near him yet not *with* him.

It didn't even matter anymore that they would only be lovers. If she could have him for a brief while . . . "Do I look presentable enough?" she asked as she tucked a strand of hair back into her coiffure.

He bent to pick up her spectacles, which had landed on the floor. "I doubt we'll come across anyone this late," he murmured as he settled them on her nose. "Besides, I'm just going to tear your clothes off as soon as we're in the room."

The excitement that bolted through her leveled all her doubts. She'd never had a man desire her so fiercely—it was incredibly enticing.

They headed for the door and were a short distance from it when it opened.

To her horror, a small voice said, "You didn't put me to bed, Mama, and then I got up to use the chamber pot and Maisie was asleep and you were gone and . . ."

Jasper trailed off as he saw Pierce. "Oh no," he whispered, his eyes wide. "I woke up the great earl."

15

Pierce just stood there, shocked. A small, brown-haired, blue-eyed boy was standing in his drawing room, wearing a nightshirt and clutching something in both fists. And he was looking at Pierce as if he'd just seen the devil himself.

Then he began to cry. "M-Mama!" he blubbered. "I–I don't want to be s-sent away!"

Camilla hurried to his side and caught him up in her arms. "It's all right," she said soothingly as she pressed his head to her shoulder. "I'm sure it will be fine, muffin, just fine."

She wouldn't meet Pierce's eyes. She just kept cradling the boy, whose little frame shook from the force of his fear.

"Your son, I take it," Pierce managed to croak.

Oh, God, she had a child whom she'd hidden from him. And

here he'd been thinking that he meant something to her, that they meant something to each other, when all the while . . .

"Don't let the g-great earl send me away!" the boy wailed, and Pierce got ahold of himself. At the moment this concerned a child, and only a child.

A child who was Camilla's *son,* for God's sake.

"No one will send you away, lad," Pierce said hoarsely.

The boy stopped crying to peer at him through red-rimmed eyes. "But . . . but her l-ladyship said I h-had to keep out of s-sight or—"

"Mother knew?" Pierce asked Camilla, his chest tightening painfully. "You've both been keeping this from me?"

Camilla's gaze shot to him at last, a look of pure panic in her eyes. "Please, you have to understand." Hitching the boy higher on one hip, she clutched him close as if he might be snatched from her at any moment. "I needed to work to support Jasper, and my employers expected me to be unencumbered, so I always told them I was. Then I sent Jasper to live with Kenneth's brother and his wife."

"They don't like me," the boy muttered.

"That's not true, Jasper," Camilla chided gently. She met Pierce's gaze. "They're very Scottish, you see, and very religious. And they already had three young children of their own." She stroked the lad's curls. "But even so, I wouldn't have brought him here if your mother hadn't found out about him and asked me to."

"*Mother* asked you to bring a child here?" he echoed, incredulous. She wouldn't keep her own son, but she'd had some stranger's boy brought to Montcliff?

"Yes," Camilla said warily, no doubt guessing the source of his incredulity. "Why do you think it was so hard for me to believe that she could ever have been cruel to you? She's been very kind to me and Jasper."

He took a step toward them, and the lad squealed and grabbed his mother. "It's all right, lad. I won't hurt you." He glared at Camilla. "What the devil have you been telling him about me?"

"You're the g-great earl," Jasper whispered, his eyes wide with fright. "I'm not s-supposed to let the great earl see me, or I'll be s-sent away."

"You won't be sent away," Pierce bit out. When the boy flinched, he modulated his tone. "No one will send you away from your mother, boy, least of all me." He cast Camilla a hard look. "I can't imagine why you would tell him such a thing."

She lifted her chin. "Mr. Fowler was very clear in my interview—he said that you required that I be childless," she said defensively. "I needed the position. I wasn't about to tell him I had a little boy."

"Well, I don't know why he would think—" He groaned. "Damn. It must have been the day we talked about children. I let it slip that I didn't intend to have any. Since I didn't want to elaborate on why, I told him some nonsense about not liking them."

When Jasper looked horrified at the thought, Pierce caught the boy's gaze and said firmly, "But I never meant that last part." He shifted his gaze back to Camilla. "And I never gave Fowler any specific rule about not having children on the estate, either, I swear. He came to that conclusion on his own."

Great God, they must have been keeping it secret from Fowler, too. From the beginning? How had they managed it?

Then something else occurred to him. "It was Jasper I heard yesterday in the drawing room."

Swallowing hard, Camilla nodded. "We had to send him off with Maisie in a bit of a hurry. You gave us quite a fright coming home early."

The thought of the two women living in fear that he might send the lad off made his heart wrench in his chest. "Do *all* the servants know?"

"Just the ones here. We dared not tell anyone else, for fear that Mr. Fowler would find out. And as you may have noticed, there's a bit of rivalry between the manor servants and the dower house servants, so the latter were more than happy to keep the secret."

He hadn't noticed any rivalry. Bloody hell, he was oblivious. He'd been thinking he had a firm grasp on everything regarding his estate, not to mention his life and his relationship with Mother, when the truth was, he didn't know a damned thing.

Even Camilla was a stranger to him again. But despite the betrayal he felt over the secret she'd been keeping from him, he couldn't blame her. At least she fought for her son. It was more than he could say for his own mother.

Except that Mother had fought for *this* boy. Pierce didn't know whether to resent her or respect her for that.

The boy was staring at him less fearfully now. "So you're not . . . going to send me away?"

"No," he managed to say past the lump in his throat. Memories of that day in the carriage with Titus swamped him. Jasper couldn't be much younger than he'd been, and he remembered only too well how much it had ached to be separated from his parents. "You're safe here, Jasper. It is Jasper, right?"

The lad bobbed his head.

"How old are you, lad?"

Jasper glanced to his mother, and she nodded encouragement. His eyes still held a hint of wariness as he stared up at Pierce. "I'm six and three-quarters."

Pierce bit back a smile. "As old as all that, are you?" He ventured nearer, relieved when Jasper didn't recoil from him. He kept his voice soft and unthreatening. "What's that in your hands?"

Jasper eyed him a long moment before opening them to show three tin soldiers in each. "Her ladyship said that for every day I kept out of sight, I could have one. I've got seven now." He frowned. "Well, six. I lost one yesterday."

The lump in Pierce's throat thickened. "Here in the drawing room." It took all his effort not to react to the fact that his mother had been giving this lad *his* soldiers. It wasn't as if he needed them anymore.

Camilla's gaze on him softened, became apologetic. "She said there were a lot. I hope you don't mind."

"Of course I don't mind." Somehow he forced humor into his voice. "I'm a bit old for them now, don't you think?"

Jasper hesitantly held out a hand. "If you want, you can have one of mine. I can share."

The peace offering from a reluctant six-year-old was nearly more than he could take. "You keep them," he rasped. "You've been a brave lad, and you deserve them."

That actually got a smile out of the cherub. And he really was a cherub, with reddish-brown curls and sky-blue eyes that saw too much. Rather like his mother's.

"What do you say?" Camilla prompted.

"Thank you, sir," he mumbled.

"You call him 'my lord,' dearest," she corrected him.

"'Sir' is fine," Pierce interjected.

Jasper gave a big yawn, and Camilla looked at Pierce. "I should probably put him back in bed."

Pierce nodded. My God, what a nightmare it would have been if the lad had wandered in while they were in the midst of . . . "You should stay with him," he said gruffly, even as his body still ached for her. "He needs you right now."

The grateful look in her eyes cut him to the soul. "Thank you."

She had already started for the door when the boy said, "Wait! I got to ask the great earl something."

Pierce went up to them. "What is it, lad?"

"You're more important than Mr. Fowler, right?"

Pierce stifled a smile. "You could say that."

Jasper tipped up his chin in an unconscious imitation of his mother's usual gesture of defiance. "So if Mother and me and her ladyship wanted to go to the fair tomorrow, you could tell Mr. Fowler it was all right, and we could go."

Camilla sighed. "Jasper heard me tell your mother that we couldn't take him there because Mr. Fowler might see."

"But her ladyship *said* we could go, before Mother said we couldn't," Jasper went on in a rush, "and I really, really *want* to go, in case they have a sleigh there. I want to see a sleigh, and the fair is tomorrow, and—"

"I'll tell Mr. Fowler myself that you're allowed to go anywhere you wish. You needn't worry about that."

The beaming smile that spread over Jasper's face made Pierce's heart tighten. It was so easy to please a child. And yet so easy to bring his world crashing down around his ears, too.

"Are *you* going, my lord?" When Pierce stiffened, Jasper added hastily, "Because if *you* went, Mr. Fowler couldn't do anything to stop it. And none of the boys would bother me or Mother."

"What boys are bothering you and your mother?" Pierce asked, more fiercely than he'd intended.

"He's thinking of London," Camilla explained. "You know how it can be in the city for a woman and a boy alone—just the usual nonsense. But nothing has happened here. Jasper hasn't even been to town yet, because I didn't dare risk his being seen by Mr. Fowler. I'm sure everyone in Stocking Pelham will be perfectly polite."

"Especially if *you* went with us," Jasper persisted.

"Jasper!" his mother chided. "His lordship has more important things to do than to squire you to a fair."

"Do you want me to go?" Pierce heard himself ask.

The boy's eyes lit up. "That would *grand*."

"Really, you don't have to," Camilla put in hastily, her voice low. "It's kind enough of you to overlook the fact that—"

"It's not kind of me," he clipped out. "It's the right thing."

She dropped her gaze. "Of course."

He hated seeing her so cautious around him, so worried

that he would somehow send her boy away from her. *Him*, of all people. She ought to know better.

"We'll all go, Jasper," he said, though it also meant spending the day in Mother's company. "We'll leave first thing in the morning—you, me, your mother, and her ladyship."

"And Maisie, too?" Jasper asked, rubbing his sleepy eyes.

"Jasper!" her mother said, obviously exasperated.

Pierce couldn't help laughing. The lad was certainly adept at getting what he wanted. "Maisie, too."

"I'm so sorry, my lord," Camilla said. "I swear, I don't know what's gotten into him."

"Don't apologize," he said, hating how formal she was being with him, but understanding why. "He's a good lad and deserves a reward."

Even if it meant that Pierce spent a day in hell.

"Thank you," she said softly. "You have no idea what it means to me. And to him."

He stared at her. "I have some idea, believe me."

She flushed. "Forgive me for not trusting you with the truth. You deserved better."

"It's all right—I understand. When a child is involved, nothing can be left to chance."

A sweet smile, the very twin to her son's, spread over her face. When she glanced down at Jasper, who'd fallen asleep on her shoulder, her expression grew pensive. "My lord, I think perhaps it would be better if after this we did not . . ."

"I know." She had come to her senses, realized how unwise it would be for her to share his bed when she had her son to consider. Not that he relished the idea of making love to her, knowing that she'd be doing it out of gratitude for his not sending her son away. But he still wanted . . . still yearned . . .

It didn't matter what he wanted. The boy was what mattered at the moment. "Besides," Pierce added with a forced smile, "you have an early day ahead of you tomorrow. I believe Mother mentioned that the two of you had to be at the fair with the servants to help set up the booth."

"Yes, we do. Thank you for understanding."

But as she left the room with her lad in her arms, he realized he didn't care if she had a son. He didn't care that it meant she might be looking for a husband, something he didn't intend to be to *anyone,* even her. Nor did he care that getting intimately involved with a woman in her situation was unwise at best and dangerous at worst.

Like the devil that he was, he still wanted her in his bed.

The question was, what the bloody hell was he going to do about it?

16

At seven the next morning, Camilla hurried a very excited Jasper down the stairs. She was already late—her ladyship had risen at six and was hoping to leave by seven thirty. But wrangling a six-year-old into his first skeleton suit took some doing, even for a woman who'd done it countless times with young lads in the orphanage. And Maisie hadn't been able to help, because she was busy helping her ladyship.

The countess met them at the bottom, a look of worry on her face.

Camilla immediately launched into an apology. "I know we're running late. Do Jasper and I have time for breakfast?"

"Of course, my dear. It's going to be a long day, so he definitely needs fortification." She took his other hand as they started for the breakfast room. "But are you sure you understood Pierce correctly? He doesn't mind about Jasper?"

This morning, Camilla had given her ladyship a highly edited version of the previous night's events, leaving out all the parts about Pierce's jealousy of Mr. Fowler and . . . other things.

"His lordship agreed to take us to town for the fair," Camilla said. "I'd say that's a strong indication that he doesn't mind."

And that still surprised her. Pierce had been so good, so kind to her son. Given his look of shock and betrayal when Jasper first appeared in the drawing room, Pierce's behavior was nothing short of astonishing. How she wished she'd confided in him sooner. But then, until last night she hadn't realized that he cared for her even a little. Or that she would have learned to care for him, too. That she might consider doing something as reckless as going to his bed.

A blush heated her cheeks. For pity's sake, Jasper had nearly found them together! That would have been horrible.

At least the near miss had brought her to her senses. Or as much of her senses as weren't still aching for him. He made her blood sing, and that had never happened to her before. The part of her that yearned for more in her life was desperate for the next time they could be alone together.

I want to see you come. I want to see you break apart in my hands, right here in this drawing room. And then I want to take you upstairs to my bed and have my wicked way with you.

She shivered every time she thought of it. Every time she thought of *him.* How he'd touched her. How he'd stoked a fire that Kenneth had never even acknowledged was there.

But she couldn't take a lover, not with Jasper to think about. What if she found herself pregnant again? It didn't bear thinking on.

They entered the breakfast room to find Pierce standing by the sideboard. As he turned to smile at her, her heart gave a ridiculous leap. He'd never joined them for breakfast before—he'd either had a tray brought to his room or waited to eat until he'd gone over to the manor house to handle estate business. Was this all for her and Jasper's benefit?

If so, it made her absurdly happy, especially when he trailed his admiring gaze down her lavender-blue morning dress. She was so glad she'd taken extra care with her appearance this morning, even adding a few sprigs of holly to her hair.

And he looked rather fine himself, in a morning suit of bottle-green cashmere with a striped waistcoat and Hessian boots polished to a high sheen. She hoped the snow had melted enough so he wouldn't ruin them, for they looked costly.

The moment Jasper spotted the earl, he let out a cry of surprise and went running up to the man as if they were grand friends. "Good morning, sir!"

Pierce ruffled Jasper's hair. "Good morning, lad. You're looking very well."

"Mama said I had to wear my new clothes." He pouted as he scratched one leg. "They itch."

Camilla sighed. Jasper had only just gotten too old for skirts, and he wasn't fond of being buttoned up tight.

"I wore a skeleton suit, too, when I was your age," Pierce said confidentially. "You'll get used to it. And only big boys wear breeches, so when they see you in your new clothes in town, they'll be impressed by how old you are."

"I hadn't thought of that." Jasper glanced at Pierce's Hessians. "They'd really be impressed if I wore boots like you, sir. And I'd be ever so much *taller.*"

"You would indeed," Pierce said with a chuckle. "Although you'd be even taller if I did this." And without warning he hoisted Jasper up onto his shoulders.

Jasper squealed with delight as he grabbed the earl's head. "Look, Mama, at how tall I am!"

"Yes, very tall indeed," Camilla managed through the lump in her throat as Pierce marched about the room with him. Pierce looked as carefree as she'd ever seen him, his eyes twinkling and his face wreathed in smiles as he hefted Jasper off his shoulders and into a chair at the table.

"Oh, Lord," Camilla murmured to her ladyship. "I believe we've opened a Pandora's box by introducing them to each other."

"I don't know," Lady Devonmont said softly. "Pierce hasn't looked this happy since he was a boy. Perhaps it will be good for him."

Perhaps so, but it could be very difficult for Jasper. Pierce might not even stay at the dower house beyond today. And if Jasper grew attached to him—

"You do have a winter coat, don't you?" Pierce bent to ask Jasper.

"Oh, yes, my lord," Jasper said as a footman placed a full plate of food in front of him. "Her ladyship bought it for me. It has fur on the inside and everything."

"That sounds warm enough," Pierce said, slanting an enigmatic glance at his mother. "I hope she bought a hat and gloves for you, too."

Annoyed that he might think she and Jasper had been taking advantage of his mother, Camilla stepped in. "Her ladyship has been very kind, but I supplied those items myself. I do look after my son."

"Of course," Pierce said.

"Good morning, everyone," said a deep voice from the doorway.

Camilla's stomach clenched. What was Mr. Fowler doing here?

"Ah, Fowler, there you are!" Pierce said, keeping one hand on Jasper's shoulder. Jasper's eyes widened in alarm, but before he could say a word, Pierce added, "Let me introduce you to my young friend, Jasper Stuart. Master Jasper, this is Mr. Fowler, my estate manager."

As Jasper mumbled a greeting, with his small brow creased in a frown, Camilla watched Fowler. Oddly, he betrayed no surprise. "Good morning, Master Jasper. His lordship was telling me all about you earlier."

Pierce had risen that early? Heavens.

"It seems I've been remiss in welcoming you to Montcliff," the man went on, his cool, remote tone belying his genial words. Camilla tensed. No doubt Pierce had lectured him about his stringent rules. She had better tread carefully.

"Of course," Mr. Fowler continued, "if I'd known of your presence here, I wouldn't have been so remiss." But it wasn't

Camilla he glanced darkly at. It was her ladyship. "Apparently, I wasn't to be trusted with such a valuable secret."

Lady Devonmont flushed. "I've learned through the years to be careful whom I trust with valuable secrets, sir. So has Camilla. And you mustn't blame her. It was my idea to bring the boy here and my idea to keep him to ourselves."

Anger flared briefly in Mr. Fowler's features before he masked it. "I don't blame Mrs. Stuart." He tore his gaze from the countess. "I don't blame anyone. I was merely making an observation."

Into the heightened tension came Jasper's small voice. "We're going to the fair today, Mr. Fowler. Are you going, too?"

Mr. Fowler drew himself up with a sort of stiff pride. "I wouldn't wish to intrude."

"Nonsense," her ladyship said, her color deepening. "It's no intrusion. We'd be quite pleased if you would join us. Wouldn't we, Camilla?"

"Of course. Do come with us, sir."

He tipped his head at Camilla, carefully avoiding her ladyship's gaze. "Very well. Given such a cordial invitation, I can hardly refuse."

Camilla sighed as Pierce invited the man to fill a plate at the sideboard. Mr. Fowler was clearly wounded by the lack of trust she and her ladyship had placed in him. But given his firm stance on children, he could hardly be surprised.

It *was* surprising, however, that her ladyship had invited him to join them. Camilla lowered her voice to murmur, "Mr. Fowler took that very well."

The countess gazed at the man's broad back. "He'll take it even better once he gets to know the boy."

"That depends entirely on how well Jasper behaves, I fear," Camilla said. "Look at him—he's about to burst out of his chair from excitement."

"If Mr. Fowler gives you any grief about Jasper, you let me know," her ladyship said with a sniff. "I may not be mistress of this estate, but I can still set a man straight if I'm pressed to it."

Camilla watched as the countess headed over to coddle Jasper, which as usual had him beaming with pleasure. More and more, the woman presented a conundrum. Clearly she had *not* stood up to her husband on behalf of her own son. Was that why she was so protective of Jasper?

Watching her with the boy must pain Pierce. Though if it did, he gave no evidence of it as they ate a quick breakfast and headed out the front door to find both her ladyship's barouche box and a massive coach-and-four awaiting them.

"Would you like to ride with me?" Pierce asked Jasper.

"Can Mama come, too? And Maisie? And her ladyship?"

Pierce looked amused. "Do the three of them go everywhere with you?"

"Well . . ." Jasper thought a moment. "Mostly. When I don't have to stay with Maisie on account of nobody wanting me seen by—" He shot Mr. Fowler a furtive glance, then added in a whisper, "By You Know Who."

Fortunately, Mr. Fowler was engrossed in helping the countess determine which items were to be loaded onto the top of the coach-and-four.

"You needn't worry about that anymore," Pierce said in a confidential voice. "You can be seen by anyone you please. And if we can fit everyone inside the coach, they're welcome to ride with us."

In the end, the servants were put into the barouche, leaving the six of them to be crammed inside the coach.

As they set off, with Camilla, Maisie, and her ladyship on one side and the two gentlemen and Jasper on the other, Pierce turned to Mr. Fowler. "Are there usually many people at this fair?"

"I don't know," the estate manager answered. "I've never been."

They both looked at her ladyship. "There's generally a few hundred at least," she said.

"The Christmas one is the most popular," Maisie put in, then reddened as she realized she shouldn't speak among such lofty personages.

Pierce smiled encouragingly at her. "Is it because of the horses? As I recall from my childhood, a great deal of horse selling went on during this particular fair."

Feeling Lady Devonmont stiffen beside her, Camilla shot her a quick glance but could tell nothing from the woman's smooth expression.

"Oh, yes, my lord, they still sell a great many horses," Maisie said. "And cattle and cheese, too."

"And reindeer?" Jasper asked hopefully.

"Reindeer?" Pierce echoed in obvious bewilderment.

"It's in the poem, you know," Jasper said, "the one about St. Nicholas."

Pierce glanced at Camilla. "Is this the famous poem that has enraptured the females of Stocking Pelham?"

Camilla smiled ruefully. "I'm afraid so. He's quite taken with it."

"I know it by heart," Jasper said. "I can say it if you like."

"Oh, by all means, let us hear the blasted thing," Mr. Fowler mumbled.

Taking him at his word, Jasper cheerily began to recite it, and Camilla didn't have the heart to stop him. Besides, she was having fun watching Mr. Fowler look so stoic about the matter.

When Jasper got to the part about the "eight tiny reindeer," Pierce interrupted. "I'm afraid I can't show you any of those, lad, but we can have a look at some regular deer, if you want."

Jasper's eyes went wide. "I guess they don't *have* to have reins on them."

Camilla stifled a laugh. Until now, she hadn't realized what Jasper thought reindeer were.

Pierce said very soberly, "Well, they only need reins when they're pulling a sleigh, but in this case, the deer are just lying about and eating. Would you like to see them?"

"Oh, yes, sir, very much!"

"I don't know if we have time," Camilla put in.

"It will only take a few minutes. It's not much out of our way." Pierce looked at his mother for the first time since they'd entered the coach. "If that's all right with you."

"It's fine. Tell the servants to go on to Stocking Pelham, and they can start helping set up the booth without me. Other ladies will be there, after all."

Pierce opened the panel at the front and called up some orders to the coachman, then settled back into his seat.

"I assume you're talking about the deer in the park?" Camilla asked, wondering how he could produce wild deer for Jasper's benefit, especially in a two-hundred-and-fifty-acre park.

"Actually," Mr. Fowler said, "his lordship keeps some for winter."

Lady Devonmont said, "What do you mean, 'keeps some'?"

"I got the idea from the Earl of Clarendon," Pierce explained. "He weeds out those deer among the herd that would never make it through the winter on their own. Then he pens them, coddles them, and fattens them up, so that by spring, his estate has venison without having to slaughter the strong breeders of his herd."

"Thanks to his lordship," Mr. Fowler put in, "we've been doing it for the past two years and we find that the herd has swelled admirably. It only takes a bit of feed and the gamekeeper's occasional attention to take care of the ones we pen. We sometimes have so much venison, we have to sell the meat."

"And there they are now," Pierce said as he hauled Jasper onto his lap so he could see out the window better. "Look, lad—all the deer you could want."

"Ohhhh, look at them!" Jasper exclaimed. "They're bigger than I thought they would be. I'll bet they could pull a *big* sleigh!"

They really were healthy-looking. Camilla shoved her spectacles up as she gazed out the window. She'd never been on this part of the estate, since she rarely left the dower house and couldn't ride. So she hadn't before seen the large pen, with a lean-to at one end to help protect the animals from the weather, hay strewn across the ground, and troughs that must contain feed.

Pierce's industrious use of the estate's resources astounded her. She would never have thought him that sort of owner—willing to try improvements, interested in new ideas. She would have thought him the sort to leave everything to his estate manager.

"Perhaps later, on our way home," Pierce said, "we'll stop and you can look at them up close."

"Oh, that would be *grand*!" Jasper said, his eyes huge as he watched out the window.

They drove slowly past the pen, and Camilla noticed something odd. "Why is the pen covered with netting?"

Jasper eyed her askance. "To keep the deer from flying away, Mama," he said, as if anyone would have known that.

When Pierce shot her a questioning glance, Camilla laughed. "If you had let him keep reciting the poem, you would have discovered that the reindeer in it actually fly. So since my son is a city boy and doesn't know about such things, he assumes that all deer fly."

"No kind of deer flies, boy," Mr. Fowler said firmly.

Jasper glanced darkly at him. "Reindeer do."

"Only because the poem is about magical deer," her ladyship put in gently. "They're distant cousins to regular deer. I'm afraid that regular deer don't fly."

"Oh," Jasper said, nodding at her as if that explained everything. "I have cousins in London. They don't fly, either."

They all laughed, which apparently hurt Jasper's feelings, for he settled into a sulk.

Pierce shifted him on his lap and said kindly, "I have cousins in London, too. Or rather, not far from London. They own a stud farm with lots of horses. I spend every Christmas with them."

Jasper gazed up into his face. "But not this Christmas. You're going to spend it here at Montcliff. Right?"

Pierce stiffened, his smile growing forced. "I don't think so, Jasper," he said tightly. "My uncle is expecting me."

Before Camilla could jump in to smooth over the moment, Lady Devonmont surprised her by saying, "His lordship is a very busy man, lad, with a great many duties. He can't spend all his time in the country with us."

Pierce's gaze shot to his mother. "Good of you to understand."

Despair swept over Camilla. Her ladyship might make excuses for her son, but she very obviously did *not* understand. The countess really thought that Pierce could just leave everything in the past and start anew.

Little did she know her son. Pierce and her ladyship might be able to be civil and even spend time together now without too much strain, but they still had a large past lying between them like some immovable boulder, and it became clearer by the day that no amount of pushing was going to roll it away.

So it was time for Camilla to be sensible. He soon would be leaving for London or Waverly Farm, and when that happened, she would have to go on without him, no matter what she was beginning to feel for him.

Because once he was gone, she doubted he would ever return to the dower house.

17

Memories swamped Pierce the minute he disembarked at the fair. Just as it had been twenty-three years ago, the village green was packed with canvas tents and booths, and the snow-crusted ground had already been trampled by man and beast alike. The smell of hot beef pasties mingled with the scent of the festive greens that were twined about a few booths as decoration.

For a moment he stood frozen, lost in his childhood. Then the others swung into action under his mother's commands, and he forced himself out of his trance and into service carrying items to the church's booth, alongside Mr. Fowler, Camilla, and the dower house servants.

His mother took charge of little Jasper, holding the lad's hand as they all swept through the fair toward her booth. When she pointed out various sights that might interest the boy, Pierce shot right back to the day when she'd done the same with him.

That's when it finally dawned on him—the reason Camilla championed his mother. It was because of Jasper. Because Mother had brought the boy to live at Montcliff, when apparently none of Camilla's other employers had cared if the child lived or died. Because Mother treated the lad kindly.

Because Mother treated Jasper like a son.

Pierce choked down the bitterness rising in his throat. It spoke well of Mother that she'd behaved so graciously to Camilla and her child. And Pierce refused to envy a six-year-old boy for his hold on Mother's affections.

When they arrived at Mother's booth and were surrounded by the village church's ladies' committee, something else dawned on him. Young Jasper was a surprise to more than just him.

He should have expected that, given what Camilla had said last night about the secrecy they'd deemed necessary. But Pierce hadn't considered the ramifications—that until now no one had known that the child even existed. So there had to be explanations and introductions, not to mention a great deal of fuss from the six women running the booth.

Pierce hung back to watch. He knew better than to launch himself into a gaggle of hens fawning over a little boy.

"He's your son, Mrs. Stuart?" one lady exclaimed. "How delightful! Isn't he just adorable?" She ruffled Jasper's curls, which the boy seemed to take offense at, pulling closer to his mother.

"He looks cold," another lady said, and promptly wrapped a

scarf tightly about his neck. "He should go stand by the brazier, where it's warm."

As Jasper tugged at the scarf, yet a third lady thrust out a plate of what looked from a distance like burned cakes. "Have a treat, my dear. I'm sure you're hungry."

"No, thank you," Jasper mumbled, clearly wary.

At least he was polite. Pierce wasn't sure *he* would have been at six. And Camilla was doing nothing to stop the ladies, obviously worried about offending them.

"Look at those chapped lips," said yet another female. "What you need, child, is my balm of juniper oil and honey water." She removed a vial from her reticule and, after pouring a bit of the contents onto her handkerchief, leaned toward Jasper's mouth with her hand outstretched. The poor lad started back in alarm.

"Excuse me," Pierce broke in, stepping up to place his arm about the boy's shoulders, "but Master Jasper and I were just heading off to take a look at the horses for sale."

Every female eye turned to him. And that's when something else dawned on him: None of them knew who he was. It wasn't surprising, given that he hadn't attended church in Stocking Pelham since he was eight, but it was unnerving.

"Ladies," Mother said into the curiosity-laden silence, "you may remember my son, the Earl of Devonmont. Though it's been some years since he has visited Stocking Pelham, he was kind enough to help us transport items for the booth in his coach-and-four this morning."

The ladies gaped at him, obviously unsure what to think. They must have heard he was estranged from his family. But what had his parents said about it, if anything? Generally the heir to a title and a great house was known at least a little in the local village. They must think him quite full of himself, that he hadn't come to town in twenty-three years.

While he was still wondering about that, Mother said, "Pierce, I'm sure you remember . . ." and rattled off a list of names.

To his shock, he recognized a few. "Mrs. Townsend," he said, bowing to the chubby-cheeked lady with the balm. "I do hope your husband is feeling better." Townsend was one of Montcliff's most successful tenants. Pierce had spoken to the farmer several times, though he'd never met the wife.

Mrs. Townsend brightened. "Indeed, he is, my lord, thank you for asking. He was laid low for nearly a week, but yesterday he began to feel better and managed to get out of bed to come today. My son is helping him oversee the sale of our two sows."

"With any luck, they'll fetch a good price." Pierce turned to the gray-haired woman with the plate of treats. "Mrs. Wallace, please tell me those are your famous gingerbread nuts. Mr. Fowler brought me some once, and I've been craving another taste ever since."

Beaming at him, she held out the same plate she'd offered to Jasper. "That's exactly what they are, sir, and you're quite welcome to have some."

He took one of the round, dark brown treats for himself, then handed one to Jasper. "Here you go, lad. I promise you'll find them delicious."

Jasper skeptically took a bite, then his face lit up. "They're as good as sugarplums!" he announced.

As Jasper accepted another gingerbread nut from the plate, Pierce fielded a flurry of questions about the estate that soon turned to queries about how long he meant to stay in Hertfordshire and what the news was from London. He answered as best he could, reminded of what village life was like and how much of it centered around news, gossip, and the local landowners' lives.

Then, of course, he had to endure a tour of the booth. At every table, the ladies had placed a handwritten copy of the poem that Jasper was so enamored of, so that potential buyers understood the purpose of what the women were selling. Next to it was a pretty display of ornamental stockings. Apparently the ladies had each made several, which were flounced and furbelowed to excess.

Great God, how many would he be expected to buy? And how could he purchase only a few without insulting those ladies whose stockings didn't meet with his favor?

He knew how this worked. Whatever choice he made, they would talk for weeks about whose stockings his lordship had bought and whose he had ignored. There was only one safe avenue—to buy a stocking from each of the ladies. Perhaps he could use them as gifts, though even he didn't have that many female friends. Not respectable ones, anyway.

Still, it was for a good cause, he supposed.

By the time he'd made his purchases, he was ready to escape the cacophony of chatter. Since Jasper had been following him about the whole time, Pierce used the lad as his excuse.

"Forgive me, ladies, I hate to abandon you, but Jasper and I must get a look at the horses before the good ones all sell. I'm sure you understand."

The ladies were quite effusive about how well they understood, but not so much that he didn't notice Camilla in conversation with a sly-faced young buck who'd just entered and was examining the stockings at her table.

Pierce's eyes narrowed. Judging from the fellow's smiles and smooth compliments, he was shopping for something other than Christmas stockings.

"Mrs. Stuart!" Pierce called above the din. "I was hoping you would join me and young Jasper on our tour of the fair."

The booth went completely quiet. Camilla colored and darted a glance at his mother from beneath her bonnet. "I promised I would work here, my lord. But if you need someone to help you with Jasper, I'm sure Maisie will go."

He didn't need anyone to help him with Jasper, and he sure as hell didn't want Maisie to come. He wanted Camilla. Or rather, he wanted to save Camilla from being bothered by every country bumpkin who fancied a taste of the pretty London widow.

He thought it rather admirable of him, to be so concerned, too. It wasn't a mark of jealousy at all. Merely consideration of her position as a member of his staff.

"Let Maisie help here, and you can come with us," he said, unable to keep a peremptory note from his voice.

"You don't need Camilla *or* Maisie," his mother broke in, her voice oddly steely. "Jasper is a good boy. He won't give you any trouble. And if you don't think you can manage him, leave him here."

Pierce was already bristling at his mother's interference when Jasper chimed in. "I want to go with his lordship! And I want Mama to go, too!"

That seemed to startle Mother, then worry her. "Well, then, I suppose . . ."

"I'll go," Camilla said tightly, setting down the stocking she'd been showing to the bumpkin. She glanced at his mother. "That is, if you're sure you'll be all right without me."

"We'll be fine for an hour or two. We have plenty of ladies to help."

"And I'm happy to be of service where I can, too," Fowler put in. He shot Mother a soft glance that reminded Pierce of Camilla's suspicions about the man.

Poor arse. Mother had married an earl for money; she wasn't likely to marry an estate manager without it.

Then with a jolt Pierce remembered what he'd learned about the circumstances of his parents' marriage. He would have to start thinking of Mother in different terms. Unfortunately, he still wasn't sure what those terms were.

"Go on, enjoy the fair with your son," Mother told Camilla.

With a nod, Camilla came toward him, but she wasn't smiling, which put him on his guard.

As soon as they had left the booth, he offered her his arm, and she laid her gloved hand on it so lightly that he could tell at once she was angry. "What's wrong?"

"Nothing, my lord."

The "my lord" made him bristle. "For God's sake, I thought you'd be happy to get away from the old ladies for a while and enjoy yourself."

"You do realize what those 'old ladies' are thinking now, don't you?" She stared straight out to where Jasper was skipping along ahead of them.

"I don't give a damn what they're thinking," he snapped, irritated by her reproving tone.

Her gaze shot to his. "Exactly. Because you spend one day out of twenty at Montcliff and don't venture into the town even then. You don't buy ribbon at the shop on the green, or attend the church, or stroll past the farmers in the fields. *I* do."

Two spots of color appeared on her cheeks as she shifted her eyes forward. "And given the difference in our stations, not to mention your well-known reputation and the fact that I'm a widow with a child, everyone will assume the worst about your intentions toward me."

"That's quite a leap," he bit out, even as the sinking feeling in his gut told him she was right. Village gossip was a vastly different animal than London gossip. It didn't take much to start the wheels turning. And by singling her out, he might as well have placed a brand on her forehead.

What the devil was wrong with him? He knew better.

"I hope it's a leap," she said mournfully. "I already gave the ladies one shock by turning up with a son they didn't know about. Let's hope this doesn't convince them to start speculating about who Jasper's father might really be."

The words set him back on his arse. Great God, he hadn't even thought of that. And he hadn't helped matters any by paying such marked attention to both her and Jasper. No wonder Mother had tried to stop him.

What had Fowler said in the study that day? *Lady Devonmont thinks the world of the young widow. She's very protective of her and would be most upset if she thought that you . . . that is, that anyone might try to take advantage of the lady.*

Bloody hell. "Surely my long absences would squelch any such speculation. You've been here for months, while I've been in London."

"You were here this summer," she pointed out in a dull voice, as if she'd now resigned herself to her fate. "And for all they know, before that I'd been living under your protection until you hired me as companion to your mother."

"That's absurd," he said, though his stomach knotted at the idea that it might *not* be so absurd. With a glance at Jasper, he lowered his voice. "They couldn't possibly think I'd insult my mother by parading a mistress in front of her and her friends."

"No, why should they?" she said bitterly. "You've only been estranged from her for years, which everyone in the county is aware of, even if they don't know the reason. They only know you by what they read about you in the paper."

He flinched as her barb hit home. Though his record as a good landlord would give him some credit with the townspeople, it could easily be overshadowed by his more spectacular record as a London rakehell. Especially since the latter was much longer than the former. This was the stodgy country, not sophisticated London.

Besides, even if his neighbors didn't construe his actions as unfavorably as *she* feared, they could still think he was starting up with her now. That would be little better. Once he returned to London, she'd have to endure the gossip. And the scandal.

"What a selfish arse I am," he muttered.

He hadn't realized he'd said it aloud until she said primly, "Well, I wouldn't go quite that far."

Glancing over, he noted that the tightness around her mouth had eased. "An oblivious clodpate?" he offered.

"Somewhere between arse and clodpate, I should think," she said with less temper, though he still hadn't managed to wipe the frown from her brow.

"An arse-pate, then."

That startled a laugh from her, which she instantly stifled. "More like a complication."

"Ah, yes. A complication. I'm used to being *that*." He slanted a glance at her. "I can't undo what I did, but is there any way to mitigate the damage?"

She sighed, her breath making small puffs of frost in the air. "The gossip will die down when you leave, especially if you're gone for months again and I'm still here with your mother."

"Of course." It would die down . . . as long as she lived an exemplary life.

As long as he stayed away from her and her tart opinions. And her attempts to smooth over every difficulty between him and

Mother. And her bright smile and sympathetic ear . . . and the sweetest mouth he'd ever tasted.

The thought depressed him.

"Is that a sleigh?" Jasper asked, running back to them to point it out. "It looks like the one in the picture."

Pierce followed his gaze. "Afraid not, lad. That's a sledge used for harvesting rapeseed."

As Jasper ran up to get a better look at it, Camilla eyed Pierce closely. "How do you know about farming equipment?"

He cast her a sardonic smile. "What do you think I do all day in that study at Montcliff Manor? Read naughty books?"

She flushed. "No, but I just assumed . . . that is . . ."

"That I twiddle my thumbs and take naps," he quipped. "Sorry to disappoint you, but I only do that every other day."

"Pierce," she chided, "be serious."

He searched her face, then let out a breath. "All right. Once I came of age, I started reading up on husbandry and planting and anything that might pertain to estate management. I figured I ought to know something about my inheritance for when I gained it, even if I didn't get to have any part in running it for a while."

"For a while? You never visited Montcliff as an adult, either?"

He'd forgotten that he hadn't told her about that awful confrontation years ago. "That should have been obvious from the ladies' reactions earlier."

"Yes, but you said you returned to Montcliff when you came into your majority."

"Briefly." Not wanting to dredge up that painful part of his past, he pulled away from her and strode over to where Jasper was attempting to climb onto the sledge. "Now, now, lad, that's a good way to break your head."

He dragged the wriggling boy off it and set him down in front of his mother, catching the boy's hat as it fell off. After Jasper clapped his hat back on, he raced off to look at a pen of cows.

Pierce shook his head. "That's one busy lad you have there."

"He's been cooped up in a house for weeks, remember?" she pointed out, though her tone had softened.

"Right." Out of fear that Pierce might send him away. The thought of it still sent a punch to his gut. "A lad like that needs the outdoors and plenty of space to run."

"True." She stared up at him with a gentler gaze than before. "Thanks to you, he'll have it now."

He offered her his arm again, and this time she curled her fingers about it with far more intimacy. It made his blood race. Apparently he'd been forgiven for his blunder with the ladies' committee.

Good. He would make the most of that while he had her to himself.

18

They wandered leisurely toward the end of the fair where the horses were kept. A month ago, Pierce would have found a country fair boring. But it was hard to be bored when a little pistol like Jasper was dragging you from here to yon, his face rapt at first one wonder, then another. Almost an hour had passed, and they still hadn't reached the horses.

"Maisie said they sell cheese here, right?" Camilla removed her spectacles and cleaned them with her handkerchief. "I want to buy a wheel of cheddar for Mrs. Beasley for Christmas. It's her favorite."

"That area over there seems to hold the food booths."

She called out, "Jasper, come here! We're going to get some cheese!"

Jasper frowned as he skipped back to them. "I don't like cheese."

"That's a good thing, muffin," she said as she took his hand, "since it's not for you."

"They have roasted chestnuts," Pierce pointed out. "Do you like those?"

"I *love* chestnuts!" Jasper cried.

"Ah," Pierce said as something dawned on him. "You must have been the one eating all the nuts in the drawing room the other day."

Jasper nodded solemnly. "When I lost my tin soldier."

"I almost forgot." Pierce drew the one he'd found out of his coat. "Is this your missing man?"

"Prancer!" Jasper cried as he took it. "You found Prancer!"

"Strange name for a soldier," Pierce muttered to Camilla.

"He's named after one of the reindeer in the poem," she explained. "They all have strange names."

"The only one I'm missing now is Blixem," Jasper said. "Then I'll have eight to pull St. Nicholas's sleigh."

Pierce couldn't help smiling. The boy's enthusiasm was infectious. "I tell you what. Tonight, when we get home, I'll give you one to serve as Blixem."

"Yay!"

"But first we have to find a good round of cheddar for Mrs. Beasley and some chestnuts for you. And perhaps some ribbons for your mother so she won't have to go buy them at the shop on the green."

As Camilla blushed, Jasper said, "Or we could get her a 'kerchief. Like in the poem."

"There's 'kerchiefs in the poem, too?" he asked as they headed for the food booths.

"Don't you remember?" Jasper said in that condescending tone boys used when they were impatient with grown-ups. "I recited that part. 'And Mama in her 'kerchief and I in my cap—'"

"Right, I forgot. That's where the reindeer came in." He stared down at Jasper. "What else is in this poem?"

"St. Nicholas comes down the chimney."

"Great God, that sounds dangerous," Pierce said. "I am going to have to read this thing for myself. Between the stockings and the 'kerchiefs and the flying reindeer, it sounds like something straight out of a fairy tale."

"Except there's no girls in it," Jasper said cheerily. "That's the best part."

"I beg your pardon?" Camilla said, feigning a deeply wounded tone. "*I'm* a girl."

"No, you're not. You're a lady. Girls are silly." He lowered his voice confidentially. "One of my cousins is a girl. She's *very* silly."

"She's only three, Jasper," his mother said.

Pierce chuckled. "I think you'll find her less silly as she gets older. Trust me on this—girls make life more interesting." He cast Camilla a meaningful glance. "We would miss them if they weren't around."

As a shy smile lit her face, it hit him like a bolt from heaven—he would miss *her*. And there was no solution for that.

He couldn't stay here, being the "complication" in her life. He wouldn't want to.

Would he?

They found the booth selling cheeses and took their time selecting one for Mrs. Beasley before stopping at a booth that sold roasted chestnuts. The one next to it sold cherry tarts, so while he purchased bags of nuts for him and Jasper, Camilla went to buy a tart.

As he watched her making friendly small talk with the booth owner, an idea occurred to him. If the ladies were going to make a scandal out of her association with him anyway, why not give them something to be scandalized about? Camilla could come to London. With Jasper. Pierce could put them up in a house somewhere, make her his mistress. . . .

He groaned. Was he mad? Aside from the fact that she would never agree to it, she was decidedly *not* the kind of woman he chose for a mistress. She knew too much about him already, saw too deeply. She was the kind of woman who would demand everything from him. And he couldn't give it to her.

Yet the idea continued to tantalize him as he watched her eat the cherry tart. Her blue eyes lit up, and her mouth—her rich, full mouth—was stained with cherry juice as she savored every morsel of the sweet treat.

He wondered if she would wear that same expression when he took her to bed in a neat little town house he'd pay for in London. Jasper would be off with a nanny whom Pierce would hire—perhaps Maisie, since she already knew the boy well—and . . .

No, impossible. Hadn't he already realized that?

But Camilla had a tiny smear of cherry at the corner of her lips, and he wanted desperately to lick it off, then lick a path down the soft silk of her skin to—

"When are we going to see the horses?" Jasper asked, pure trust shining in his gaze as he looked up at Pierce.

It jerked him back to the real world, the one where he had to keep his hands off the lad's mother. Pierce stifled an oath. He had to get control of himself. "Horses," Pierce choked out as he wrestled his urges into submission. "Certainly. If I remember correctly, they're this way."

At every step, Pierce was aware of her soft hand curled about his arm and her faint scent of cinnamon and honey water. But as they approached the paddock and saw a man putting a horse through its paces for a prospective buyer, a memory stirred that drew his attention from Camilla.

This felt familiar—the paddock, the horses, even the horse trader.

Then he recognized the man. Ah, *that's* why it felt familiar. "I bought a mare from this fellow last year." They came up to the paddock's makeshift fence, and Pierce hoisted Jasper up onto it so the lad could see everything. "It was a wedding gift for my cousin Virginia, who married into the infamous Sharpe family."

"Oh, yes, I remember reading about that," Camilla said lightly as she gazed up at him. "They're the ones people call the Hellions of Halstead Hall, right?"

Pierce arched an eyebrow. "There's not much hellion left in them these days. Marriage seems to have knocked it right out."

Her smile looked forced as she returned her gaze to the horses. "Marriage has a way of doing that to some people."

"True. That's why I've never married."

"You don't want to give up reading naughty books and drinking until dawn," she said dryly.

"Exactly." He wasn't about to give up control over his life to someone else ever again. "I like my fun." Except that his life wasn't much fun anymore. Not that he would ever admit that to *her*.

"But you'll have to marry one day," she pointed out.

"Why? So I can bear an heir to continue my cursed family line? No, thank you. It can die with me, as far as I'm concerned."

She gave him a sad look. "I see. You're not marrying because you want to punish her."

"I don't want to punish anyone," he snapped. He didn't need to ask who "her" was.

"Don't you? It's the only way to strike back at her for what she did. If you don't marry and don't have children, then she has no grandchildren to look after her in her old age."

"Given how little of my life she took part in, I wouldn't think she'd *want* grandchildren."

That was partly true. But what Camilla said made a certain sense, too. *Was* that the real reason he'd balked at marriage? To keep from giving Mother grandchildren?

No, the idea was absurd. He couldn't be that petty, surely.

Thrusting the lowering picture of himself from his mind, he leaned toward where Jasper was drinking up every sight in the paddock from his perch on the fence. The same sense of familiarity hit Pierce again, but he ignored it. There must be hundreds of these paddocks in fairs across England.

"Which of the horses do you like best, lad?" he asked Jasper. "The black gelding perhaps? Or the gray stallion?"

"I like the little brown one over there," Jasper said, pointing to a Shetland.

"Ah, the pony. I have a Welsh pony in my stables at Montcliff. You should ride it sometime."

"He doesn't know how," Camilla said.

"Why don't you teach him?"

"Because I don't know how, either."

Pierce gaped at her. "You don't know how to *ride?*"

She eyed him askance. "Until six months ago, I lived in London all my life. I didn't need to ride there. Mostly I walked. If my destination was too far away, there was always some equipage to take me long distances."

"But when you were a child, surely—" He broke off, cursing himself for being oblivious. "No, I don't suppose there are many mounts for children in an orphanage."

"None, actually," she said with clearly pretend nonchalance.

He always forgot how different her life had been from his. And suddenly it seemed a damned shame. "You should ride at Montcliff."

"Someone would have to teach me. Besides, I spend my days with your mother, and she has difficulty riding." Her tone turned wistful. "No, I think riding isn't destined to be one of my abilities."

"The hell it isn't. *I'll* show you how to ride."

She uttered a sharp laugh. "You're returning to London soon, remember?"

And you'll be going with me.

He'd nearly said it aloud. Damn it, but he couldn't let go of the idea of making her his mistress. It tantalized and intoxicated him. Ah, the things he could teach her, introduce to her . . . do with her.

And the first thing would be to buy her whatever damned horse she desired. She'd be a glorious rider; he was sure of it. He could easily imagine her riding to hounds, her hair streaming out behind her and her cheeks flushing with pleasure.

But first he had to convince her to go with him, and that would take some doing.

"Mama can't ride—her spectacles would fall off," Jasper announced. "But *I* want to learn."

"Of course you do," Pierce said, biting back a smile. "And you shall. I'll speak to Fowler about it." He cast her a long glance. "About both of you learning."

"Pierce—" she began in a low voice.

"Good morning, my lord, and welcome!" cried the horse trader, who'd finished with his customer and had now spotted Pierce. The man hurried up to them. "Looking for another horse to buy?"

"Perhaps, Whitley," he said with a smile. "My cousin was quite pleased with the purchase I made for her. So was her new husband."

"Good, good. That bay mare was an excellent choice. Glad she went to a good home."

Pierce laid his hand on Jasper's shoulder. "We're here because my young friend Master Jasper wanted to see your stock."

"Did you, now, lad?" Whitley said with a toothy smile. "And are you fond of horses?"

Jasper's eyes were huge. "I like that pony over there."

"I see," Whitley said with a covert glance at Pierce, who nodded. "Would you like to try it out for me? I could use an expert opinion."

"He's not old enough," Camilla broke in.

"Nonsense." Pierce patted her hand. "I'd been riding for a year by the time I was his age."

"I don't know, Pierce, I—" Realizing she'd used his Christian name, she said quickly, "My lord, perhaps it would be better if he just looked."

Whitley was a sharp fellow and instantly assessed the situation. "It's a good pony, madam. The young master would get great enjoyment out of it."

She blinked. "Oh, I'm not planning on purchasing—"

"The boy wants a ride, that's all." Pierce cast Whitley a warning glance. Later Pierce could point out to her the advantages to being his mistress, for Jasper as well as her. But no need to spook her now.

Pierce looked at Jasper. "Would you like to ride the pony?"

"Oh, yes, my lord. Ever so much."

"Good, then it's settled."

Camilla's grip tightened on Pierce's arm. "Are you sure he'll be all right?"

"He'll be fine just riding about the paddock, won't he,

Whitley?" Pierce said in a voice that conveyed what would happen if the boy was harmed.

"I'll treat him like me own, madam," Whitley said, obviously used to anxious mamas. He helped Jasper down from the fence, then ordered his youthful helper to fetch the pretty little Shetland from the pen. As Whitley brought Jasper over to the pony, Pierce felt that same persistent nagging at his memory.

It wasn't because he'd bought a horse from Whitley; that had happened in a barn. It was this particular situation—a paddock and a boy going to ride.

"Oh, I do hope Jasper doesn't get frightened," Camilla said. "He's so young."

He scarcely heard her. "Camilla," he said as his mind sifted through his memories. "I think I might have ridden a horse at this fair, too, years ago."

She looked up at him. "What do you mean?"

"When I came here with Mother. I remember it." More of the past came into his mind, and he closed his eyes, trying to summon up the scene. "She told me . . . yes . . . she said she wanted to purchase a real horse for me. Not a pony."

His eyes shot open. "No, that can't be right. It was only after spending so much time at the stud farm that I started enjoying riding. Before that, while I was still at home, I wasn't fond of it and Mother knew that. She would never have considered buying me a larger horse."

"Then why would she have said it?" Camilla glanced over to where Jasper now sat in the saddle, looking like a sultan on the throne, his hat perched rakishly to one side. Apparently reassured that he was all right, she added, "Why would she have had you ride at all, if not to try out a horse for purchase?"

He shook his head. "I don't know. I just remember being led around the paddock while Mother watched." He caught his breath as memories flooded him. "No, she didn't only watch. She argued with her cousin."

"Her cousin?"

"A second cousin, if I remember right." He shook his head. "I'd forgotten all about that. He was standing near the fence. At the time, I didn't think it odd, but now . . . Why was Mother's cousin at the fair? To my knowledge, he didn't live nearby."

"You're sure it was him?"

He nodded. "I'd met him at Grandfather Gilchrist's funeral tea when I was six. One of Mother's aunts introduced us. I only knew him as Mr. Gilchrist. That day at the fair, Mr. Gilchrist stormed off before I was done riding, and when I asked Mother about it she said they were arguing because he wanted to buy the horse, too. Only . . ."

Oh, God.

"Only what?" she prodded.

"I never made the connection before—it was so long ago. But a few days later, he showed up at Montcliff. I heard a servant tell Father that Mother's cousin was waiting for him in the drawing room. Father went in and Mother followed him, and there was a great row with the man. I couldn't hear what it was about."

His stomach clenched, just as it had then. "But I do remember that Father was furious. He threw Gilchrist out and ordered him never to return. Said he wasn't welcome at Montcliff."

Camilla shot a quick glance to where Jasper was waving at her. She waved back as she asked in a low voice, "Did your parents explain what the problem was?"

"I asked Father. He told me to mind my own affairs." A chill swept through him. "Since he was always saying that, I thought it was just grown-up business. He'd always hated Mother's family. But now I wonder if it might have been more than that."

"Why?"

"Because just a few weeks later, I was packed off to school. And I didn't see my father again for thirteen years."

19

Camilla stared at Pierce, worried by the way he'd turned still as stone. Glancing over to where her son was happily riding, she forced a smile for him, but her blood was pounding so fiercely she could hardly keep her countenance. The same idea as before leaped into her head, but this time she felt she should mention it.

"Have you considered the fact . . ." She paused, wondering how someone suggested such a thing to an earl. "Is it possible that—"

"I'm not my father's son?" he finished in a strangled voice.

She nodded.

"I never considered it before." A muscle ticked in his jaw, once, twice. "But it would make sense. It would explain why he hated me, why he banished me from my home after that day

Gilchrist came to see him. Perhaps Mother's cousin knew who the man was. Gilchrist might have tried to blackmail her or threatened to go to the scandal sheets with his knowledge if Father didn't pay him."

"Or Gilchrist might himself have *been* the man."

He sucked in a breath. "I hadn't thought of that."

"Cousins are often thrown together. Look at you and your Waverly cousins. He might have seen her at any family affair."

"Except that I was definitely born after my parents married—ten months after the wedding." He blinked. "Or so I've always been told. But a few weeks might have been glossed over. It wouldn't surprise me to learn that I was born earlier than they said. And that's easier to swallow than the possibility that Mother—"

"I know. It doesn't seem like her to break her marriage vows."

He cast her an earnest glance. "You've considered this before."

She reddened under his gaze. "Only after she told me that your father kept her from you. But you look so much like him."

"That's what everyone says. I can't see it, though. Aside from our coloring being the same, I don't think we look alike in any other way."

She wasn't so sure about that. She'd have to get another look at his father's portrait. And portraits weren't always true, either. "Still, I just can't imagine that your mother . . . would take a lover."

"Nor can I. She would have risked much to have an affair. If I am a bastard, I had to have been conceived before the marriage. And he would have known she wasn't a virgin on their wedding night."

"There are ways to . . . well . . ."

"Yes, I know. To disguise it. Because surely if he'd guessed it then, he wouldn't have waited until I was eight to banish me." He drew in a deep breath. "And there's another flaw in this theory."

"What's that?" she asked. Mr. Whitley was drawing the pony to a stop; it appeared that Jasper's ride was just about over.

"I can see how Father would hold her sin over her to keep us apart, especially if I wasn't his son and he couldn't stand the sight of me. But why did she go along so completely? She never wrote, never visited. I didn't see her for thirteen years."

"Perhaps he threatened to divorce her."

He stared blindly at the horses. "Divorces aren't easy to gain, especially if he had no proof that he'd been cuckolded. And it would have created a huge scandal, even if it could be done. He wasn't fond of scandal, trust me."

"Besides," she said, "given the choice between a divorce and losing her son, I can't imagine your mother choosing to lose you, especially if the earl wasn't really your father. Although if she knew she couldn't support you . . ."

"All right, let's say he threatened to divorce her and leave us both destitute. She might have done as he demanded to prevent that, but it would only have worked until I was grown. Once I reached my majority, I inherited money from my grandmother, and that would have kept us both comfortable enough until Father died and I could inherit the estate."

"Could he have threatened to disinherit you?"

"No. The estate is entailed, and both it and the title go to his heir. The law says that his heir is the eldest son born into the marriage, and I was born on the right side of the blanket. Even if he divorced her, I would have inherited everything eventually." His voice grew choked. "So why would he let the bastard he hated inherit, while he got rid of the wife he wanted to keep under his thumb? No, divorce couldn't have been what he threatened."

"He must have threatened *something* to make her comply."

"Yes, but what? And why did she *keep* complying even after I had come into my majority?" He swallowed convulsively. "Why did she choose him over me?"

"How do you know that she did?"

His face clouded over. "Because of what she said to me when I was twenty-one and traveled here to confront Father."

"What was that?"

But he didn't answer. He merely nodded to where Jasper was running toward them.

"Mama, Mama, I rode the pony! Did you see?"

"Yes, muffin, I saw!" she said with a tremulous smile. She caught him up in her arms, and tears started in her eyes as her gaze met Pierce's haunted one.

She hugged Jasper tight to her breast. How could a mother ever give her child up? It was unfathomable. It would kill her to lose Jasper.

If it had been *her*, she would have run off with her son and never come back.

Camilla sighed. Easy for her to say. She wasn't a countess with a husband who had riches and power beyond measure.

"Stop squeezing me, Mama!" Jasper exclaimed, wriggling out of her embrace. "I'm not a baby anymore. I rode a pony!"

She let him slip to the ground, though her heart was in her throat. "Yes, you did. You rode it very well."

"Did you enjoy the pony, lad?" Pierce asked, obviously attempting to hide the strain in his voice.

"Oh, yes, my lord. He comes from way up in Scotland, and his name is Chocolate because he likes chocolate drops." As Pierce went over to Mr. Whitley and had a short, murmured conversation with the man, Jasper added, "Do you think he could pull a sleigh, Mama?"

"Probably not by himself," she said absently, preoccupied by Pierce's tale.

When Pierce returned to her side, he looked solemn. "We'd better go back. They'll wonder what has happened to us."

She nodded, but she knew that wasn't why he wanted to return to the booth. He wanted to question his mother. To get answers.

As Jasper skipped ahead of them, she said in a low voice, "I know you want the truth, and I don't blame you. But you mustn't question your mother about this until you can do so in private, preferably back at Montcliff."

"Why?" he ground out. "No matter how I look at it, she made the choice to abandon me, at least after I was grown. Because *he* demanded it. Perhaps she felt some ridiculous guilt over going into the marriage with a babe in her belly. Or perhaps Gilchrist threatened a scandal. Either way, she acquiesced to his separating her from her own child."

"You can't be sure of that. You can't be sure of any of it."

"I know that she didn't fight for me, and if I'm to believe that she wanted to, then he must have threatened her with something. What? Or was she just too spineless to stand up to him? Damn it, I want to know. I deserve to hear the truth."

"Yes, but not now," she chided. "She's part of a community here. Surely you're not so angry at her that you would wish to see her shamed in front of people who respect her." When he said nothing, she added, "And whether you like it or not, you're part of the community here, too. You have to behave with decorum, if only because you're the Earl of Devonmont."

He walked on in silence for a few moments, then scowled at her. "I hate when you're sensible."

She let out a relieved breath. "What a pity. Because I love when *you* are."

"Do you?" He gazed, unsmiling, at her and lowered his voice to a husky murmur that made her pulse quicken. "Last night I wasn't being sensible, and you didn't seem to mind *that* too much."

Feeling the heat rise in her cheeks, she jerked her gaze from his. "That shouldn't have happened."

"Yet it did." He looked as if he was about to say more. Then he glanced down to where Jasper had slowed to listen to them, and he seemed to think better of it.

They walked in silence a few moments, picking their way over the slushy ground and trying to keep Jasper from getting his little shoes too wet in the icy weather. With only a week left until Christmas, there were holly berries adorning every other booth, and pitchmen trying to coax young men into buying gimcracks and scarves and such for their sweethearts.

But Camilla wasn't feeling very festive at the moment. The

impending storm between mother and son had put her in a quandary. She cared deeply about them both. They would expect her to take a side, but how could she?

Pierce stared ahead at the booth offering ballad sheets for sale. "I suppose there's another reason I shouldn't confront my mother before God and everyone."

She glanced at him. "Oh?"

"If I shame her publicly, you and Jasper will suffer embarrassment, too."

"I don't care about that," she said.

"I know you don't," he said irritably. "You never care about yourself. But that doesn't mean I should allow it. I may be a selfish arse, but considering the damage I've done to your reputation already by singling you out in front of the old ladies—" He halted at the ballad sheet booth. "Great God. I have an idea. Wait here."

He disappeared into the booth and came out a short while later with a package wrapped in brown paper. "Come on," he said brusquely. "And let me do the talking when we reach the booth."

That sounded worrisome. But now they were headed into the most crowded part of the fair, and it was hard to converse, especially since the number of fairgoers had increased substantially, undaunted by the winter chill.

Up ahead, she could see Lady Devonmont and the ladies inside the church's booth. They looked to be doing a brisk business in stockings.

As soon as they entered, he took Mrs. Townsend aside and said in a low voice, "Is there somewhere I can hide my package until we leave? It's a Christmas present for my mother."

Mrs. Townsend blinked. "Oh! Give it to me, and I shall put it under my basket behind the table."

"I hope she likes it," he said conversationally as he handed it over. "It's an assortment of broadsides for the pianoforte, since she enjoys playing and singing so much. Mrs. Stuart helped me pick out pieces my mother doesn't already have."

"Oh, yes?" Mrs. Townsend said, and offered Camilla a faint smile.

Camilla tried to look as if she was in on the secret.

Pierce cast the woman a knowing glance. "I did have some trouble extricating Mrs. Stuart from here so she could advise me. Since I couldn't say why I needed her, Mother proved stubborn. You know how she can be."

"I do, indeed," Mrs. Townsend breathed, obviously delighted to be included in the subterfuge. "Your mother worries overmuch about propriety, my lord."

Her heart swelling at his ingenious solution for tamping down the gossip, Camilla stepped forward to do her part. "I told his lordship that her ladyship would be happy with anything he gave her, but he insisted on the music."

"Certainly," Mrs. Townsend whispered. "Very thoughtful of him."

"You mustn't say anything to her," he cautioned the woman.

"I won't breathe a word—you may depend on me. I'll just put this under my basket now."

As she scurried off, stopping every foot or so to relate this new information to the other ladies, Camilla said, without glancing at Pierce, "Thank you."

"It's the least I could do," he murmured. "Not the best story, I suppose, but it will hold."

"On the contrary, they'll find it convincing. It was clever of you to think of it."

"One might even call it 'sensible,'" he said dryly. He raised his voice just enough to be heard by two ladies standing near. "Thank you for your help, Mrs. Stuart."

"You're welcome, my lord." She pasted a smile onto her lips, bowed to him, and then carried Jasper to the other end of the booth. Now that he'd gone to the trouble to mitigate any damage to her reputation, she wasn't going to ruin it by standing with him and giving rise to more speculation.

She spent the next few hours helping the ladies at the booth. Maisie took Jasper off again to see more of the fair, while Pierce disappeared entirely. Was he touring the fair again, looking at horses and cattle to buy? Or was he just shopping for Christmas gifts to give his Waverly cousins?

Or his mistress.

Her stomach roiled at the thought. As far as Camilla knew, he was still involved with that famous courtesan mentioned in the scandal sheets, and she had no reason to think he wasn't eagerly anticipating returning to her.

That possibility was certainly lowering. Still, it reminded her that he had no ties to her and Jasper, no reason to involve himself with her. The only association they could ever have was an illicit one. Earls, no matter how unconventional, did *not* marry paid companions.

And she didn't think she could stand having the other kind

of relationship with him. To be his, but only in some secretive, shameful fashion . . .

Sweet heaven, she was getting ahead of herself. He might not even want that. There was nothing keeping him at Montcliff, so she simply *must* resign herself to his leaving. Otherwise, she was going to find herself quite heartbroken when at last he did.

Still, her spirits lifted shamelessly when he sauntered into the booth in the early evening. The sun had set, but the fair was still going, lit by oil lamps and moonlight. He'd brought a large bag of beef pasties with him, for which all the ladies were grateful. It was well past dinnertime for most of them, and they hadn't taken a break to eat.

As they shared the food, the ladies discussed when to close the booth. People were still wandering in, though traffic had subsided in the past hour. They'd sold nearly all the stockings, and it was getting quite a bit colder now that the sun had gone down, so it seemed unnecessary for them all to remain there on the off chance that they would sell every stocking. After another hour passed and they sold only one more, they decided to close up.

Pierce had stayed out of the discussion, talking to Mr. Fowler instead. To Camilla's astonishment, the estate manager had spent the entire day helping in the booth. The ladies had been quite impressed, and one of the widows had even flirted with him, which her ladyship had frowned over. Perhaps she *did* have a spark of interest in the man.

Maisie had brought Jasper back not long ago, and after eating his share of beef pasties, the boy sat in a corner playing with Prancer.

As they began closing up, Pierce went over to watch Jasper play. He looked pensive and somber, and said little as they packed up. He accepted his package from Mrs. Townsend with a word of thanks, then gave commands to the servants about moving the items into the two carriages.

Jasper started to whine, but before either Camilla or Maisie could tend to him, Pierce hefted him onto his shoulder, which managed to cheer Jasper enough to stop him from being *too* querulous as his lordship walked back to the carriage beside Mr. Fowler and Maisie.

Her ladyship walked with Camilla, far enough behind the men to be out of earshot. "We did very well today," the countess said. "I believe we raised enough to not only refurbish the church's organ, but perhaps repaint the vestibule."

"That's good," Camilla said. "It badly needs it."

Lady Devonmont glanced ahead at her son. "Did you have fun earlier when you were going about the fair?"

Camilla tensed. "Yes. Although Jasper ran us both a merry chase."

Her ladyship cast her a shuttered look. "I overheard one of the ladies explaining that Pierce took you off so you could help him pick out a Christmas gift for me. Is that true?"

"Of course," she said lightly.

"Come, my dear, you and I both know Pierce is not buying me any gifts."

Camilla thrust out her chin. "You might be surprised."

"I doubt that." The countess lowered her voice. "Take care, Camilla. Judging from London gossip, I gather that my son has long been used to making free with women's hearts. Pierce may be charming, but he's still a rogue."

Because you made him into one by abandoning him.

No, it would be cruel to say such a thing. And it might not even be true. Pierce might be a rogue by nature.

"He's not as much a rogue as you think," Camilla said, remembering the pain in his eyes whenever he spoke of his past. "He has a lot of good in him."

"Yes, but that doesn't mean his intentions toward you are honorable."

"I would imagine they aren't." At her ladyship's look of alarm, she added hastily, "That is, *if* he had any intentions at all toward me. Which he doesn't."

"Are you sure?"

No. But she wasn't about to tell his mother that. "Trust me, you don't need to warn me that a man like him would never marry so far beneath him. I am well aware of that."

"It has nothing to do with your situation in life, my dear. I don't think he cares much about such things." She squeezed Camilla's hand. "And I would personally be delighted to have you as my daughter-in-law. But Pierce doesn't strike me as . . . well . . ."

"The marrying kind?"

The countess sighed. "Exactly."

"He doesn't strike me that way, either," she said with forced nonchalance. "I know the situation, and I'm fully armed. You mustn't worry about *me*."

Her ladyship gazed earnestly into her face. "I don't want to see you hurt, that's all."

"I understand. I'm safe, I swear."

She *was* . . . because even if she did indulge in an affair with him, she would go into it knowing fully what would happen in the end. Knowing and accepting it.

But that was a very big *if.*

It became even bigger when they climbed into the carriage and headed home. Pierce looked grimmer than she'd ever seen him. He didn't speak, just stared out the window as the carriage trundled along.

Jasper fell instantly asleep in her lap, and she was glad of it. She doubted that Pierce—or even his mother—had the patience to deal with a six-year-old's questions just now.

As they approached the estate, her ladyship said, "You should stay for some supper, Mr. Fowler. I know it's late, but it's the least we can offer after all your hard work today."

Before Fowler could answer, Pierce said, in a tone that brooked no argument, "Fowler has a great deal to do for me this evening, since he's been busy elsewhere today."

"But, Pierce, surely it can wait until tomorrow," his mother said.

"No, his lordship is right," Fowler said smoothly. "I'd already planned to return to Montcliff Manor for a couple of hours before I headed home."

It was clear from the quick glance he shot Pierce that the two of them had worked that out before they'd entered the coach. Camilla stifled a sigh. It was going to be a long night.

"Oh, very well," Lady Devonmont said, clearly unaware of the ambush being prepared for her.

As soon as they arrived, Jasper woke up enough to climb down from the carriage. While the rest of them headed inside, Mr. Fowler rode off in Pierce's coach-and-four to Montcliff Manor.

The footman took their coats, and Camilla told Jasper to go upstairs with Maisie to have his supper. "I'll be up in a bit to tuck you in, muffin," she said. He looked too tired to complain that she wasn't joining him.

"I'm sure they held dinner for us," her ladyship said as soon as Maisie and Jasper left. "It may be a bit cold, but—"

"Mother, I wish to speak to you in the study," Pierce interrupted.

Her ladyship blinked. "In the study! About what?"

"About something we should have discussed years ago."

That put her fully on her guard. "I don't think this is the time or place."

"It's either in the study now, Mother," he said firmly, "or else here in front of the servants."

The two footmen who'd been helping them with their coats exchanged furtive glances, and the countess paled. With a tight nod, she swept ahead of him down the corridor that led to the study.

Camilla stood there, uncertain what to do.

Pierce turned to her. "I want you there, too."

"Are you sure? She might be more honest with you if I'm not."

"I doubt that. She told you more of the truth the other night than she's said to me in my entire life." He offered her a rueful smile. "Besides, if you're there, I might actually keep my temper long enough to get at the truth."

"If she's being her usual stubborn self, I may not keep my own temper."

"It's a risk I'm willing to take." He held out his arm. "Come, it's time to ask her the hard questions. I don't think I can do it alone."

"All right." She took his arm, but her heart flipped over in her chest. What did it mean, that he wanted her with him at such a moment? She tried not to read anything into it, but it was hard not to.

As they walked down the corridor, another thought occurred to her. She'd never been in his father's old study. She'd asked her ladyship about it once, and the countess had said she didn't like to go in it. To her knowledge, Pierce never went in it, either. So why had he picked it for this discussion?

When he opened the door and they walked in, Camilla felt an instant chill, and it wasn't just from the lack of a fire in the room. What little furniture there was lay under canvas cloths, and the place looked as cold and barren as a mausoleum. His mother stood with her back to them, staring at the shrouded desk. Pierce visibly stiffened and cast a quick look around, as if even being in the room caused him pain.

Apparently the same was true for his mother, because as soon as he closed the door, she shuddered before she faced them.

When she saw that Camilla was with him, she gave a start. Avoiding Camilla's gaze, she said, "She shouldn't be here."

A dark scowl knit his brow. "I wouldn't be in this house at all if not for her. I wouldn't have spent the past week here, nor would I have considered, even for a moment, dining with you or spending time with you or even going to the bloody—" He caught himself. "She has championed you and fought for you from the beginning. So she at least deserves to know why."

His mother swallowed hard. "Pierce, I do not wish to—"

"Why did your cousin come to the fair to see you twenty-three years ago?" he asked bluntly.

The color drained from his mother's face. "What do you mean?"

"You know what I mean." Pulling away from Camilla, he approached the countess. "I remembered something today at the fair. I remembered seeing you argue with Gilchrist. Barely two days later, he was here at the house and Father was arguing with you about it. And not long after that, I was banished."

He stared her down. "So I ask you again, Mother, why was he here? What did you argue about? What did he tell Father that day?"

She tipped her chin up. "Nothing. Not a blasted thing."

"I don't believe you," he said. "Gilchrist obviously knew *something* about you—or perhaps about *me*—and whatever it was held enough power to give Father a hold over you that caused you to give up your only son. So damn it, I deserve to know what the man said!"

"I did not give you up!" she cried. "Not in my heart. Not for one day."

His eyes were ablaze. "It certainly felt that way to me."

Her face crumpled. "I know. But we can start anew, forget the past—"

"Not until I have the truth from you."

"My cousin said nothing, I swear! You know how your father always was."

"Yes, but he only banished me from this house after Gilchrist came here. That can't be a coincidence." Pierce set his shoulders. "So tell me this. Am I really Father's son?"

Camilla groaned. Pierce knew nothing about subtlety, at least when it came to his mother.

Her ladyship gaped at him, then lowered her brow to a fierce glower. "If you are implying what I think you are—"

"I'm not implying anything," he snapped. "I'm trying to get at the truth. And it seems to me that the one thing Father could hold over your head, the one thing that would make him banish me from this house, is that you bore him some other man's child!"

"Some other man's—" She muttered an oath under her breath. "Anyone can look at you and tell that you're his son!" She drew herself up with all the dignity a countess could muster. "And how dare you accuse me of . . . of . . ."

"I wouldn't blame you for marrying with a babe in your belly, especially given what I've learned of your situation. I only seek the truth—the reason for why Father hated me so much that he sent me away. The reason for why you *let* him send me away, and keep me away until his death. And the only reason I can come up with is that I wasn't his."

Casting him a blistering glance, she turned for the door. "I'm not going to stand here another moment and be accused of such a thing in my own home."

"It's *my* home now, remember?" he cried as he followed her, his face alight with righteous anger. "Mine. The house is mine.

The estate is mine. It's *all* mine. You may be queen of this particular part of it, but it's only because *I* allow it. So the least I deserve from you is the truth!"

She paused in her march to the door to glare at him. "And the least I deserve from you, as the woman who brought you into this world, is a modicum of respect."

That seemed to stymie him. He stood there a moment, his jaw taut and his manner stiff. When he spoke again, his voice was laden with pain. "I'm not asking this because of the years that you left me in the care of my relations, nor even because of the letters I wrote to you that remained unanswered." There was a sharp hitch in his tone. "I'm asking because ten years ago, I stood in this very room and told you and Father that I wished to come home so I could learn how to run the place that would one day be mine."

Her face turned ashen.

"I see that you recall that day, too. You may also recall his response." He glanced over at Camilla with anger glittering in his eyes. "My father told me that if I didn't get my 'damned arse' out of his house and his sight, he would have the footmen forcibly remove me."

Camilla's heart lodged in her throat. She could easily imagine a twenty-one-year-old Pierce, determined to demand his due, being confronted by such a blatant rejection from his own father.

How had he stood it? How could he even stand to speak of it now?

With his hands curling into fists, he turned back to his mother. "If you recall, I told him I wouldn't leave unless he let me speak to you alone. He laughed, but he allowed it. He walked out and left us together." His face darkened. "Because he was sure of you, wasn't he? Sure of his hold on you even then."

"Pierce, don't," her ladyship whispered. Her gaze, torn with agony, flitted briefly to Camilla. "Please don't talk about this in front of her. Leave it between you and me. I beg you."

"I won't leave it," he said hoarsely. "Not unless you tell me the reason for all of it. That's the only thing I want. An explanation. *Any* explanation."

Camilla's heart sank. He'd brought her in here only to use as a weapon against his mother. "Pierce, leave it alone," she said in a low voice.

"She won't tell me!" His gaze locked with his mother's. "So I have to *make* her tell me."

"Not like this," Camilla begged.

"If you insist on revealing to her the awful things I said that day, then go ahead." His mother's shoulders were shaking. "But I won't stay here to witness it."

As she turned again for the door, Pierce cried, "If you walk out on me again without giving me an explanation, Mother, I swear to God, I'll leave for London in the morning, and that will be the end of anything between us!"

She halted at the door to glance back at him with a look of pure torment. "All I can tell you is this," she choked out. "I love you, son. No matter what I did or said during all those horrible years, no matter how things might have appeared to you, I never stopped loving you."

And with that, she walked out.

Camilla whirled on him, unable to blot out his mother's

tortured expression. "How could you be so cruel? Clearly she can't talk about this, and you only make it worse by bludgeoning her with words and accusations!"

With her heart in her throat, she headed for the door, wanting to do something, anything, to help his mother face her pain.

"Cruel?" he called out as she reached it. "You have no idea what cruel is."

When Camilla glanced back at him, his face had gone dead and cold. And when he spoke again, his voice echoed hollowly. "You find her words of 'love' convincing because you don't know what went before." He fisted his hands at his sides. "But the last time I stood in this study, the woman you're so eagerly defending told me to my face that she never wanted to see me again."

20

Perhaps Pierce shouldn't have revealed it, but right now he would say almost anything to keep Camilla from running to Mother and pandering to the woman's refusal to face up to what she did. And where else should he say it but in the place of his shame? The place where his parents had both demonstrated how thoroughly they hated him.

Camilla eyed him warily from behind her spectacles. "Your father must have forced her to say it."

"How, damn it? She was alone with me, right here in this study. She looked me in the eye, her face as cold as a corpse's, and said that if I ever came within a mile of the estate, she would have me thrown off of it. She told me I wasn't welcome here and I wasn't to come back. Ever."

He saw the shock on her face and felt a moment's guilt. But damn it, it was time she recognized that he wasn't at fault. Mother had *chosen* to evict him from her life. And he had every bloody right to hate her for it.

Except that he didn't.

Bile clogged his throat. He'd thought he did. He'd thought he had shut Mother out of his heart completely. But now he realized he'd left a window open somewhere, and she'd found it and was trying to crawl back in.

All these years, he'd fought so bloody hard to protect his heart. To be as cold as Mother was. Yet all she'd had to say was "I love you, son. . . . I never stopped loving you," and the wound was torn open again.

How dare she spout such a lie? It wasn't true. It *couldn't* be true. Because if it were, if he'd been unfair to her, if he'd been wrong to despise her . . .

"Perhaps your father was listening, and she knew it," Camilla said, obviously desperate for a way to vindicate his mother. "Perhaps he was waiting in the hall."

"I considered that at the time." He stared at the window, remembering the agony coursing through him when he looked out of it and realized . . . "But then I saw him riding away, as if he hadn't a care in the world, even as she said those horrible things to me."

His throat felt raw. He couldn't stop the words from flowing as they never had before. "So I took advantage of his absence. I just couldn't believe that she wasn't the same mother who had . . . held me as a boy and comforted me when I suffered from asthma and—"

He choked back a vile oath, struggling to gain control over his riotous emotions. "I grabbed her by the arm and said, 'I can protect you. I have the inheritance left to me by Grandmother. Come with me now, and we'll say to hell with him.'"

Camilla approached him, but he couldn't look at her. He hated her pity almost as much as he hated this weakness, this need to unburden himself to her. To show her what a pathetic excuse for a man he was, that his own parents could toss him aside like so much rubbish.

"And do you know what her response was?" he ground out. "She shoved me away and stood there, hands clenched, while she told me she didn't want or need my protection, that she wanted only to be free of me. Then she walked out."

He stood there as he had then, hearing the crackle of the fire, the distant peal of the case clock. Tasting the bite of unshed tears as it dawned on him that he really had no parents. Not anymore.

"The footmen entered a few minutes later," he said, "but I had already gotten the message. I left. I went back to London, and I began a systematic course of study in the art of pleasure. I got drunk and I gambled and I had a string of mistresses as long as my arm. It was the only way to show them that they hadn't broken me."

The only way to obliterate the memory of that day. For a time, anyway.

But not anymore. Even before he'd responded to Camilla's damned summons, Mother's weekly letters had started to crack his armor despite his refusal to read them. That was the reason for his restlessness. He could see it now.

"Was that the last time you saw her?" Camilla asked softly.

"Until Father's funeral." He whirled on her, steeling himself for anything, but though pity glimmered in her gaze, it was mingled with something greater. Understanding perhaps. Even empathy.

And more words spilled out of him. "So now you see why I assumed it was all about the money. I thought she wanted me back here because she'd decided she had a use for me at last."

Camilla's heart shone in her face. "I suppose you had good reason to think so ill of her. What she did, what she said, was awful." She spoke slowly, cautiously, as if choosing her words. "But surely now that you've spent time with her and seen what she's really like, you realize that matters couldn't have been what you thought, that nothing was as it seemed."

"I don't know a damned thing anymore."

"Then know this." She came up to him, her eyes bright. "Having sat with that woman for six months and having heard her go on about her fine son for every day of them, I can assure you that she loves you. As I suspect she did then, no matter what she said that day."

"If she loved me," he growled, "she would explain herself!"

"Perhaps. Or perhaps it's *because* she loves you that she won't. She may just be too ashamed of whatever brought her to that pass. I understand why it drives you mad. It drives me a little mad myself, and I know her better than you." She met his hard gaze unabashedly. "But you may have to resign yourself to never knowing the truth."

"The hell I will," he bit out.

"Listen to me, Pierce," she whispered, her voice so full of compassion, it made him tense up.

Because he didn't know if the compassion was for him or for his mother. And it couldn't be both. "If you're going to argue for *her*—"

"I'm going to argue for *you*. Whatever happened in the past can't be erased. And clearly she won't explain it. But she might in time, if you can bring yourself to put your anger aside for a while." She gave him a sad little smile. "Speaking as someone who never had parents, I can promise that even having an imperfect one who loves you is better than having none at all."

He gritted his teeth. Camilla wanted him to forgive and forget. Why couldn't she see that it was impossible? "You don't understand. *Your* parents were taken from you by a force of nature or illness or . . . or something." It occurred to him suddenly that she'd never said how. Not that it mattered. "Whatever it was, it was comprehensible. You knew from the beginning that you were an orphan, whereas I—"

"I'm not an orphan," she broke in.

He narrowed his gaze on her. "Of course you are. You told me all about the orphanage." As she tensed, his blood began to pound in his chest. "Your letters of reference were from St. Joseph's Home for Orphans." His voice rose. "Are you saying they were lies?"

She didn't flinch from his angry tone. "No, they're all true. I was raised at St. Joseph's, and I worked there later. That's how I found out that I had no parents. Or rather, none who would claim me." With color suffusing her cheeks, she dropped her gaze to her hands. "I'm not an orphan, Pierce. I'm a foundling. And as I'm sure you know, they're very different things."

For a moment, he could only stand there speechless. They were indeed. "Is that why you *lied* to me about it?" he snapped, his heart thundering in his chest.

Her gaze shot up to his face. "I never lied to you. You made an assumption and I let it rest, as I've let it rest for years with everyone. Because I had to. Because it made it easier for me to be hired."

Her words gave him pause. He thought through every conversation they'd had, then groaned. She was right. She'd never claimed to be an orphan. She hadn't spoken of her parents at all, obviously because she didn't know anything about them.

He'd looked at her on the surface, just as he had with the matter of her son. He hadn't delved any deeper, too absorbed with his own pain to see hers.

She went on in a leaden voice. "I suspect that my parents, whoever they were, personally knew one of the people who managed the orphanage and convinced that person to take me, despite my bastardy." Anger flared in her face. "Otherwise, you and I both know I would never have been admitted. Even the Foundling Hospital, with its rich patrons, has been forced to limit the number of babies it will accept. Every charitable institution is afraid that taking in bastards will encourage the lower orders to leap into bed with each other willy-nilly." She snorted. "As if a woman would *choose* to gain nine months of discomfort, would risk losing her life bearing a child, just for one night's pleasure. People are fools."

"They are indeed," he said hoarsely, still trying to comprehend this new facet of her.

She shot him a look of pure defiance. "My point is, my parents wanted to be rid of me from the moment of my birth. I may not know who they are, but I know that much about them. They couldn't get me into the crowded Foundling Hospital, so they got me into the orphanage."

Her voice turned bitter. "Either way, they had to know I would never be adopted. No one who is willing to take in someone's bastard wants a redheaded, freckled child—they all want pretty children, with blond curls and porcelain skin."

"Camilla—"

"Don't say it!" she snapped. "Don't try to claim that I *am* pretty, that anyone would have been lucky to have me. Don't tell me all those nice things people say to children who nobody wants."

"All right," he said, taken aback. He'd never seen her like this, at least not on her own behalf.

"Even my husband wanted me only for what he could get out of me." She was shaking now, her temper higher than he'd ever seen it. "Your mother may have abandoned you at eight, but you had her until then. And when she gave you up, she made sure you were put in a safe place, a comfortable place, with good people who cared about you. You weren't left to the indifferent care of an institution. The orphanage wasn't a bad place, mind you, but it wasn't a home, either."

Anger and anguish twisted into one thread in her voice. "So don't tell me how justified you are in throwing away a mother who loves you. Whether you accept it or not, you have her in your life now. You have your cousins and your great-uncle." She set her shoulders like a fierce lioness preparing to fight. "I have no one but Jasper."

He stared at her, unable to look away.

All this time, he'd seen her as sensible, forthright, impossible to ruffle. But beneath that sensible exterior she was a cauldron of righteous fury, a roiling mass of seething emotion. She wanted, she needed . . . she burned every bit as much as he did.

She was magnificent.

As if aware of how much of herself she'd revealed to him, she started to turn away, but he caught her by the arms to hold her still. "You have me," he said hoarsely. "You bloody well have me."

Shock lit her face. Then she gave a mocking laugh. "And what is that supposed to mean? You're going back to London tomorrow, and you made it clear you won't be returning to the dower house. I don't have you in any sense of the word."

When she tried to wrest free of him, he wouldn't let her. Instead, he dragged her closer, his pulse pounding madly. "You would if you came with me."

Her eyes widened. "What do you mean?"

"To London. You and Jasper could return with me." When her brow lowered to a scowl, he added hastily, "Hear me out. I could take a house for you, for us. The two of you would be under my protection."

Her gaze turned wary, like that of a cornered hare. "Let me make sure I understand you correctly. You're offering to make me your mistress, my lord?"

"Yes," he said, ignoring the frosty edge she gave to the words *mistress* and *my lord*. "That's exactly what I'm offering."

He ought to have been surprised that she had leaped right to that conclusion instead of assuming that he meant marriage. But he wasn't surprised. She knew him, understood him, as no woman ever had. So of course she understood that, too.

But that didn't mean she would accept it. He would have a fight on his hands to make her agree.

And he was prepared to fight. He wanted her that much.

This time when she jerked free, he let her go, though he was ready to snatch her back if she tried to flee.

Instead, she went to stand before the dead hearth. "You have a mistress already," she pointed out dully.

"I gave my last mistress her congé before I even came here."

She whirled on him, face ablaze. "So now you need a substitute, is that it?"

"Damn it, no! That's mere coincidence." He approached carefully, not wanting to spook her again. "If all I wanted was a substitute for her, I'd take one from among the demimonde as I always have. But that's not enough for me anymore."

"I see. You want a change of pace," she said bitterly. "You think to try your hand at a respectable woman, someone who might actually care about you. Is that it?"

As always, the depth of her perception surprised him. But she didn't have the whole story by far. "No. That's not it." Then the rest of her words dawned on him. "Wait, you *care* about me?" And why did that make his pulse quicken? It was only words.

Except nothing was ever "only words" with her.

"Of course I do," she choked out. "I certainly care enough not to want to be your temporary diversion."

"You're more than that to me," he said fiercely, and realized, to his shock, that it was true. When had that happened?

"You say that now, but how long will it be before you tire of me?" She crossed her arms over her chest. "Especially when I have a child in tow."

For some reason, that sparked anger deep inside him. "It's not like that between you and me," he bit out.

"Isn't it?" Sorrow glinted in her eyes. "You're hurt and lonely, and you have no one waiting for you back in London. So you've decided I will do in a pinch."

"No. That's definitely not it."

He stalked her now, determined to make her understand. When she blinked and started to back away, he caught her about the waist and pulled her to him. "Don't you see?" he murmured. "We're alike, you and I. We both show a carefree face to the world while we keep our private torments hidden."

She swallowed hard, showing that she knew exactly what he was talking about. "That merely makes us liars."

"To the world perhaps, but not to each other. We see each other for what we are, and understand each other down deep." He lifted one hand to cup her cheek. "*That's* why I want you to be my mistress."

21

Camilla knew she ought to be insulted. But staring up into the face that had become much too dear in the past week, she ached to accept his offer.

And that made him dangerous.

"We aren't alike at all," she shot back, trying to convince herself of it. "You despise respectability while I—"

"Want it? Really?" He searched her face. "Admit it, dearling, the only thing respectability has gotten you is years of waiting on other people's leisure."

She uttered a harsh laugh. "And I wouldn't be doing that with *you?*"

He scowled. "It wouldn't have to be like that."

"Oh, really. Then tell me what it *would* be like." When he

drew breath to explain, she touched a finger to his lips. "You don't have to—I already know."

With his dark eyes alight, he moved her finger aside, only to catch her hand and press his lips tenderly into her palm. "You don't know anything," he rasped, then kissed her wrist. "We would make our own rules."

Her pulse raced beneath his caress despite her determination to stand firm against him. "I doubt that," she said shakily. "Living in the corners of society as I have, I know how these things work. Nobody makes their own rules."

He trailed kisses up her forearm to the soft skin of her inner elbow.

She fought the desire bolting through her. "If I were your mistress, I would see you at *your* leisure. You would send word that you wished to see me whenever you wanted female companionship, and I'd stop everything to be ready for you. I'd send Jasper to his room with orders not to come out, and I'd—"

"No," he said firmly, pausing to stare at her. "We'd hire Maisie. She would take care of him when we were together."

"When we were fornicating, you mean."

Anger flared in his features. "Damn it, don't make it sound sordid. It won't be that way."

"You can't stop it from being 'that way.'" Pulling free of him, she turned for the door, but he caught her from behind, keeping one arm about her waist as his hand swept up to caress her throat, her jaw, her mouth.

He pressed a hot kiss to her cheek. "It will be what we make of it."

"Not for me, it won't," she choked out. "You can play with me for a while and no one will care, but once you're done, I'll no longer be able to find a post as a companion. The only thing left to me will be other liaisons for hire."

"I wouldn't let it come to that." He nuzzled her ear, and a sensual shiver rocked her.

"I'm sure men have been saying that for centuries," she managed to gasp, though every inch of her wanted to turn and lose herself in his arms. Curse him for that. "I realize you're too far above me for a respectable connection, but that doesn't mean—"

"It's not about that," he hissed. "It's not about your station or your birth. For all we know, I might very well be a bastard, too, no matter what Mother claims." He kissed her neck with such tenderness that it melted all the cold parts of her. "But as you well know, marriage can rapidly become a prison which neither party can escape. I've no desire to let it do that to us."

He pulled her around to face him, his gaze boring into her. "What did your respectable marriage ever gain you? Happiness? We both know it did not. A sense of fulfillment? Not that, either."

"It gained me my son," she whispered. "And it's for him that I must remain respectable."

"And sacrifice your happiness for it? He won't thank you for that, trust me."

"He won't thank me for dragging his name through the mud, either."

"No one's name would be dragged through the mud, I promise you." He slid his hands up her arms to grip her shoulders. "We would be discreet."

"I'd like to see you manage that," she countered. "Especially when I'm heavy with *your* child."

He stared at her as if thunderstruck. Then he shook off his surprise. "There are ways to prevent that."

So she'd heard, while working in Spitalfields. But she'd also heard that men weren't fond of such preventatives. "And you, of course, would be perfectly willing to use them," she said, unable to keep the sarcasm from her voice.

"For you, I would. I have no desire to shame you by forcing you to bear my bastards. I know how you must feel about that." His face was alight now, the face of a man who always got his way, at least where his bed partners were concerned. "And as for the son you already have, only think what I can offer him. I can give him more than you ever could on a companion's wages. You know that's true."

She caught her breath. Oh, he was playing dirty now. "Leave Jasper out of this."

He ignored her. "He'd go to the best schools, eat the finest food, have as many damned tin soldiers as he could cram into his room. He'd have servants at his beck and call, and a pony of his own if he wanted. He'd have a chance at being someone important."

Heaven save her, he knew just what would tempt her. He didn't try to offer her great riches or fine gowns for herself—he knew that wouldn't sway her. But for her son, she would do much.

His gaze was full of promise. "I'd give Jasper anything his heart desired."

"Until you tired of me," she whispered.

"Stop saying that!" He fixed her with a glittering stare. "I would never tire of you. How could I?" He reached up to remove her spectacles and set them on the desk nearby. "You're the only one who sees me for who I am, the only one who knows my secret shame and isn't repulsed. Who wants me in spite of it."

"I don't want—" She halted, realizing the trap he'd laid for her. If she denied wanting him, she'd be saying that his "shame" repulsed her, which simply wasn't true. "It doesn't matter that I want you," she managed in a last desperate effort to resist temptation.

It didn't work. Triumph lit his gaze. "It bloody well matters to me."

Then his mouth took hers, and she was utterly swept away. Because she'd been craving his kiss, his touch, his heat, ever since last night.

No, she'd been craving it far longer than that. Fool that she was, she'd spent half her life wanting someone to desire her, to find her irresistible. Pierce was right—she'd learned to hide that aching need from everyone.

Except him. He did see her, with all her imperfections and seething urges, and he still wanted her. It was so enticing that she couldn't resist him. Not right now.

Then it dawned on her, as he rained kisses over her lips and cheeks and brow, that she had a third choice beyond being his mistress or staying here.

She could have him for tonight. Store up every moment with him for the time when he left.

"I want you, dearling," he rasped as he filled his hands with her breasts.

She hesitated, wondering if she was mad even to consider such a thing. But she would regret it if she didn't take this chance. For once in her life, she wanted to know what passion was like, what having a man desire her felt like. She wanted something real to fuel her dreams for the empty years to come.

The choice was easier to make than she'd expected.

She looped her arms about his neck. "I promised Jasper I would put him to bed, but after that . . ."

Fire blazed in his face. "You'll come to my bed."

It was more an order than a question, but she nodded anyway. For tonight, she'd be his.

"Swear it," he growled.

"Don't you trust me?" She stroked back a wayward lock of his hair.

Foolish question. He didn't trust anyone—his mother had made sure of that, whether she'd meant to or not.

Which was probably why he avoided answering the question directly. "I won't risk having you run up to see your son or console my mother and then changing your mind." His brooding gaze fixed on her as he caught her hand and kissed the back of it. "Swear it."

She couldn't breathe, couldn't think. "Very well. I swear I'll come to your room as soon as I've seen to my son."

That answer gained her a hot, ravening kiss that sparked her need for him into a bonfire, even in the chill of the room. When he finished and she was breathing hard and heavy, he reluctantly released her. "Go. But don't be long."

With a nod, she put her spectacles back on and hurried up

to her room. As she passed the floor with the bedchambers, she wondered if she *should* check on the countess. It seemed cruel to leave her alone tonight.

But she just couldn't face the woman right now, given what she was about to do. So she continued up to the room she shared with Jasper. She walked in to find him sound asleep and Maisie waiting for her.

"Her ladyship sent a note for you by one of the footmen," Maisie said, looking up from her sewing. "It's over there on the dresser. I'm surprised she didn't bring it herself—she does enjoy being here when you put Jasper to bed."

"Yes," Camilla said as she read the note, relieved but not unsurprised to hear that the countess wanted to be left alone for the evening.

"I suppose she's having another of her headaches and wants you to read to her," Maisie said, obviously fishing for information about what was in the note.

"I have to go," Camilla said, and shoved it into her pocket, hoping that Maisie would assume the reason for it without her having to lie. "I won't be back too late."

"Oh, it don't matter." Maisie yawned. "I'm going to bed soon as you leave. I'm near as tired as the poor lad was."

"I suppose he ran you ragged today."

"Not a bit. He was right happy to be outside, even in the cold. It was a joy to watch him." The maid smiled. "This afternoon, he couldn't stop talking about his lordship and the horses and how he was going to learn to ride a pony. It was very kind of his lordship to say he'd give the lad lessons."

"Yes, very kind indeed," Camilla managed. That was precisely why she couldn't become Pierce's mistress. Once he ended their liaison, it wouldn't just be *her* heart that was broken.

She shook off that thought. Tonight, she was going to enjoy her time with him. Though she would make him do as he promised and use measures to prevent children. "Good night, then," she told Maisie with a twinge of guilt for misleading the poor girl.

As she headed out of the room, she reminded herself that this was how it would be if she went to London with Pierce. She'd always be leaving Jasper with a maid while she went to meet her lover.

But even that observation didn't dampen the anticipation she felt as she rushed down the stairs and headed to his room.

Before she could reach it, the door opened, and he halted on the verge of coming out. He looked startled. "I was going to fetch you. You were taking too long."

She felt a sudden perverse need to tease him. "I was just passing by, my lord, on my way to the kitchen. Since I was hungry, I thought—"

He yanked her inside the room, then shut the door and backed her against it. "I'll take care of your hunger," he rasped, and covered her mouth with his.

Every inch of her responded, leaping to be touched by him. She craved his kisses, relished the heat and pressure of his hard body. She could feel his arousal against her belly, and it incited her own desire. Even the smell of brandy on him and the taste of—

She tore her lips from his. "You had supper," she accused.

He laughed. Jerking his head toward the table behind him, he said, "I told you I'd take care of your hunger."

Sliding out from between him and the door, she walked to the table and her eyes went wide. Somehow, in the brief time she'd been upstairs, he'd fetched enough food for them both: slabs of cold ham and cheese, thick slices of bread, pears and walnuts, and something in a bowl that looked like . . .

"Almond blancmange?" she exclaimed as she whirled on him.

With a smile, he stripped off his coat and tossed it over a chair. "I know how much you like it. And fortunately Cook does, too, so she had it waiting in case we wanted a good supper. I stole it for you." Eyes gleaming, he strolled over to pick up the bowl and slide a spoon into it.

"How very wicked of you," she said as a thrill went through her. No one ever did such things for her. "Though it shouldn't surprise me that you're a thief as well as a rogue."

"Don't forget 'seducer.'" He handed her the bowl, and as she took a bite of the blancmange, he circled around to stand behind her. Tugging her back against his firm body with one hand, he removed her spectacles with the other and set them on the table. "I'm rumored to be quite accomplished as a seducer."

"Are you?" she murmured, and took another bite of blancmange. Then she offered him some, and when he bent his head over her shoulder to eat off her spoon, she twisted her head to kiss his cheek. "Even you, who don't like desserts, must admit that it tastes very good."

He caught her mouth in a long, hot kiss, then drew back. "Not as good as you taste, dearling." Her blood quickened, especially when he cupped her breasts and fondled them shame-lessly through her clothes, thumbing the nipples into fine points. "Though I'm happy that *you* enjoy it."

"Oh, I do," she said, savoring another bite of blancmange as he slid one hand down over her belly. She undulated against it, wanting it lower. "Keep feeding me blancmange," she gasped out, "and you won't need to seduce me. I'll fall into your bed of my own accord."

He chuckled. "You may not know this," he murmured as he continued his roguish caresses, "but I'm famous for paying my chefs very well." He nipped her earlobe, then soothed it with his tongue. "So even the most celebrated would happily come to work for my mistress. You could have all the rich desserts you could dream of."

She nearly choked on her blancmange. Wily devil. Leave it to Pierce to try tempting her into accepting his offer with a promise of fine food.

But did he really believe he could gain her only by buying her? Did he think so little of himself?

She set the bowl on the table. "I don't need a celebrated cook. I'm quite happy with the usual fare."

He worked loose the buttons of her day dress. "Ah, but are you happy wearing another woman's cast-off gowns? Because as my mistress, you'd never have to again. You'd have clothes made specifically to show off your spectacular figure."

"I don't need false flattery, either," she said tartly, annoyed that he would stoop so far. "I know I'm plump."

"It isn't flattery, and it certainly isn't false. I like women who feel like women, not lampposts." Sliding her gown off, he began to unlace her corset. His breathing grew rough. "The first time I saw you, I desired you. And yes, you *are* pretty. It would give me great pleasure to dress you in clothes that convinced you of that."

The idea enticed her in spite of herself. Sweet heaven, how could she be that shameful? This was why the local rector always railed against the temptations of the flesh. Because they were so very tempting.

As her corset came free, she wriggled out of it and turned to face him, wearing only her shift. "You said we'd be discreet. But dressing me up and parading me about town would hardly be *that*."

His admiring gaze slid slowly down her, heated, hungry. He tore off his cravat and waistcoat, but his eyes never left her body. "We can be discreet without having to be recluses. London is large—if we choose the house carefully, we can live as we like without fearing that everyone is watching."

More temptation. The idea of being with him, of *living* with him . . .

Ah, but she knew it wouldn't be like that, no matter how much he wished it. Tonight was all they had.

So she would make the best of it. She reached up to unbutton his shirt, revealing a light dusting of dark brown curls as she opened it down to the placket, then pulled the tails from his trousers.

His voice turned ragged. "We could even go shopping and attend the theater, if we were careful about it."

He yanked off his shirt, leaving his chest exposed, and she

caught her breath. She'd guessed that he would be muscular and well-formed, but she hadn't guessed it would have such an effect on her.

Kenneth had been a bit scrawny, nothing like the feast of male flesh before her. She wanted to touch, to caress, to rub herself all over him. What a wanton she was.

As if he read her mind, he grabbed her hands and placed them on his chest. A bit embarrassed, she avoided his gaze as she spread her fingers over the now tense muscles, reveling in how they jumped beneath her touch and how his heart raced at her caress.

How that made her own heart race.

He tugged loose the ties of her shift. "We could go to the museums or . . . take a boat along the Thames in the summer . . ."

He trailed off when she slid her hand down to work loose the buttons of his markedly bulging trousers. His breath came in a harsh rasp now, yet he kept talking. "We could even . . . live close enough to the country . . . to keep horses and ride. I'd buy you the finest mount . . . with a beautiful saddle and . . . a neat little curricle for your own use. . . . Then I'd teach you to ride and drive and—"

"Shh," she whispered. She couldn't bear it anymore. "Stop trying to buy my affections." She brushed a kiss over his lips. "You already have them."

His eyes glinted obsidian in the firelight.

"Would I love for you to teach me all that, and buy me new clothes and the rest of it?" she went on, desperate to make him understand. "Yes. But if I became your mistress, it wouldn't be for any of that." Taking his hand, she pressed it against her chest where her heart pounded furiously. "It would be for *this,* for how you make me feel."

A shuddering breath escaped him. "And how *do* I make you feel?"

She stretched up to kiss his mouth. "Like I can fly."

With a groan, he caught her to him and kissed her with such fervent need that she thought her heart might explode. Oh, what was she going to do? She was falling in love with him.

And he didn't want that.

So she gave him what he did want. She let him pull her shift off her, let him carry her to his bed. She let him lay her down and run his smoldering gaze over her while he finished stripping off his clothes. She didn't flinch or blush or turn away from that hot, riveting stare.

Until he was naked. Then she had to look at *him.* And what a sight he was, all lean muscle and fine lines, a sweet symphony of a body that she wanted nothing more than to play.

He reached over to pull out the drawer to the little table beside the bed. "Since I promised you I'd take preventative measures . . ." He drew out a long sheepskin tube, then held it out to her. "Would you like to do the honors?"

She sat up to gape at it. "Do you carry such devices about with you as a matter of course?"

He laughed. "No. But after what happened last night, I figured you might be more amenable to sharing my bed if I could promise to protect you. And you'd be surprised what the tinkers at a county fair have for purchase, if you know how to ask the right questions."

"*That's* what you were doing this afternoon?"

"Among other things."

With a shake of her head, she took the tube from him. "You really are quite a wicked fellow." Though the fact that he was willing to wear such a thing touched her deeply.

"That's what you like about me," he drawled.

"Hardly," she said with a sniff. "I like you in spite of that."

But as she smoothed the covering onto his thick, jutting member, so much larger than her late husband's, and he hardened even more, it dawned on her that their positions resembled those of the characters in that shocking drawing from *Fanny Hill.*

That's when she finally blushed.

With a chuckle, he tied off the tube, then slid onto the bed and pulled her down to lie next to him. "For a widow, you sometimes seem very innocent."

She frowned at him. "Forgive me if I don't have *your* vast experience. I had only the one husband, and he mostly touched me in the dark when I was half asleep. I hardly ever saw him like . . . well . . . this."

His gaze turned positively carnal. "You'd best get used to it," he said in a husky murmur as he filled one hand with her breast. "Because I intend to be naked with you every chance I get."

Then his mouth was on hers—as was his body—and she shut her eyes to savor it, putting her late husband thoroughly from her mind. Pierce whispered admiring compliments about her hair and her breasts and her belly, kissing each part with a mix of heat and tenderness, making her want and need and yearn—

He kissed her between her legs, and her eyes shot open. "Wh-what are you doing?"

When she tried to pull her thighs together, he wouldn't let her. "You need to read more naughty books, dearling." His eyes glittered. "You had your dessert. Now let me have mine."

And he lowered his mouth to her most private part again.

"But . . . but . . . Pierce . . . ohhh . . ."

She'd had no idea. The way he was kissing her . . . *there* . . . seemed decadent and wild and . . . so very delicious that she curled her fingers into his hair to hold him close.

His response was to kiss and suck and tease until she thought she'd go out of her mind with need. It wasn't long before she could feel her release building, feel it growing and lifting . . . "Pierce . . . oh, dear heaven . . . please . . ."

"Not yet, dearling." Dark eyes alight, he moved up over her. "This time we'll go there together."

And he entered her with one silken thrust.

Oh, it was magic. He was inside her, around her, driving her once more toward a glorious madness. How would she give this up? How would she give *him* up? He felt part of her. With him, she was herself and it was right. He liked her just as she was.

But he didn't love her, and that would kill her in time. Because she could never be with him, day in and day out, without telling him she loved *him*.

She did. She loved the dear, complicated man. And she knew, just as she knew everything else about him, that he wouldn't want to hear it. So she would show him tonight, instead.

As he drove into her over and over, she kissed his chin, his throat, his mouth . . . anything she could reach. She wrapped her legs about his hips when he urged her, and she gave herself up to the act that until now she'd always thought awkward and embarrassing. Because with him, it was neither of those. It was like . . . like . . .

"Are you flying yet?" he rasped as he thundered into her, each stroke bringing her nearer loftier heights.

It *was* like flying. Exactly. "Yes . . ." she choked out. "Oh, Pierce . . ."

"Fly then, dearling," he murmured as he drove her higher and higher. "As high . . . as you can . . ." He stared down at her, his eyes darkening with an emotion she'd never seen in them before.

Longing. She recognized it because that's what she felt, too.

He brushed his lips against hers, then whispered, "Just make sure you take me with you . . ."

And with one great plunge, he sent her soaring into the heavens.

She clasped him to her as he, too, reached his release, and for one precious moment, they vaulted into the highest heights together, wrapped in each other's arms without a care in the world.

Then slowly they tumbled to earth. And to her surprise, that was precious, too—for although he rolled off her, he didn't turn over and go to sleep. He drew her close, then held her and kissed her and made her feel like something more than a bedmate.

And as he nuzzled her neck with infinite tenderness, the words she'd fought not to say just spoke themselves.

"I love you," she whispered into his ear. "I love you, Pierce Waverly."

22

To Pierce's shock, his heart sang at the words. He would never have expected them to sound so wonderful. Then again, he hadn't expected sharing a bed with Camilla to be so wonderful, either.

It made no sense. He'd been with plenty of women—more experienced women, younger women, more accomplished women. He'd shared the beds of actresses and whores, opera singers and duchesses, and never once had it been an act of such sweetness that it damned near brought him to tears.

Never once had any of them said those words to him afterward.

Oh, God, didn't he know by now that love was just a word? That it meant nothing?

Except that he couldn't believe Camilla would lie to him. He knew who she was, from tip to toe. She would never say such a thing lightly.

But that didn't mean it was real.

He drew back to stare at her. "Don't."

The pain in her eyes was swiftly covered by belligerence. "Don't what? Love you? Or *say* that I love you? I can stop the latter, but I can't stop the former. It's too late for that."

With his blood pounding through his veins, he took her hand and kissed it. "Look, I know that you think you feel something—"

"I don't *think* I feel anything." She snatched her hand from his. "I know what I feel, Pierce. Don't try to tell me otherwise." Pulling out of his hold, she sat up to throw her legs over the side of the bed.

He looped his arm about her waist to keep her there, then pressed a kiss to her back. "Don't go. Not yet."

She sat there, her body stiff against his arm, but as he sat up beside her, she let out a long, shuddering breath. "I'm sorry. I knew you wouldn't want to hear it. But I couldn't help myself." A wry note entered her voice. "It's been the curse of my life that I speak my mind even when I shouldn't."

"That's what I like about you," he assured her. Even when what she said set him on his ear. He stared down at her bent head, feeling a welter of confused emotions, not the least of which was hope, damn it. "But I can't . . . I don't . . ."

"I know, my lord," she said, the formal term cutting him to the heart. "It just had to be said."

She started to rise from the bed, but he pulled her down onto his lap. "It's not what you think." When she wouldn't look at him, he turned her face up to his. "I'm not capable of loving anyone."

She cupped his jaw, her hand infinitely gentle. "I don't think that's true."

"Ah, but it is."

He debated a moment, but the melting look in her eyes decided him. She deserved to know what sort of man she was taking up with. Reaching over to open the little drawer by the table, he drew out a much-creased and worn letter and handed it to her.

When she cast him a quizzical glance, he said, "It's the last letter my mother ever wrote me at school, right after I was sent away."

Paling a little, she opened the fragile parchment and read the lines that had been etched on his soul for years. The lines that ended with *And always remember, I love you very, very much. With many kisses, Mother.*

"I kept it at first to sustain me through the difficult times." His voice hardened. "Then I kept it to remind me how little the words mean."

She glanced at him, tears filling her eyes. "I'm not lying to you when I say them, and I suspect that neither was she."

"Perhaps not," he managed. "But that makes it even more obvious that love is just a meaningless fiction. At least I'm wise enough to understand that. And I can't feel something I don't believe in. I might have believed in it once, but not anymore."

"Because of your parents abandoning you, you mean."

"Not just that." There were times he hated how deeply Camilla saw into him. "But I've experienced too much in my life, witnessed too many unhappy marriages, and . . ." He forced a smile. "It's like Jasper believing in flying reindeer. Once you're around real deer enough to know they don't fly, the magic disappears."

"On the contrary," she said softly. "Believing in love isn't like believing in flying reindeer. It's like believing in rain. Or summer. Or Christmas. Love is real and steady and absolutely essential to any kind of life. Not believing in it doesn't make it any less so."

Fighting the seductive appeal of her words, he rasped, "For me, it does, and that's what matters."

He braced himself for more of an argument, but she merely shook her head at him. "I know. That's why I didn't intend to say the words."

The regret in her voice knifed through him, and he caught her by the chin so he could kiss her, soft and deep. "It doesn't change anything. Wanting you, having you want me, is more than enough for me."

"Is it?" She stared into his face, her eyes luminous in the firelight. Without her spectacles, she looked even more like a maiden waiting for love.

And it hit him suddenly how unfair he was being, to ask her to give up a future with any other man just to be his mistress.

But she'd had her chance at marriage, and she hadn't liked it. That's what made the two of them so perfect for each other. They were peas in a pod and wanted the same things, whether she admitted it or not.

Didn't they?

"Camilla, I—"

A knock came at the door, and he froze. A glance at the clock told him it was long after midnight. No servant would be up here at this hour.

Camilla leaped from his lap. "Oh, Lord, Maisie must have guessed I was here. Something must be wrong with Jasper!" Guilt suffusing her features, she hurried to put on her shift, then her drawers.

Swiftly, he rose and began to dress, too.

The knock came again. "Open the door, Pierce!" his mother's voice commanded. "I wish to speak with you!"

As the blood drained from Camilla's face, he cursed under his breath. The main rooms downstairs in the dower house had special servants' passages, but none of the bedchambers did. There was no escape.

"I'll be there in a moment, Mother!" he called out as he jerked his trousers on. Somehow he had to draw her away so Camilla could leave without being seen.

Camilla was still frantically gathering up her clothes and grabbing her spectacles when the door swung open, and his mother entered.

Bloody hell. He'd forgotten to latch the door.

Mother took in the scene with a look of pure horror. "I knew it!" she cried. "I went looking for Camilla, and Maisie said she'd thought she was with me. So I went to the drawing room and the study and found no trace of either of you. That's when I knew." Her gaze met his accusingly as Camilla stood fixed in the middle of the room. "How could you?"

"My lady, please, it's not how it seems," Camilla said.

"No?" she choked out. "Because it appears to me that my son has just finished seducing you."

Pierce glared at her. "How dare you—"

"You have every reason to be angry with me, Pierce," his mother went on fiercely. "But to use Camilla as a weapon against me is—"

"A *weapon?*" Only with an effort did he keep from tossing her bodily from his room. "Not that it's any of your concern, Mother, but she *chose* to be here. We chose to be together."

"A woman in Camilla's position is unable to choose such a thing," his mother protested. "Do you really think she could refuse you? You're her employer, so any association of that kind between you gives you all the power, and you know it."

He stiffened. He did know it. And the worst of it was he would do it again if he had the chance.

"You paint your son more ill than he is, my lady," Camilla put in. "He never demanded anything of me, never took advantage. I really *did* choose to be with him. I know you probably think it very wrong of me, but—"

"I don't blame you, my dear," his mother told her softly, then nodded to Pierce. "I blame *him.*"

That was the last straw. "You have no right to blame me for anything, ever," Pierce hissed as he advanced on her, not caring that he wore only his trousers. "You gave up the right to dictate to me when you abandoned me."

"I did not abandon you!" Mother cried. "I acted in your own interests."

That was a new twist, and the ludicrousness of it infuriated him. "Oh? How so?"

Her lips tightening, she glanced away and said nothing more.

His temper rose into fury as the festering sore of twenty-three years erupted. He bore down on her with ruthless intent. "Were you acting in my interests when you ignored the letters where I begged to be allowed to come home? Or when you kept me from learning how to run the estate I would one day inherit? Or even when you shattered every real feeling I ever had by telling me—"

He broke off with a curse. "I refuse to do this anymore. I don't care what your reasons were. Nothing you say can make up for what you did." He turned to where Camilla was watching them both, her expression clearly torn. "Camilla, go gather your things and Jasper's. We're leaving for London now."

His mother turned ash white, which gave him a moment's twinge of conscience, but he ignored it. She had no say in this. She'd given up that right years ago.

But Camilla hadn't moved.

"Go on, dearling," he commanded her. "I know it's late, but you and Jasper can both sleep in the carriage. Bring Maisie, too, if you need to."

She swallowed hard, then said, barely above a whisper, "I'm not going with you."

He gaped at her. He couldn't have heard her right. "Of course you are."

"I can't," she said, her voice a little firmer. "My place is here."

"Your place is with me!" he ground out.

A tear escaped her eye, then another. "Pierce, you have to understand—"

"No!" he cried as the bottom dropped out of his stomach. "Damn it, no, I don't have to understand a bloody thing!"

She couldn't be doing this. He wouldn't let her.

He strode up to grab her by the arms. "You belong with me. We belong together. You owe her *nothing,* no matter what you think."

Tears were streaming down her face now, and she clutched her pitiful bundle of clothes closer to her chest, as if to use them as a shield against him. "It's not about your mother."

"The hell it isn't! You're choosing her over me, because you've got some idea in your head that being at her beck and call is more respectable, more—"

"I'm not choosing either of you," she said in a tortured whisper as she pulled free of his grip. "I'm choosing my son."

That caught him by the throat. It was an argument he felt powerless to refute. But he tried anyway. "You know he'll be better off in London."

"As the scorned son of your mistress?"

He glowered at her. "No one would *dare* to scorn him, or you. Not with my power and fortune behind the two of you."

"And after we no longer have you?" she asked softly. "What becomes of us then?"

Her logic was inescapable, and he hated her for it.

"Or what happens when you marry?"

"I will *never* marry," he vowed.

Tears sparkled in her eyes. "You say that now, but you can't promise it."

He scowled. "If you want promises from me, then come with me to London. I'll have my solicitor draw up whatever legal document you require to ensure that you—"

"It has nothing to do with money!" she cried. "I can't risk your coming in and out of Jasper's life at your leisure. Small children don't understand such things. You of all people should know that."

The words hit him like a blow to the gut, making him want to strike back. "I know that you said you love me. You *claimed* that the words were real."

Though the blood drained from her face, she didn't waver in her stance. "They are, and I do. Which is precisely why I can't go with you. I love you too much to be just your toy for a while."

"You wouldn't be my toy, damn it!"

But he could see from her face that no argument would sway her. Once Camilla made up her mind to do something, she stayed the course, even if that course drove a stake through his heart.

How *dare* she show him heaven for one brief, glittering moment, and then snatch it away, leaving him alone once more?

Always alone.

"Fine," he choked out, steeling himself against the hurt that rent his heart.

She thought to force him into marriage, did she? Well, the days when he could be jerked about by other people's whims were long gone. Never again would anyone force him into doing anything.

"To hell with you." He looked beyond her to where his mother had gone still as death. "To hell with both of you. I'm leaving this house, and I'm not returning. So I hope you're both very happy together. Now get out of my room."

When they just stood there, staring hollow-eyed at him, he marched toward them. "Out, damn you!"

His mother fled at once, but Camilla paused in the doorway to glance back at him. "I know you're angry, Pierce, and I understand why. Your parents tore a hole in your heart when they abandoned you, and you've been trying to mend it ever since. That's why you've had a string of mistresses—not because you wanted to show your parents they hadn't broken you but because you kept hoping to find someone who really did care about you."

"Shut the hell up!" he cried, fighting the truth in her words as furiously as he fought to ignore the compassion on her face.

"Well, you've found that someone. I truly do love you. But until you put the past behind you, you won't be free to love me or anyone else." She hitched up the bundle of clothes in her arms. "If you've learned anything from your parents, it ought to be this—love works only when it's mutual. Otherwise, eventually it becomes exactly what you call it—a meaningless word. For both parties."

Then she walked out.

He stared blindly at the door, willing her to come back through it, to change her mind, to throw caution to the winds.

But he knew better. She would never do that. Not for *him*. No one ever did.

And it was time he stopped waiting for it.

* * *

Camilla stood in the countess's sitting room as the house was thrown into an uproar. Pierce had given orders for his coach-and-four to be readied, and the entire cadre of servants had been roused to do all the myriad tasks required for a trip.

His mother wouldn't look at Camilla, and Camilla wasn't certain if it was embarrassment or disgust that kept her so distant.

At the moment, she didn't care either way. She was numb from the inside out. She should have known that her heart-stopping plunge into pleasure would end like this. Anything that wonderful never lasted.

Ruthlessly, she stifled the tears that kept threatening. She refused to cry in front of her ladyship. That would come later, when she was alone. No doubt, regret would come with it, too.

But right now she didn't regret her few stolen moments with Pierce. They would sustain her for years to come.

They would have to. Now that she knew what love was like, she didn't want to go through it with anyone else. She didn't think she could bear this pain more than once.

Tears threatened again, and she lifted her handkerchief to blot them before they could fall.

"Perhaps you should have gone with him," the countess said in a ragged whisper.

The words, sounding like a dismissal, startled her. "Will it be so hard for you to endure my presence now?"

"No! Never, my dear, never. But I hate to see him go off alone." Her ladyship seized Camilla's hand and squeezed it. "And I hate to see you so unhappy."

The countess's words made Camilla want to cry even more. She squeezed her ladyship's hand back. "I'll be fine."

One day perhaps. But at the moment, it didn't feel as if she'd ever be fine again.

"I suppose you did the right thing. It wouldn't do for Jasper—"

"No, it wouldn't," Camilla said firmly. It wouldn't do for her, either. Spending her life as Pierce's sometime lover would have drained the heart out of her.

"He shouldn't have asked it of you," her ladyship said. "It was very wrong of him."

"He was just being Pierce."

And yet . . .

She kept seeing the look of betrayal on his face. He'd been sure she would go with him, especially since she'd been foolish enough to tell him how she felt about him.

Of course, then the wretch had tried to use that against her. Anger coursed through her, and she choked it down. What else had she expected? That he would profess his undying love? She should have kept her feelings to herself.

The door burst open, and Maisie rushed in with a wide-awake Jasper in her arms. "What's going on, milady? The poor lad woke up in a fright at all the noise."

Lady Devonmont drew herself up, becoming her usual restrained self once more. "His lordship is leaving."

"In the middle of the night? But why . . . what . . ." Maisie glanced to where Camilla stood, now dressed but with her hair still down about her shoulders and her eyes teary, and Maisie's lips tightened into a line. "I see."

"You are not to say a word about this," the countess commanded. "Not to anyone, do you understand?"

"Of course, milady," Maisie said fiercely. "I would never do anything to harm you or Mrs. Stuart."

Camilla cast the maid a grateful smile.

Sudden silence descended on the house, and her ladyship sighed. "He must be gone now."

"Yes." Camilla's stomach plummeted. Oh, how would she bear it?

Jasper reached for Camilla, and she took him from Maisie. He stared up at her sleepily. "Why did his lordship go away, Mama? And why didn't he say farewell to me?"

"I'm sure he wanted to, my dear boy," Lady Devonmont put in, "but he was in a very big hurry. He has a lot of important matters requiring his attention in London, you know."

Jasper stared at the countess. "Because he's the great earl, you mean."

"Yes, exactly," Camilla choked out. The great earl who equated believing in love to believing in flying reindeer. Because if he believed in love, he'd have to put the past behind him, and he just couldn't.

"But what about Christmas?" Jasper asked. "And what about Blixem? He said he'd give me Blixem when we got home, and he forgot."

"I'll give you Blixem," her ladyship answered. "Don't you worry about that."

"And if you'll recall," Camilla added, "his lordship did say he wouldn't be here for Christmas. He has to go to Waverly Farm."

"I remember." Jasper pouted. "I just thought he might change his mind."

Thank heaven Pierce had left when he had. Right now Jasper was merely intrigued by the man, but many more encounters and his leaving would have hurt the boy deeply.

Rubbing his eyes, Jasper stared into her face. "Does this mean I don't get to learn to ride a pony? His lordship said there was a Welsh pony in the stables, and I could learn to ride it."

"And you shall." Lady Devonmont's voice was firm. "I'll speak to Mr. Fowler about it tomorrow."

"I don't know if I want to anymore." Jasper laid his head on Camilla's shoulder. "It won't be the same without his lordship. Will it, Mama?"

"No, muffin, it won't," she choked out.

Nothing would ever be the same again.

23

Pierce tried to sleep on his way back to London, but it was impossible. He couldn't cast Camilla from his mind. At first all he could do was rage at her for her small-mindedness. How could she not see the value of what he offered? And how could she claim Jasper would be harmed by their association? He would never hurt the lad. Never!

Jasper would gain advantages beyond her wildest imaginings: schools and money and—

And after we no longer have you? What becomes of us then?

He clenched his hands into fists. The words rankled. Yet as his temper cooled, his rational mind reasserted itself, and he recognized that her words were fair. She had every right to worry about the future. Her idiot husband had died unexpectedly, and she and

Jasper had been left with nothing. It could happen to Pierce just as easily.

All right, perhaps that was true. But he would make provisions, *legal* provisions.

It has nothing to do with money! I can't risk your coming in and out of Jasper's life at your leisure. Small children don't understand such things. You of all people should know that.

He did. God, how he did.

His heart pounding, he stared out the coach window at the pre-dawn darkness. The snowy fields glowed white beneath the waning moon, reminding him of the day he'd left home for school, not knowing it would be his last day at Montcliff for years to come.

And he realized with a jolt that if Camilla had chosen him over Jasper, she would be no better than his own mother, who'd chosen Father over him.

Or had she?

He'd scoffed when Mother had said she'd acted in his own interests, but now he had to reconsider that possibility. If Father had held something over Mother's head, as he and Camilla had postulated, what if it really *had* been something having to do with him? Pierce couldn't see how that was possible, but then, he couldn't see straight when it came to the past.

Camilla had recognized that.

I truly do love you. But until you put the past behind you, you won't be free to love me or anyone else.

Try as he might, the words kept thrumming through his brain. It was easy for her to say—she didn't have his past.

No, he thought wryly, she merely lived with the daily realization that her parents hadn't wanted her at all. That she'd been born destitute in ways he couldn't begin to understand, even with his own painful situation.

He let out a long breath. No wonder she couldn't accept his offer to make her his mistress. She yearned to be wanted for herself, as she never had been, and what he was offering was a poor substitute.

But could he offer her more? Did he dare? Or would he be better off not risking it?

He still had no answers by the time the coach arrived at his town house shortly after dawn. The servants were prepared for him since he'd sent word ahead, but even their presence couldn't liven a place that felt like a tomb after the bustle and cheer of the dower house. He hadn't realized until now how sterile his life had become, with his mistress relegated to her own lodging.

Indeed, even before he'd gone to Hertfordshire, his most pleasant days had begun to be the ones spent with his cousins and their friends the Sharpes. What did it say about him that he increasingly found enjoyment only with happy couples and relations?

He ought to go to bed—he hadn't slept in twenty-four hours. But he was too restless to sleep. And a few moments playing the pianoforte in his drawing room gave him no comfort, either.

The brandy decanter tempted him briefly, but he'd gone that route three days ago. It had been oddly unsatisfying.

Thinking that losing himself in work might be the best alternative, he headed for his study. But as he stood behind the desk, sifting through the pile of mail that Boyd had left for him, he was arrested by the sight of the infamous box of Mother's letters.

Pierce's throat tightened as he stared at them.

Then he sat down, dumped out the box so that the very first letter was on top, opened it, and began to read.

> *My dearest son,*
>
> *You cannot know how much I have missed you all these years. You probably have trouble believing that, but it is the absolute truth. Being with you at the funeral, even with you so very angry at me, made all the rest of it bearable.*
>
> *May I say that you were dressed very well? I was glad to see it. Your great-uncle always said that you wore a fine coat better than any man he knew, and I quite agree.*

The nine-page letter went on in that vein, mixing her observations of him from the funeral with information she had apparently gleaned from his great-uncle. He hadn't known that his uncle wrote to her, but it wouldn't have mattered if he *had,* for apparently she hadn't written back to Uncle Isaac, either, since she made no mention of it.

But here and there her letters to Pierce contained a reference to this or that anecdote Uncle Isaac had written about him. Some events she described had so faded into the distant mists of his memory that he was astonished anyone remembered them, especially her.

As he tore through letter after letter, she commented on her daily life, but the accounts always rambled into memories she'd stored up of him from myriad sources. Some were gleaned from the newspapers—in one letter she waxed on for pages about how Eugenia wasn't worthy of him—and some were taken from his great-uncle's and the late Titus Waverly's letters.

Occasionally she would recount something that Fowler had told her of Pierce's work at the estate. She even offered advice, and he realized with faint amusement that although he hadn't read any of it, it had still filtered to him through Fowler, and he'd often taken her advice secondhand.

It took him several hours to read all of her letters, and when he was done, he sat back with a tightness in his chest. Years of tales of him were recounted, some that he couldn't believe she'd even heard about. It was as if she'd stored up his entire life for the day when she could relive it with him. The day when she could be with him again.

And he had spurned the gift without even giving it a glance. Why? Because she wouldn't explain herself or her actions.

She didn't do it in the letters, either, just as Camilla had predicted. There were no references to his years of banishment, no mention of that horrible day in the study. She barely spoke of Father at all. It was as if the man had disappeared from her thoughts and memories on the day of his death. Clearly, there'd been no love there.

Yet love for her son shone in every word.

He sat there with the last letter in his hand, his blood thundering and his eyes misty with tears, and read the last line. It was the same last line of every single letter in the box:

Even if you can never forgive me, my son, know that
I will love you until I die. And beyond, if God would
allow it.

He stared blindly across the study, and Camilla's words came
to him.

Your mother may have abandoned you at eight, but you had her
until then. And when she gave you up, she made sure you were put in
a safe place, a comfortable place, with good people who cared about
you. . . . So don't tell me how justified you are in throwing away a
mother who loves you.

Mother *had* loved him. He could see that now.

Camilla had said that the very fact of her love might have to
be enough for him. That he might never know the truth about
why she'd banished him for so many years.

But could he put the past behind him and just go on, build a
relationship with his mother outside of the past?

He didn't think he could. Not because he didn't want to but
because he didn't think *Mother* could, either. No matter how they
tried to ignore it, those years of pain would taint every encounter.

If Camilla was right, however, and Mother would never reveal
the truth, then he'd have to discover it on his own. He knew more
now than when he'd gone off to Hertfordshire. He might even
know enough to get him started solving the puzzle.

Because it was time he got to the bottom of things. Since she
wouldn't reveal it, he would unveil it. It was better than sitting
around brooding over Camilla, better than parsing his wreck of a
life for what he might have done differently.

And he knew just the man to help him do it, too.

A few hours later, fueled by coffee and a fresh purpose, Pierce was being shown into Sir Jackson Pinter's grand new office in Bow Street.

The famous former Bow Street Runner had been knighted for solving the twenty-year-old murder of the Sharpe siblings' parents. Thanks to that—and other celebrated cases—he was now chief magistrate, but as far as Pierce knew, he still did investigative work. At least Pierce hoped so. Because if Sir Jackson couldn't find out the truth, no one could.

But only when the former runner greeted him with a decidedly cool manner did Pierce remember that the fellow didn't *like* him. Unbeknownst to Pierce at the time, the woman who was now Sir Jackson's wife had briefly used Pierce as a pretend suitor in part of a scheme to thwart her grandmother's edict of marriage.

He'd forgotten that rather sticky point.

"Have a seat, Devonmont," Sir Jackson said with a jerk of his head toward the chair before his desk.

As Sir Jackson sat down, Pierce did the same. "You look well," Pierce said, figuring he'd best smooth the past over if he could. "Marriage suits you."

A smile stole over the man's face, softening what were generally rather harsh features. "Marriage and fatherhood. I have a son now, you know."

"I heard. Congratulations. Did he come out brandishing a pistol?"

Sir Jackson blinked, then laughed. "No, but if Celia has her way, he'll be learning to aim one by the time he's three."

"If anyone could teach him how to shoot, it's your wife. And if anyone could teach him *when* to shoot, it's you."

"Thank you, my lord." Looking a bit more genial, Sir Jackson settled back in his chair. "Now tell me, what brings you to Bow Street?"

Pierce got right to the point. "Actually, I have need of your services to find out information about a cousin of my mother's."

"Your estranged mother?" Sir Jackson said.

"You know about that?"

"Aside from the fact that the Sharpes are notorious gossips, I . . . er . . . did a bit of research into your background for Celia."

"Ah." Pierce wasn't surprised. He wasn't even annoyed. Since Sir Jackson seemed a bit embarrassed by it, he might be willing to make up for it by helping Pierce now. "Well, that's all water under the bridge." He arched an eyebrow at Sir Jackson. "As long as you're willing to take the case."

"Willingness has nothing to do with it, I'm afraid. I don't do that sort of work anymore. Between serving as chief magistrate and being asked to supervise a number of criminal investigations, I have no time."

Pierce sighed. "I was afraid that might be the situation."

"However," Sir Jackson continued, "I've passed off the private investigations part of my work to a new fellow. He's very competent, worked for me for years, and has now struck off on his own. And you're in luck—he just happens to be here today, questioning some fellow in our custody. If you can wait a minute, I'll have him fetched."

"Thank you," Pierce said.

Sir Jackson rose and headed for the door. "You'll like the man. He was a Harrovian like yourself, though in a younger class, I believe. His name's Manton. Dominick Manton."

And before Pierce could react, Sir Jackson was out the door.

Manton? The brother of George Manton did investigative work? How the devil had that come about? Viscounts' sons, even younger ones, didn't do work for hire. And certainly not *that* kind of work for hire.

He vaguely remembered Dominick Manton—a sullen, quiet chap with a passion for dogs and mathematics, who was two years Pierce's junior. While George had stalked about bullying all the younger boys, including Dominick, his little brother had sat in the corner reading tomes by Sir Isaac Newton. Strange fellow.

But as Sir Jackson brought Manton in, Pierce had to acknowledge that he'd grown up well enough. Nor did he much resemble his brother. George, now the Viscount Rathmoor, was beefy and hard-faced, though handsome enough to have snagged himself a very wealthy wife. The last time Pierce had seen Rathmoor, the man still had a body like a mastiff, all head and brawn.

Manton, however, had a body like a Labrador—leaner and sleeker, with intelligent eyes. His black hair was unfashionably short, and a light scar crested one cheek, giving him a rakish appearance.

"My lord," Manton said after Sir Jackson introduced them.

Pierce found the formal address ironic, considering they were both gentlemen. "You may not recall, but I went to school with you and your brother."

The tightening of Manton's lips at Pierce's mention of Rathmoor told Pierce a great deal. The brothers clearly didn't get along.

Which was fine by him. Anyone who hated Rathmoor was a friend of Pierce's.

"I remember," Manton said. "You had asthma."

"For a while, yes."

"If you gentlemen don't mind," Sir Jackson broke in, "I'm expected at a meeting down the hall. But you're welcome to talk in here if you like." He sighed. "The only thing I hate about being chief magistrate is all the damned meetings."

Pierce chuckled. "Not as exciting as running after nefarious criminals, I would expect."

"Not even as exciting as eating supper," Sir Jackson said wryly, before he disappeared out the door.

Once again, Pierce took a seat in front of the desk, but Manton took the chair next to his.

"What can I help you with, sir?" he asked.

Pierce found it easier than he expected to lay out what he wanted from Manton. With Sir Jackson he might have been less forthcoming, since the man was now related indirectly to Pierce's cousins.

But Manton, with his efficient manner and thorough questions, put him at ease.

When Manton had finished asking everything he needed to know, he said, "So you want me to find out what I can about this Mr. Gilchrist and the rest of your mother's family, especially her relationships with all of them. Is that correct?"

"Yes. And I'll pay you whatever it costs to have it done quickly. Preferably before Christmas."

The man started. "That *is* quick. Today is Thursday, and Christmas is next Monday."

"I realize that." But he couldn't bear the idea of returning to Montcliff without knowing the truth. Nor could he bear spending Christmas with the Waverlys without knowing the truth. It felt important to know it as soon as possible. "Do your best. It should help that all of Mother's relations live in London."

"Yes. Little Britain, though a shabby community, isn't that big. And I know a tavern owner on Aldersgate Street, near where your mother used to live."

It dawned on Pierce that the man hadn't taken any notes during their entire interview. "You remembered all that without writing it down?"

Manton nodded. "I never write anything down. I remember everything I hear, word for word."

"That's quite a talent."

"It comes in handy. But it can be a damned nuisance sometimes, too—all that information buzzing around in my head when I want to sleep."

"I can imagine."

Manton stood. "Well, then, if that is all, you'll be hearing from me soon."

Pierce stood, too, and held out his hand. "Thank you. I know it's not the most interesting of cases, but—"

"Actually," Manton said as he shook Pierce's hand, "this should be a nice change of pace. I spend most of my time looking into the backgrounds of prospective applicants for various posts, confirming their former places of employment, their birth records, and such. Much less interesting work."

Pierce stared at him. "Do you ever investigate a foundling's parentage, something of that nature?"

"No, but I could, if I had enough information to begin."

"Then I believe I have a second case for you. You see, my mother's companion . . ."

As he filled Manton in on the details of Camilla's background, he told himself he was only doing it for her sake. He wanted to help her, to give her some knowledge of the family she'd lost.

It had nothing to do with his own curiosity about her past. Nothing to do with wanting to be prepared for whatever surprises might lie in wait for him if he happened to marry her.

Marry her?

Ridiculous notion. He had no intention of marrying anyone. Marriage was for men who intended to bear heirs.

It's the only way to strike back at her for what she did. If you don't marry and don't have children, then she has no grandchildren to look after her in her old age.

He groaned. Camilla was right. And he no longer *wanted* to strike back at his mother. Not that way, in any case.

But did he want to marry? Did he want to risk giving up the hard-won measure of control he'd gained over his life? That was the crucial question. And he just didn't know the answer.

One thing was certain—Camilla would never agree to anything less than marriage. And he began to think that life without her might be worse than life as a married man.

The morning after Pierce left, Camilla wandered about in a fog. Her ladyship slept very late after their long night, and Jasper did, too, but Camilla couldn't. She kept replaying in her mind everything she'd said to Pierce. Should she have tried harder to keep him here? Said something different?

But what could she have said? He was too damaged by the past to be reasoned with. How was she supposed to break through that?

Now the three of them sat in the drawing room, along with Maisie. It was early afternoon. Jasper was gilding almonds under Camilla's supervision as Maisie and her ladyship made paper cut-outs of reindeer for the Christmas tree.

Though neither Camilla nor her ladyship felt like preparing for Christmas, they had to. Jasper was looking forward to it, and they needed something to keep their hands and minds occupied. Otherwise, they would both fall into a gloom from which neither was liable to emerge anytime soon.

One of the footmen appeared in the doorway. "Mrs. Stuart, there's a Mr. Whitley here to see you. He asked for his lordship, but when I said that my lord had gone to London, he said he would speak with *you*."

"Who is Mr. Whitley?" her ladyship asked.

"I don't know. The name does sound familiar, though."

Camilla frowned in thought. "Wait, that was the name of the horse trader from the fair. What would he be wanting with me?"

"I don't know," Lady Devonmont said, "but we should definitely find out. Do send him in."

The footman looked uncomfortable. "He asked that I have Mrs. Stuart come into the garden, my lady."

"This grows more curious by the moment," the countess said. "Come, Camilla, let's go find out what this is all about."

"I want to go!" Jasper cried, always eager to be outside.

So all four of them followed the footman out into the garden, where Mr. Whitley stood waiting for them in a fine suit.

And he had the Shetland pony with him.

"Chocolate!" Jasper cried as he raced over to the pony.

"Good day, madam," Mr. Whitley said, smiling. "I brought the pony over just as his lordship asked."

Camilla paled. "I believe there's been some mistake."

"No mistake. The earl said it was a Christmas present for the lad. Told me to see Mr. Fowler about payment today, and I did. It's already paid for."

"Oh, but—"

"Just take it," Lady Devonmont said in a low voice. "If it worries you, I'll pay for it." She squeezed Camilla's arm. "It's worth it to see the boy so happy."

Jasper was petting Chocolate and talking to him nonstop, and the pony was enduring it all with what Camilla thought was a great deal of patience.

"I'll fetch a groom for him," the footman said, and hurried off.

"Well, then, I wish you joy of him," Mr. Whitley said with a tug of his forelock to her ladyship. Then he left.

"I had no idea," Camilla said. "It seems wrong to accept such an extravagant gift, especially now, given what has happened between me and Pierce."

Her ladyship told Maisie to go keep an eye on Jasper, then said to Camilla in a low voice, "I think perhaps my son feels more deeply for you than he can admit."

"Because he bought Jasper a pony?" Camilla said skeptically. "It's just part of his campaign to make me his mistress."

"I don't think so. In all the time he's been taking mistresses, he's never been involved with anyone who had a child. The women have all been cold, glittering females flitting from protector to protector, not your sort at all."

"That doesn't mean anything. I just happened to be handy."

The countess shook her head. "I saw how he looked at you last night. It's not the way a man looks at a conquest." She drew in a deep breath. "I think you should go talk to him in London."

Camilla gazed into the woman's face. "There's no point. Not unless you come with me and tell him what he needs to know. Until he can put the past behind him, he can't go on, and he's never going to do that as long as you don't set things right."

Her ladyship was quiet a long moment. "What if it didn't set things right?" she finally said. "What if it made them worse?"

"How can they possibly be worse than they are now?"

"He could still come back here," the countess said, worrying her lower lip with her teeth. "He might relent in his anger, especially for you."

Camilla shook her head. "I don't think so. I think he's had enough." She tucked her arm in the countess's. "At least tell *me*. Then I can judge how he would take it."

Lady Devonmont stiffened. "You'll despise me."

"He told me what you said to him that day in the study, and I'm still here, aren't I?" Camilla's tone was gentle. "I'm willing to give you the benefit of the doubt. Because unlike him, I can see beyond the past to how much you love him."

Tears started in the countess's eyes. "All right. I'll tell you what happened."

24

Pierce kept as busy as he could during the next couple of days, while he waited to hear from Manton. The night after he'd met with the man, Pierce went to his club, but he kept running into men who unwittingly reminded him exactly how much of an arse he'd been for the past several years.

Everyone had heard of his break with Eugenia, so they were eager to find out who his next mistress would be. Was he considering the French opera singer Minette, with the fine tits? Or Nelly Banks, whose low beginnings were matched only by her astounding ability in bed?

For the first time, their coarse remarks annoyed him, especially in light of the fact that he'd meant to bring Camilla to London as his mistress. No wonder she'd refused. Even without moving in his circles, she'd known what it would mean for her and, by extension, for Jasper. And she had too much integrity to want the boy sullied by such slurs.

It began to shame him that he'd even considered it.

After spending the next day with his secretary, going over the previous week's correspondence, Pierce attended an afternoon performance of the opera, but his heart wasn't in it. He kept comparing the voices of the female singers to Camilla's, and all of them came up wanting.

Worse yet, in the theater lobby he ran into Eugenia. She'd already found a protector, whom she paraded in front of Pierce in what appeared to be an attempt to make him jealous.

He felt nothing, even when she and her new gentleman friend paused to talk to him for several minutes. Hard to believe that he'd ever been enamored of her. Now she seemed brittle as ice, her sophistication like a table that had been lacquered so many times, one could no longer see the luster of the wood.

But watching her try to rouse a response in him did remind Pierce that with him gone, Camilla was now free to take up with any damned chap near Montcliff who fancied her, especially since there was no longer any need for secrecy about Jasper. She could find a respectable husband, a farmer or a shopkeeper—or even the handsome new doctor in Stocking Pelham.

That thought succeeded in rousing his jealousy. Indeed, the idea of a horde of country doctors beating down Camilla's door so annoyed him that when the opera was over, he chose to walk home rather than ride in his carriage, hoping that the biting cold and brisk walk would clear his head.

But it merely lowered his spirits further. Since it was the night before Christmas Eve, the city had taken on a festive air. Mince pies were displayed in all the bakery windows, mistletoe was hung wherever young people congregated, and carts had begun to enter the city laden with evergreens and the occasional tree. Apparently the custom Mother had followed for so many years was beginning to catch on.

Were Mother and Camilla preparing *their* tree? Were they even now hanging evergreens on the mantel and winding them up the banisters? Jasper must be beside himself with excitement over the impending holiday.

Pierce missed the boy. No, he missed them all, every damned one of them—Mother and Maisie and Fowler. He even missed Cook, with her no-nonsense meals of beef and onions.

Most of all, he missed Camilla. And the ache of missing her, which he'd thought would diminish over time, only got stronger with each day.

He was so lost in thought that he didn't hear the voice hailing him from the street until a phaeton practically ran him down. It was his cousin Virginia's husband, Lord Gabriel Sharpe. Only Sharpe would drive an open phaeton in the middle of damned winter.

"What the devil are *you* doing here?" Pierce asked as Sharpe offered him a hand up into the phaeton.

"Looking for you." Sharpe turned the phaeton and started back for Pierce's town house. "I'd been waiting at your not-so-humble abode, but when your carriage came back without you, I gave up and headed for home. Then, as luck would have it, I spotted you on the street." Sharpe slanted a glance at him. "Good thing I did. You were so distracted, I daresay you would have gotten yourself run over."

"The only person I was in danger from was *you*," he grumbled. "Why were you waiting for me, anyway?"

"My wife sent me, what else? You know Virginia. When she didn't hear from you about whether you were coming to Waverly Farm for Christmas, she got worried. She thought perhaps with our moving into our own property outside town and your uncle Isaac marrying my grandmother . . . well, you might think you weren't welcome."

Camilla's words flitted through his mind again: *And when she gave you up, she made sure you were put in a safe place, a comfortable place, with good people who cared about you. . . .*

A lump stuck in his throat. "Your wife worries too much," Pierce said.

"As I tell her practically every week. But she ignores me, especially where you're concerned."

At his arch tone, Pierce bit back a smile. "Don't tell me you're still angry over the time I pretended to court her."

"Certainly not. I know you did it to be sure of my intentions." He grinned at him. "Besides, she has convinced me that she knows you for the arse you are, so I have nothing to worry about."

Though Sharpe was just trying to get his goat, the remark sobered him. He really *had* been an arse, and for quite some years. He'd spent nights in a drunken stupor, gambling to excess merely because he'd known it would land him in the newspapers. He'd seduced actresses and toyed with young ladies' affections so the gossips would excoriate him, and in the process had left a trail of wreckage behind him.

And for what? To strike back at his parents? It hadn't done that. It had merely obscured the past even more. He could have spent his time more usefully, but he'd been too angry to see the forest for the trees.

He was damned well seeing the forest now.

"You *are* coming for Christmas, aren't you?" Sharpe asked as he pulled up in front of Pierce's town house.

Down the street, carolers were regaling a household with a warbling version of "Here We Come A-Wassailing." His neighbors had clearly been busy this evening decking the outside of their houses with greenery, and the pungent scent of fir wafted to him on the night breeze.

"No," he heard himself say. "I'm going home."

Home?

Yes, home. He'd been banished from it for so long that he'd grown used to thinking of it as something denied to him. But it wasn't anymore.

Sharpe turned to gape at him. "You don't mean Montcliff?"

"I do. I mean to spend Christmas with my mother and her companion." *The woman I intend to marry.*

She deserved better than a life as his mistress. He could never drag her down into such a situation; he saw it now. And marriage didn't have to mean becoming some besotted fool like Sharpe and giving up control over his life. He could still protect his heart.

She won't settle for that.

She would have to. It was all he had to give.

Sharpe was looking at him oddly. "But I thought you and your mother didn't . . . er . . . get along."

"We didn't. But now . . . well . . . it's a bit hard to explain."

"Trust me, I understand 'hard to explain.' I have a family full of 'hard to explain,' as you well know." Staring ahead to where his horses were champing to be off, he frowned. "When will you leave?"

"Tomorrow morning, at first light."

Sharpe brightened. "Then you'll have plenty of time to stop at our place in the country. It's right on your way, and we're not leaving for Waverly Farm until late in the afternoon." When Pierce drew breath to protest, Sharpe said, "Virginia will never forgive me if you don't at least come by. You haven't even seen our new home yet. For that matter, you haven't even seen the baby."

Pierce winced. He'd forgotten that Virginia had recently given birth to their first child, a baby girl named Isabel. "All right. I'll stop in on my way to Hertfordshire."

The next morning, Christmas Eve, Pierce arose early and ordered the servants to pack up his bags. The very prospect of heading to Montcliff lifted his spirits, which told him he was doing the right thing.

But just as he was shrugging into his greatcoat, Manton arrived. He had information for Pierce, he said, and some of it couldn't wait until after Christmas.

Blood pounding in his ears, Pierce brought the man into his study and prepared himself for anything.

"First of all," Manton said after they'd exchanged the usual pleasantries, "I tracked down a few of your mother's relations, including your mother's second cousin Edgar Gilchrist."

Pierce blinked. "You spoke to him."

"I'm afraid not. He died a few years ago, but I was able to talk to his widow."

"He was married?"

"Yes." Manton shifted nervously in his chair. "But she said he only married her after he'd given up all hope of being with your mother."

Pierce sucked in a breath. Camilla was right—Mother *had* been involved with Gilchrist. "His wife knew about him and Mother?"

"Oh, yes. She gave me quite an earful. All about how your mother was the siren who'd broken his heart and ruined him for any other woman. According to her, he courted your mother behind your grandfather's back. It started when she was sixteen and he was twenty."

"Sixteen!" That stymied him. She'd married Father at eighteen. "How long did Gilchrist court her?"

"Up until the time they attempted to elope, shortly after she turned eighteen."

Great God, that was a serious courtship. "Attempted? How, exactly?"

"Well, as best I could determine from the man's wife, who'd been admiring him from afar all those years, your mother and Gilchrist ran off to Gretna Green and actually got across the border, before her father caught up to them and made them come back. One of your mother's other relations confirmed that. The family managed to hush it up, and it rapidly became apparent why, when the earl proposed to your mother."

"Ah, yes," Pierce mused aloud. "By then, the earl must have agreed to pay off Grandfather's debts in exchange for Mother's hand in marriage."

"That would explain why she married him."

No, Pierce thought with a sinking in his stomach. *The babe in her belly explains why she married him.*

Gretna Green was a long way off, after all. Plenty of time to consummate the wedding before it took place. Then she would have been too ashamed to admit to her father that she wasn't chaste. Or perhaps she *had* admitted it, and Grandfather Gilchrist hadn't cared. After all, he already had an earl waiting in the wings.

Or had he? "Did Mother know the earl before she eloped?"

"Yes. Apparently the reason your mother and Gilchrist ran off in the first place was because the earl had taken a fancy to her, and since her father didn't approve of her marrying Gilchrist, the couple feared they would never get to marry unless they eloped."

"Did my father—" He checked himself. "Did the earl know about her connection to Gilchrist?"

"That, I could not discover. All I know is that he met your mother at some grand ball during your mother's come-out. According to Gilchrist's wife, a friend of the family even then, the earl was instantly smitten and pursued your mother relentlessly. When she ran off, he was told she was visiting relatives, and as far as Gilchrist's wife knew, he believed it."

"But then Gilchrist came along years later and threatened to tell my father that she'd borne him a bastard," Pierce mused.

Manton snorted. "A bastard? If that's what you're worried about, my lord, you can set your mind to rest. The earl was engaged to your mother for six months before they married—it took that long to prepare the large wedding that your father insisted upon. Unless Gilchrist found a way to get around her father and see her during that time—which I seriously doubt, considering their previous attempt at elopement—you are almost certainly the earl's son."

That's what Mother had claimed, too. He'd thought she might be lying, but perhaps she hadn't been.

Still, if Mother *had* shared Gilchrist's bed while they were eloping and Father found her unchaste on their wedding night, he might have suspected her of infidelity later with *someone*. Father had to have believed Pierce wasn't his, despite all evidence to the contrary. That was the only explanation for why the man had despised his own heir.

But it still didn't explain why Father had spurned him only after Pierce turned eight. Had Gilchrist tried to blackmail Mother by threatening to tell Father that he'd been the one to take her innocence? Given the Gilchrist family's predilection for gambling, perhaps the man had needed money and had thought that a way to gain it.

And if Mother had stood firm against his threats, then he might have gone to Father, threatening a scandal if Father didn't pay him off.

But then what could Father have been holding over Mother's

head to make her cut off her son so completely? Knowledge of some botched elopement wouldn't have made any difference in their marriage.

Unless . . .

A cold chill passed through him. "Are you absolutely certain that Gilchrist and my mother didn't make it to a church or even an 'anvil priest' in Gretna Green?"

Manton's eyes narrowed. "Gilchrist's wife said they didn't."

"What else *would* she say? If Gilchrist *had* managed to marry my mother, even in one of those havey-cavey Scottish weddings, and it became known, his marriage to this other woman would be entirely void. She would be left with nothing."

Manton's gaze locked with his, reflecting the same horror Pierce felt. "And your mother's marriage to your father would have been entirely void as well."

"Exactly. Except that my mother wouldn't have been the only one left with nothing."

As the full ramifications of that hit him, Pierce's heart plummeted into his stomach. At last he knew what Father had held over Mother's head. And perhaps even what Gilchrist had told Father that day at Montcliff.

Pierce rose, his mind racing. If his theory was right, it changed everything. He had to see Mother. He still had a couple of stops to make on the way out of town, and he'd promised Sharpe . . .

That was one promise he must keep. The Waverlys were his family, too, after all, and he was just beginning to realize how important a part they had played in saving him from his father's wrath.

"Forgive me, Manton, but I have to go."

Manton rose as well. "Of course, my lord."

"You will keep this to yourself, I assume." With a sudden sick feeling in his gut, he remembered that Manton's brother had always hated him. What if Manton—

"You have nothing to fear from me," Manton said fiercely. "My clients always have my complete discretion. Sir Jackson would never have recommended me to you if he didn't trust that."

"True," Pierce said tightly, only slightly reassured.

"Besides, I know better than you think how family arrangements can destroy people's futures." Manton looked as if he were debating something, then added softly, "My father had another family, a mistress and two illegitimate children—my half brother and half sister. It is because of them that I am estranged from my brother. Father left them provided for, but George refused to honor the agreement. It has wreaked havoc on all our lives."

Pierce instantly understood why the man was telling him this family secret. Manton clearly knew that the best way to reassure a man that his secrets were safe was to offer one of his own.

Feeling more easy about Manton, Pierce turned for the door, and Manton said, "Did you wish to hear about the other investigation you charged me with?"

"Other investigation?"

"The one concerning Mrs. Stuart."

"Ah, right." He'd forgotten about that. It felt like years since he'd asked Manton to look into her background. And now it seemed rather . . . sordid.

"I don't have much to tell you," Manton went on. "When I

spoke yesterday to the couple who run St. Joseph's Home for Orphans, they were evasive. They admitted that she'd worked there and had an exemplary record but said they had to check their files concerning how she'd ended up there. They said they would report to me this morning about whether they could even speak of the matter. That's one reason I'm here. I thought you might wish to attend the meeting with me."

So he could find out if Camilla was the daughter of a whore or a princess? He didn't need to know that, because he already knew he wanted her in his life.

It didn't matter who her parents were. It didn't matter how she'd come to be at St. Joseph's. Pierce knew the kind of woman she was, inside and out. She was the kind of woman who stood up for those who wouldn't or couldn't stand up for themselves. The kind of woman who took delight in a simple pastry, who could tease a lord about naughty books in one moment and defend the man's mother in another.

The kind of woman who still believed in love. And who apparently had been fool enough to fall in love with *him*.

The least he could do was accord her privacy in her personal affairs. She had never asked him to find out who her parents were, and she could have discovered that herself when she worked at St. Joseph's, if she'd wanted. So he was far overstepping his bounds by pursuing this. He certainly hadn't asked about it for her sake. He had done so for his own, so he could feel safe in marrying her.

Well, no more. If any problems ever arose out of her murky

background, they would face them together. Assuming she gave him that chance.

When he saw her, he would tell her that if she wanted Manton to pursue the matter, he would arrange it. But it would be her private affair. Because it truly was none of his concern.

"No," he said. "I don't need to be there for the meeting. And neither do you. I'll pay you for what you've found out so far, but unless I'm directed otherwise by Mrs. Stuart, we'll leave the past in the past."

"Whatever you wish, sir," Manton said, a decided note of approval in his voice.

Clearly they were both in agreement on this—there were some Pandora's boxes that should never be opened.

"What do you think?" Lady Devonmont asked as she held up a delicate figurine in the early evening of the night before Christmas. "Too extravagant for the tree?"

Camilla gazed at the glass angel and remembered Pierce's words about angels and devils. Perhaps if she'd never looked past the flip words to the clear heartache behind them, she wouldn't now be sitting here with her own heart bleeding.

"Camilla?"

"Hmm? No, not too extravagant." She stared at the countess. "We should have gone to London. He shouldn't be alone for Christmas."

The countess sighed. "He isn't *in* London, my dear, and he's certainly not alone. He's at Waverly Farm. And it's better this way. I'm willing to take some risk in telling him all, but . . . I can't bear to do it amid all the madness at the Waverlys'. There's more of them now, and I'm sure they think I'm—"

She pasted a determined smile on her face as she turned back to the boxes of baubles. "It doesn't matter. But I would rather have him to myself when I talk to him." She cast Camilla a long glance. "And you said you didn't want him thinking you were interested in being his mistress."

"I know. We made the right decision not to go. It's just—"

"Mama, Mama!" Jasper cried as he ran in ahead of Maisie. Bored with the tree decoration, he'd gone out earlier to feed Chocolate sugarplums. "Someone's coming!"

Camilla's heart leaped into triple time, and she surreptitiously smoothed her skirts. "His lordship has returned?"

Maisie flashed her a pitying glance. "It's not his carriage. Though it's quite a fine one, I don't recognize it."

"Well, then," the countess said smoothly, "let's go see who it is."

The four of them headed out toward the entrance hall, reaching it just as two people entered. It was a gentleman about Pierce's age and a woman of about the countess's age, dressed entirely in deep mourning, down to her ermine fur muff. A very odd couple, who looked a bit startled by the foursome coming to greet them before they could even be announced.

The countess came forward with a smile. "Good day, sir. I am Lady Devonmont. May I help you?"

He gave a bow, and his gaze flicked briefly over Camilla and

Maisie. "My name is Dominick Manton, and this lady is Edith Perry, the Viscountess Hedon."

Lady Hedon gave a quick nod to everyone. Camilla couldn't tell if it was because she was haughty or shy. Mr. Manton, a rather handsome fellow with eyes of a remarkable green, seemed oddly uncomfortable with his surroundings, too.

He nervously scanned the entranceway. "I was hoping to find Lord Devonmont here. I was told, when I met with his lordship at his town house this morning, that he was heading here directly."

"His lordship is coming! His lordship is coming!" Jasper burst out.

"Jasper, we have guests," Camilla chided him. "Hold your tongue."

"Yes, Mama." But his smile didn't fade.

Camilla's heart began to pound, and her ladyship cast her a look of mingled panic and joy as she said to the man, "Are you sure he—"

"His servants told me that he was, and I saw his equipage being loaded. Plus, he said he had to head off. But perhaps I was mistaken in where he was going."

"Perhaps," Lady Devonmont said. "Is there something *I* can do to help you?"

Mr. Manton glanced to Lady Hedon as if for direction.

"I see no need in waiting for his lordship," she said, her eyes darting from Maisie to Camilla, and then settling on Jasper most oddly.

"Very well." Mr. Manton smiled at them all. "I assume that one of you other two ladies is Mrs. Stuart?"

Camilla blinked, then stepped forward. "I'm Camilla Stuart, sir."

As Lady Hedon's wan cheeks grew even more pale, Mr. Manton said, "Is there somewhere we can speak privately, madam?"

Camilla looked to the countess, who said, "Why don't you take the small parlor, dear? I'll have refreshments sent in."

"You are Mrs. Stuart's employer?" Lady Hedon asked, obviously bewildered by her ladyship's manner.

Camilla couldn't imagine what business it was of hers but was gratified when her ladyship said, "I think of her more as a friend than an employee."

"That's good," Lady Hedon said, to Camilla's surprise.

Camilla led the guests into the little parlor, burning with curiosity to know what this was all about.

After everyone was in the room, Mr. Manton closed the door. "Before I explain myself, Mrs. Stuart," he said, "I wish to assure you that I didn't intend for this to happen. After his lordship asked me to look into . . . er . . . how you came to be at St. Joseph's—"

"He did *what*?" she asked, not sure whether to be outraged or touched. It vastly depended on his reasons.

"Oh, he thought better of it later," Mr. Manton hastened to add. "He told me to halt my investigation until he could speak to you about it, but by then the wheels were turning."

"What wheels?" she echoed, thoroughly at sea.

"What Mr. Manton is trying to say," Lady Hedon put in softly, "is that some months ago, after my husband died, I went to St. Joseph's looking for you, but they weren't sure where you worked anymore. So when Mr. Manton came to the orphanage this week asking questions, they arranged to meet with him and then hastened to me to ask if I wished to be there. I said yes, of course." Her tone grew arch. "Mr. Manton didn't show up for the meeting, so I went to his office, but—"

"I beg your pardon, my lady," Camilla said, becoming more bewildered by the moment. "But who exactly are you, and why are you looking for me?"

Lady Hedon swallowed, then stepped forward to seize Camilla's hands. "I, my dear, am your mother."

25

Christmas Day

It had been snowing now for hours. It was melting almost as soon as it hit the ground, but it still made travel more difficult. And Pierce had only himself to blame for his being so late.

His stops in London had taken more time than he'd expected, and then he had stayed far too long at Virginia's. Uncle Isaac and his new wife, Hetty, had shown up for the occasion, and he'd been forced to attempt to explain what was going on between him and his mother, which he hadn't done very well.

There was too much he had to leave out, too much he couldn't say until he had more answers. He'd talked briefly with his uncle, hoping that he could shed some light on the past, but Uncle Isaac could say only what Pierce already knew. When Pierce was eight,

Mother had asked Titus to raise him with his other children, and Titus had agreed.

After Titus died, Uncle Isaac had been asked to take up the mantle, and he'd done so, hoping that Pierce could be like an older brother to Virginia and the late Roger. Pierce had done his best with that.

Indeed, it was precisely because Virginia was like a sister to him that he'd had so much trouble getting away. And baby Isabel hadn't helped matters any. The child was so amazingly winsome. He kept holding her, thinking that he and Camilla might have a little girl, too. And marveling that for the first time, the thought of having a child didn't completely terrify him.

But he shouldn't have lingered so long with his cousins be-cause he'd been forced to drive through the night. It was nearly eight o'clock on Christmas morning, and his coach-and-four was only now approaching Montcliff.

Were they at breakfast? he wondered as the carriage halted and he leaped out, carrying a box in his arms. Mother and Camilla tended to rise early, so he wouldn't be surprised. And it was Christ-mas morn, so Jasper had probably been up with the chickens.

He strode into the house and stamped the snow from his boots but found it oddly quiet. "Where is everyone?" he asked the footman who took his greatcoat.

"Her ladyship is in the drawing room, milord. And Mrs. Stuart—"

"Thank you," he said, hastening off in that direction with his box. They were undoubtedly all in the drawing room, if that's where they'd put the tree.

He couldn't remember what they'd said about that, but Mother used to put it there.

Evergreens were draped on every available space, but for the first time in years, the smell of fir and cedar didn't plague him with bad memories. Not now that he understood so much more.

He walked into the drawing room, then halted. Mother was sitting at the table alone, drinking tea and eating toast. The tree was nowhere in sight, but its absence didn't register nearly as much as Camilla's.

She must be getting dressed or something, which was just as well. What he had to say to Mother would best be said in private.

"Pierce!" she cried, a smile breaking over her face. She rose, then seemed to remember the circumstances under which they'd last parted, and her smile faded a little. "We . . . didn't expect you."

"I tried to get here for Christmas Eve, but I stopped at Virginia's and—" He was babbling, for God's sake. Fighting for calm, he set down his box and went over to her. Might as well get right to the point. "Mother, I don't know how to tell you this, but since you refused to tell me anything about Gilchrist, I had an investigator look into your friendship with him."

He expected her to try to escape the conversation, as always, but she just stared at him, her eyes wide. "I see. And what did he learn?"

"That before you married Father, you attempted to elope with Gilchrist."

She swallowed, then nodded.

"So I figured out what Father was holding over your head—

the fact that you'd married him while already married to Gil-christ."

"I did *not*!" she cried. "I was *never* married to Edgar. And Wal-ter knew it, too. His blasted investigators couldn't find one shred of evidence that I was ever married to Edgar because I *wasn't*! We didn't get that far."

"Then why—"

"Because your father never needed any proof to use some-thing to his advantage," she said bitterly. She began to pace, her color high. "You know how Walter was. He felt his honor was besmirched. He told me that if I didn't send my 'bastard' away and never see him again, he would drum up whatever evidence he needed to prove a prior marriage. He would pay witnesses and he would stop at nothing."

Tears sparkling in her eyes, she halted to gaze at Pierce. "And he was just the man to do it, too. He would have disinherited you entirely! You would have lost everything—the title, the estate, your legitimacy!"

"I wouldn't have cared," he choked out, his throat tightening convulsively. "I would have had you. I would have had one par-ent, at least."

"You say that now, as you stand in one of the several proper-ties you inherited, with the weight of your title behind you," she pointed out raggedly. "But you wouldn't have thanked me if I had let that bitter, resentful man plunge you into poverty and disgrace at the age of eight."

She lowered her voice to a hiss. "I slid from riches to poverty as a girl, my boy. I knew what it was like. And I didn't live in disgrace, as you would have had to do. No. I wasn't going to let *my son* endure any of that just because my jealous husband had some foolish notion that you weren't his. You have *no* idea how cruel life can be."

He stood there, buffeted by her words. Life had certainly been cruel to her. Who was he to sit in judgment on what methods she had taken to protect him? He had never been a woman, entirely dependent on the men in her life. Men who'd failed her, one after another.

Still, there were things he didn't understand. "So I really *am* the earl's son."

She fought to regain her composure. "I told you before— of course you're his son. You were born ten months after we married."

"There wasn't any leeway in that? Because if there wasn't, I don't understand why he thought me a bastard." That was the crux of it.

Apparently, it was the crux of it for her, too, for she'd gone white, and she wouldn't meet his eyes.

"Mother?" he prodded.

She started pacing again, this time wringing her hands. "You just couldn't leave it alone, could you? You had to start stirring up the past, looking under rocks."

This time he refused to let his temper get the better of him, though she was sorely trying his patience. "What do you expect?" he said quietly. "You stood there in the study and told me to my face—"

"Because you were going to ruin everything!" she cried. "If

I had weakened even one moment, if I had let you know how I felt and you had started coming round, he would have done as he threatened. I could see it in his face. He would have cut us both off out of sheer spite. The money you inherited from your grandmother? Gone. Your position in society, your inheritance, your title? Gone! And all because I—"

She broke off with a sob.

His heart breaking to see her so overwrought, he walked up to pull her into his arms. "Shh, shh, you don't have to tell me." He held her trembling body close, cursing himself for bringing her to this pass.

"I do have to tell you," she whispered. "Camilla was right about that." She lifted a tear-streaked face to him. "But if I had guessed for one moment what my stolen afternoons with Edgar would cost me . . ."

And that's when it hit him. They'd been wrong about her. She *had* risked it all; she *had* stood up to his father. She'd had an illicit affair with her cousin—her lover—and had paid the price. A very high price.

So had he.

That's why she wouldn't tell him this before, why she wouldn't admit the whole truth. Because she felt deeply ashamed. And obviously deeply guilty, too.

She ducked her head and pulled away from him. "Your father . . . was very enamored of me. And at eighteen I found it rather flattering, even though I was still in love with Edgar. Even though I had . . . given myself to Edgar."

Mortification reddened her cheeks. "When your father discovered on our wedding night that I was not . . ." She swallowed. "I made the mistake of confessing all, admitting to having run off with Edgar. But I told your father—and I believed it—that I was past my youthful indiscretion. That I would be a good wife to him. And he forgave me."

Her voice hardened. "Or so I thought, for he sometimes taunted me with it privately. It was like a burr under his saddle in the early years of our marriage. But we had you, and I tried to be content." She cast Pierce a quick smile. "You were the only bright spot in those years."

Pierce could hardly breathe. He knew what was coming, and he knew he should stop her from telling it. But he couldn't. She needed to tell it as much as he needed to hear it.

"Then I went to your grandfather's funeral, and Edgar was there."

"I remember," he said hoarsely. "That's when I met him, when I was six."

"We were as much in love as ever, and I was so unhappy with your father—" Her breathing grew labored. "We started meeting in a town not too far off. Your father drank a lot, as you may remember, so I would go riding when he was passed out, and . . . well, you can guess the rest."

"He found out," Pierce said, his blood thundering in his ears.

"Yes. After that day at the fair." Her expression grew rigid. "I'd begun to realize how much I was risking, and I'd stopped going to meet Edgar. But the blasted fool wouldn't be cautious. He came to the fair, hoping to see me and persuade me to run away with him. I told him I couldn't—it would mean giving you up." Her tone turned brittle. "Because a woman may leave her husband, but if she does, she can never take her children with her."

And he had worried that marriage meant giving up control of his life? What had he been thinking? A woman gave up far more in a marriage than a man ever could.

"We argued, and Edgar left, and I thought that was the end of it." She stared off beyond him, as if looking into the past. "But someone saw us, someone who knew who Edgar was. And that person, whoever it was, mentioned to Walter about seeing me with my cousin at the fair."

She pressed her fingers to her temples. "That's when all hell broke loose. Your father sent footmen to bring Edgar to the house, and told Edgar that if he ever came within a mile of me, he would kill him."

A shudder racked her. "And then he went on a rampage, convinced, no matter what I said, that we had been seeing each other all along. That's when he took the notion into his head that you weren't his."

"He never did think me worthy of his fine bloodlines," Pierce said acidly.

"I don't think it had anything to do with you, my dear. He could see that I loved you, and he knew I didn't love *him*. And he hated that. It was an easy leap for him to say that I must love you because you were Edgar's child."

That made a horrible kind of sense to Pierce. In every memory he had of his father, even as a young child, it had been Mother and him against Father. That had to have rankled.

"So after he dealt with Edgar, he laid down the rules for me. I was never to see Edgar again. I was never to go anywhere without my husband. And I was not—"

She choked back tears. "I was not to see my . . . 'bastard' child. In exchange, Walter would allow me to send you off to school and relations. If we didn't have another child, he would allow you to inherit. But I was not to write to you or speak to you. He allowed me that last Christmas with you only because the school wouldn't take you until after the holidays."

Her gaze met his, glittering with tears. "I treasured every moment of that Christmas. And even after you left, I kept hoping that once you were away, he would relent. But when he discovered I was sneaking letters out to you, he told me that if he ever saw that again, he would do as he threatened—claim I had been married before and in one fell swoop make you illegitimate."

Pierce stood there, fists clenched, wishing his father were alive so he could kill him with his bare hands.

When the tears began to fall and she patted her pockets, apparently looking for a handkerchief, Pierce stepped forward to give her his.

She took it gratefully. "He was determined to *make* me be the wife he wanted. He knew I would do anything to keep you safe, and he used that. I think he was terrified that if I ever got you to myself, I would run off with Edgar and he would never see us again."

"Why didn't you?" he rasped, his own tears clogging his throat.

"And have your inheritance denied you because that . . . that evil wretch thought you weren't his? Not on your life." She lifted her chin, her gaze fierce. "I could endure the blasted devil if it meant keeping you from losing everything. And your children and your children's children."

His children's children.

Great God. That's why she'd been so hateful to him that day in the study. Because she had seen beyond him to a future that went down generations, a future she'd been bound and determined to save for him. Always stubborn to a fault, she was not going to let Pierce "ruin everything" in a fit of pique at his father. Not after what she'd already suffered to gain it.

The fire suddenly went out of her face. "So now you know. You were punished because I was an adulteress."

And she clearly believed he would hate her for it. But how could he? It was monumentally unfair that she had been forced to give up the man she loved because her father couldn't control his gambling. That she'd suffered because she'd confessed all to her husband on her wedding night.

Snatching something precious for herself shouldn't have brought her to this. "I don't blame you for what you did."

"You should," she choked out. "If I hadn't taken up with Edgar again—"

"Father probably would have found some other reason to suspect you. Men like that often do." He pulled her into his arms, his eyes burning with unshed tears. "I don't blame you for wanting a few moments of happiness in such a miserable marriage."

"Even if it meant that you—"

"Yes," he choked out. "Even then." He held her close, his

heart in his throat. He still thought she would have been better off throwing Father's rules in his damned face and running off with her true love, taking him with her.

But that was a man's way of thinking. He wasn't a woman. He wasn't a mother, who would do anything for her child.

"I wish you'd told me sooner," he whispered into her hair.

"And have you learn . . . that I was a vile adulteress? That I risked your entire future for . . . for a sordid affair?"

"With the man you'd always loved?" He drew her back to stare at her. "It wasn't you who banished me, Mother. It was Father. And I think I'm wise enough to place the blame squarely where it belongs." He swallowed. "Though I wasn't always." He brushed a tear from her cheek. "I'm sorry I didn't read your letters. It was wrong of me."

Tears threatened to overthrow her again. "You're here now. That's all that matters." She stepped back and forced a bright smile as she dabbed at her eyes. "And it's Christmas! I have you for Christmas. At last."

He choked down his own tears. "Yes, you do," he managed. "And you always will." Before she could start crying again, he added, "Which reminds me, I brought you a couple of presents. But one in particular I wanted to give you privately."

He went over to where he'd set down the box and brought it back to her, then opened it to reveal all her letters. Unsealed. "I want you to know that I read every one, from beginning to end. I only wish I'd read them sooner."

"Oh, Pierce . . ." That brought the tears back, and he had

to set down the box to hold her again and comfort her until she stopped crying, all the while cursing himself for not starting to repair their relationship the very day of Father's funeral. For being so angry that he hadn't looked beneath the surface.

Once she got control of herself and pulled back from him again, he glanced around them with a frown. "But where is the tree? I thought it would be in here, and young Jasper would be fighting to get at it by now."

"Oh no, it's in the nursery," she managed as she blotted her face again. "Jasper begged us to put it there once he saw it all decorated." She beamed at him. "He and Camilla are up there now, with Lady Hedon. I came down to give them some time to themselves after we opened our gifts this morning."

"Who the devil is Lady Hedon?"

Her smile faltered. "You didn't know? It was your man Manton who brought her here—oh, right, he hadn't had the chance to tell you." She took a heavy breath. "Lady Hedon is Camilla's mother."

Pierce stared at her, thunderstruck. "Her mother."

"Yes. Thanks to you, Manton found her." She gave a small frown. "And now I'm going to be hard-pressed to keep Camilla here. The woman wants to take her back to London and make her part of her family."

Pierce turned to the door. "The hell she does!"

His mother caught his arm. "Don't spoil this for her. She has a chance to make her own way for once. To be her own person. Lady Hedon is a widow with no other children and plenty of money, and she says she wants to leave it to her daughter. Camilla will be able to live as a lady, with her son alongside her."

"You mean, instead of living a life of degradation and shame as my mistress."

Mother colored. "Exactly. She deserves better."

"I know," he said tightly. She deserved much better than what he'd offered. She deserved what Lady Hedon was apparently willing to offer—freedom. The right to live her life as she chose. He should let her have that.

And he would, if that's what she really wanted. But he prayed to God that it wasn't. "You'll be happy to know that I've seen the error of my ways. I've come to offer Camilla marriage."

He would have thought that would make his mother ecstatic, but she merely stared at him with a worried frown. "Why?"

He blinked. "Because I want to marry her, of course."

"Yes, but *why* do you wish to marry her? If it's just because you think that it's the only way you can have her in your bed—"

"No!" He stopped, then said more firmly, "No. That's not why."

It dawned on him—that really *wasn't* why. He did want her in his bed, of course; he'd always wanted that. But there were other things, too. He liked that she smiled at his wit, even when he was being an "overgrown child," and that she listened to him with an intensity that showed she cared what he said.

Yet it went beyond enjoyment of her very amiable self. For the first time in his life, he was willing to give up a bit of control to be with someone forever. To be with *her.* Because he didn't mind giving up control to the woman he knew he could trust absolutely. With his life, his soul . . . his heart.

"I want to marry her because I love her," he told his mother.

"Well, then," his mother said with a brilliant smile. "That's a different matter entirely, isn't it?"

He damned well hoped so.

26

The Christmas tree sparkled in the nursery corner where they'd placed it. With the candles lit, Lady Devonmont's ancient glass baubles glittered from every branch, reminding Camilla of a bejeweled music box she'd seen once in a London shop.

She glanced over to watch as Lady Hedon showed Jasper how to tie a ribbon into a bow. This was what she'd always wanted—a family. And now she had it. Yet something was missing.

The viscountess—her *mother*, of all things—caught her staring and smiled. "I still can't believe I have a grandson."

"And I still can't believe I have a mother," Camilla choked out.

She'd expected to feel more of a connection, an instant visceral recognition of the person who had borne her. But Lady Hedon still felt like a stranger. Far more than Lady Devonmont did.

When Jasper took the bow and ran off to show Maisie, Lady Hedon said quietly, "I didn't want to give you up, you know."

"Yes. You said that last night."

Lady Hedon cast her a sad glance. "But you don't believe me."

"On the contrary. Working at the orphanage, I've seen how hard the world makes it for a woman having a child outside the confines of marriage."

"I was so young, only sixteen," Lady Hedon said, wistfully watching after Jasper. "My parents gave me little choice. It was either relinquish you or be cast out." Her clasped hands tightened into a knot in her lap. "And having grown up very sheltered as an earl's daughter, I didn't know how I would take care of myself and an infant, too."

"I understand," Camilla said, though she was really only beginning to. After hearing Lady Devonmont's horrific story, she no longer felt qualified to sit in judgment of other women's decisions about their lives.

She did have one question she burned to ask her mother. The entire time since last night that they'd spent coming to know each other, she'd wanted to broach it, but it was a delicate subject, and since Lady Hedon hadn't brought it up yet . . . "If you don't mind me asking," she blurted out, "who is my father?"

Lady Hedon blushed. "I am almost ashamed to tell you. When I do, you will know exactly how much a slave to my passions I was." She hesitated, then said, "He was one of my father's footmen." Pain slashed over her face. "And he happily took a nice sum of money from Papa to make himself scarce."

"I'm sorry," Camilla whispered.

"I'm the one who's sorry. I wish I could have given you better news on that score, but I don't even know where he is now. I haven't seen him since the day Papa paid him to leave."

Camilla reached over to squeeze her hand. "It's all right. One parent is more than I had two days ago."

Camilla started to pull her hand back, but Lady Hedon caught it and held it. "I never stopped thinking about you. My late husband and I tried to have children but couldn't, and though I would have suggested looking for you then, I would have had to admit what he never realized—that I wasn't chaste when we married."

Thank God she hadn't admitted it—he might have been the cruel sort of fellow Lady Devonmont's husband had apparently been.

"In any case, he . . . he wasn't the sort of man who would have wanted to take in my . . ." She sighed. "He was a very upright sort. Don't mistake me, he was a good man, and I loved him, but I just couldn't tell him *that*. I couldn't risk my marriage."

Camilla understood all too well after Lady Devonmont's tale. Was it any wonder that Pierce couldn't find any path to happiness when he had such a skewed blueprint to follow?

Pierce. She sighed. *He* was what was missing.

As if she'd imagined him, the door to the nursery opened, and his painfully familiar voice said, "There you are, lad. I was wondering where you'd gone off to."

"Lord Devonmont!" Jasper cried, and ran over to him. "Look, Mama, who's come for Christmas!"

"I see," she managed, trying to keep her heart from shining in her eyes as they all rose to greet him.

There was a shadow over his features and a hint of uncertainty in the way he stared at her. She didn't know what to make of that, but she took some reassurance from the fact that Lady Devonmont stood beside him beaming. Had he talked to her already? Had she told him all?

Pierce lifted Jasper into his arms, but his eyes never left Camilla. "Merry Christmas, Mrs. Stuart."

"Merry Christmas, my lord." She dared not say more. She was afraid her every word would trumpet her feelings.

"I understand that we have guests," Pierce said.

With a groan, Camilla realized she'd been so flustered that she hadn't made the necessary introductions.

As she did so, she could feel her mother's eyes on her. No doubt she was curious about why the atmosphere between Camilla and his lordship was so charged.

"I'd like to thank you, sir," Lady Hedon said, looping her hand through Camilla's arm. "If not for you sending Mr. Manton to St. Joseph's, I would never have found my daughter."

"You're welcome," he said, his voice now decidedly strained.

"I got a lot of Christmas presents, my lord!" Jasper said, always wanting to be the center of attention.

"Did you, indeed?"

"Oh, yes! Her ladyship gave me a box of brand-new tin soldiers, and they even have a fort! And Mama gave me a stocking to hang by the fire, that she made all by herself, and it's full of nuts and oranges and sugarplums. Oh, and she gave me a wooden boat, too. And Maisie gave me a cap for Christmas and it's like the one in the poem and I'm supposed to wear it when I sleep and—"

"I brought you a Christmas present, too, my boy," Pierce said, staving off what was promising to be a long recitation.

"Oh no, my lord, please," Camilla protested. "You already gave him a pony. And you really shouldn't even have done that."

"Nonsense. Besides, this is just a small gift." Setting the lad down, he motioned a footman forward who was carrying several wrapped boxes. Pierce pulled one out and offered it to Jasper with a flourish. "Here you go."

Jasper looked to her. "Can I open it, Mama?"

"Of course," she said.

Tearing off the paper, Jasper pulled out what looked like a framed picture. He stared hard at it, then broke into a smile. "It's the poem, Mama!" he cried, running over to her. "Look, it's the poem about St. Nicholas!"

It was indeed. Pierce had gotten someone to write it out on vellum and then frame it.

"Now, it will be preserved for whenever you want to read it," he told the boy.

Camilla's heart caught in her throat. "It's a very lovely gift," she choked out. "What do you say, Jasper?"

"Thank you, my lord!" Jasper said. "Thank you very much!" Then his face fell. "I don't have a present for you." He glanced over at his eight tin soldiers, lined up in front of the tin cup that was serving as a sleigh. "Unless you want my old soldiers."

Pierce walked up to ruffle his hair. "You keep those. But there *is* a gift you could give me." He lifted his gaze to Camilla. "I'd like to steal your mother for a short while, if you don't mind. I won't keep her long. Is that all right?"

Jasper bobbed his head. "I'll stay here with Maisie and her ladyship and my grandmama. I have a grandmama now, you know."

"I heard," Pierce said tightly.

"I never had a grandmama before." Kenneth's parents had been long dead when Jasper was born. The lad smiled over at Lady Hedon. "She's nice."

Lady Hedon chuckled. "And you, my boy, are quite the little charmer. In fifteen years, you'll be breaking every heart in London. Now come here and sit with your grandmama and show me your new poem, while your mother goes to speak to his lordship."

Pierce held the door open, and Camilla went out with him, her heart hammering so hard she was sure the world could hear it.

He led her down the hall a short way to where a big box sat. "I brought you a present, too," he said.

She wanted to cry. "Pierce, you can give me and Jasper as many gifts as you like, but it's not going to change my mind about—"

"I know. That's not what I'm trying to do." He gestured to the box. "Just open it."

With a lump in her throat, she opened the box, then stared in bewilderment at what was inside. It was a miniature sleigh with handles on the back, for a doll or a—

Her gaze shot to his.

"It's for the children I hope we'll have. At Montcliff. If you'll consent to be my wife."

When she just stood there, gaping at him, hardly able to believe her ears, he added, "You told me once that I make you feel like you could fly. Well, I'm hoping perhaps we can fly together as one big family. You, Jasper, our children—"

"Your mother?"

"Yes, her, too," he said, his eyes misty. "She told me everything. I'd already figured out most of it, yet when I heard it from her, I realized that you were right—about a great many things, but one in particular. I *was* trying to punish her by not marrying. All I ended up doing, however, was punishing myself, denying myself the family I'd never had, because I was sure that if I tried to gain it, I would fail. And I knew I couldn't endure that pain a second time."

She was crying now, silently.

"Hearing how much she risked for me made me see that love has risks at every turn. She risked so much for love—love of Gilchrist, love of me, love of the children I haven't even had yet. So I told myself that the least I could do to honor that sacrifice was risk my own heart."

He smiled and reached up to rub her tears away. "There was only one problem with that," he said, his voice hoarse with emotion. "I'd already lost my heart. I think I lost it the moment you showed up in my bedchamber, demanding that I give my mother her due, telling me that absurd tale about how you would readily jump into my bed because I was 'rumored to be quite good at that sort of thing.'"

"And justifiably so," she managed to tease through her tears.

"You see?" he rasped. "That's why I love you, Camilla. You are the only woman who simply laughs at me when I try to be an arse. And somehow, in doing so, you make me not want to be an arse at all."

"You're not an arse," she said, lifting her hand to cup his cheek.

He covered her hand with his. "Oh, I am sometimes. And I know that you have other choices now that you have a mother who wants to make you an heiress, and you are free as a bird for the first time in your life. I realize what an incredible gift she is offering you. But if you marry me, I promise to spend the rest of my life giving you every possible chance to fly."

"I don't want to fly, my love," she whispered, sure that her heart would explode at any moment. "Not unless we fly together."

The smile that broke over his face was so unguarded that it made her want to drag him downstairs and right into bed. But she settled for letting him pull her into his arms and kiss her as if she were the only woman in the world. The woman who'd miraculously captured his heart.

When he had her pulse racing and her toes curling, he tucked her hand in his elbow and said, "Now let's go tell Jasper that he's just gained himself a papa and another grandmama."

She gazed up at him with a happy smile. "That might actually render him speechless."

He eyed her askance. "I would sooner believe that reindeer fly." Then his gaze warmed until she could see his heart, his true feelings, shining in his eyes. "But after today, I might actually believe that, too. Because if I can fall in love, dearling, then anything can happen."

Epilogue

A year and a day later, Pierce sat in the big chair in the nursery at Montcliff Manor with Jasper, dressed in his nightshirt, in his lap. His wife sat opposite them, nursing their two-month-old daughter, Gillian, while Maisie, who'd proved to be an excellent nursery maid, was tidying up.

Beyond them, the tree in the nursery sparkled and gleamed in the firelight. It was one of three at Montcliff this year, with a larger one in the grand drawing room downstairs and one at the dower house.

It was amazing how Montcliff Manor had become so dear to him. But it didn't take long for him to realize that it hadn't been the house that was cold and sterile. It had been the people in it.

The nursery was an excellent example. His father had built it with an eye toward having an heir one day to supplant Pierce. The fool had fitted the room with austere paintings and a tall table and unforgiving chairs that would make any child squirm.

Camilla had thrown all of that out. Now cheerful scenes of boys riding ponies and children gamboling through a wood hung on the wall. The chairs were smaller and adorned with brightly colored cushions, and the table was lower to make it easier for little ones to write.

Pierce chuckled. Father was probably turning over in his grave to see it being inhabited by the likes of Jasper—the son of a vicar and a foundling—and little Gillian, the daughter of his despised son and a foundling. Every time Pierce thought of his and Camilla's children profaning Father's holy empire, running joyously about the estate, he felt a certain smug satisfaction.

Perhaps Mother was right. All the years of pain had been worth it just so they could both beat the old bastard in the end.

"I suppose you want me to read the Poem again," Pierce said to Jasper. That was what they all now called "A Visit from St. Nicholas."

"Oh no, not tonight, Papa," Jasper shocked him by saying. "This is the night *after* Christmas, so I wrote a new poem for it."

Pierce blinked. "You did? When did you do that?"

"This afternoon, while Grandmama Devonmont was here. She helped me." As he unfolded a sheet of paper, he said, "Are we going to Grandmama's house for Twelfth Night?"

"I imagine that your grandmother would march over here and box our ears if we didn't."

Camilla snorted. "As if she would ever 'box' anyone's ears."

"She used to make me sit in the corner when I was a boy," Pierce pointed out. Strange, how the memories of his childhood had become less painful and more treasured in the past year.

"You probably deserved it," Camilla said with a twinkle in her eye.

"Me? I was a model child."

"Like *me*," Jasper said.

"Exactly," Pierce agreed as his wife rolled her eyes.

She claimed that he spoiled Jasper, and perhaps he did. But he certainly didn't spoil the lad one whit more than Grandmama Devonmont did. Or, for that matter, Grandmama Hedon, whom they were going up to London to visit next month.

"All right," Jasper said as he smoothed out the paper. "Here's my poem. ' 'Twas the night after Christmas and all through the manor / Not a creature was stirring, not even a grandmama.'"

"Your grandmama didn't mind that you called her a 'creature'?" Pierce interjected.

"She wanted to be in the poem. And I didn't want to put a mouse in there; they scare Mama."

"Ah, right. Go on."

"'The baby was nestled all snug in her crib, / While visions of sugarplums danced on her bib.'"

Camilla's lips were quivering, and Pierce had to bite his tongue to keep from laughing.

"'And Mama in her 'kerchief, and Papa in his cap—'"

"I don't wear a cap to bed," Pierce pointed out.

"You do in the poem," Jasper said, as if that explained everything. "'Had just settled down for a long winter's nap / When out on the lawn there arose such a noise / That it woke up the boys.'"

Pierce raised his brows. "You have a baby sister."

Jasper cut a sly glance up at him. "And now I want a baby brother."

Camilla began to cough.

Pierce grinned over at her. "I think that can be arranged."

"You do, do you?" she said coyly as she got up to put the now slumbering baby in the crib.

Jasper paid no notice and went on. "'When what to my wondering eyes should appear—'"

"Wait a minute," Pierce said, lowering his voice to keep from waking the baby. "You skipped ahead."

"I know. I couldn't think of anything for that stuff about the 'breast of the snow.' It's silly." Jasper took a deep breath. "'When what to my wondering eyes should appear / But a really big sleigh and eight giant reindeer.'"

"Why did the reindeer get so big?" Pierce asked curiously.

"So they'll be like *our* deer." He gazed up at Pierce. "You know, the ones in the pen. Besides, if St. Nicholas is carrying presents, he needs *lots* of room. A miniature sleigh isn't nearly big enough."

"Excellent point," Pierce said.

Jasper folded up the paper. "So that's it."

"What about the rest of it?" Camilla asked in a whisper as she came up to perch on the arm of Pierce's chair.

"Mama, the Poem is *really* long. It took me all afternoon to write this part out." He snuggled closer to Pierce. "Okay, now you can read me the real Poem."

"Oh no, lad," she said as she picked him up and headed off. "No more stalling. It's time for bed."

Jasper cast Pierce a beseeching glance over his mother's shoulder, and Pierce threw up his hands with a rueful smile. He knew better than to gainsay Camilla when it came to bedtime.

Besides, once the children were in bed . . .

A short while later, he had *her* in his lap as they sat in the drawing room looking at the tree. This one had ribbons and bows and lit candles, as well as a number of new baubles from the London shops. Camilla wasn't one to spend buckets of money on anything, but she did like a pretty Christmas tree almost as much as his mother did.

He propped his chin on her head. "Fowler informed me today that he is planning to ask for Mother's hand in marriage. I think he was rather surprised when I told him I'd be delighted to have him in the family."

"He certainly waited long enough in getting around to it."

"You know Fowler. It took him six months after our wedding to work up the courage to ask her to go for a walk, and another two months before he progressed to asking her to ride with him. If I hadn't prodded him into inviting her to accompany him to that harvest assembly last fall, he would probably still be riding with her every day and giving her long, yearning glances at dinner. That man courts at a snail's pace."

"Not everyone can court at *your* manic pace," she teased. "Though I'm not sure I'd call it *courting*. More like a transparent attempt to get beneath my skirts."

"It worked, didn't it?" he said with a grin.

"Yes." She shifted in his lap so she could look up at him. "As did my transparent attempt to reform you."

"You did not reform me," he said stoutly. "I reformed myself."

"Oh, you did, did you?" she asked as she looped her arms about his neck. "I had nothing to do with it?"

"Hardly. Every time I looked at you, my thoughts were decidedly *un*reformed." He lowered his gaze to her mouth. "They still are."

"Are they, indeed?" Her eyes gleamed. "Do tell."

He brushed a kiss over her lips. " 'Twas the night after Christmas, and all through the place / The only ones stirring were the lord and his mate."

"That is an awful rhyme."

"Shh, I'm not done." He rose with her in his arms, and headed for the door. "They went off to nestle all snug in their bed / While visions of lovemaking danced in their heads."

She eyed him suspiciously. "Is this the naughty version of the Poem?"

"No." He stared down into the face of the woman who'd become dearer to him than life. Who made his life richer and fuller and decidedly more interesting with each passing day. "It's the version for men who are in love with their wives."

She smiled up at him, that same love shining in her face. "Then carry on, sir."

"And Mama, quite naked, and I naked, too—"

"Pierce!" she cried, half laughing, half chiding.

"Oh, all right," he said as he carried her up the stairs. "I suppose it *is* the naughty version."

Acknowledgments

First, to my critique partners, Rexanne Becnel and Deb Marlowe, thank you for always knowing what's wrong even when I can't put my finger on it. And Deb, thank you for finding the secret door even when I painted myself into a plot corner!

Thank you, Becky Timblin and Kim Ham, for keeping me sane during the months and months of insanity.

This book wouldn't even have been conceived without my agent, Pamela Ahearn, who has always encouraged me to push beyond my comfort zone.

And I can't do anything without my wonderful editor, Micki Nuding, who didn't even blink when I said I needed another month to finish. Thanks, Micki, for understanding that sometimes characters need time to come into fruition.

Most of all, thanks to Rene for enduring all the chaos with stoic grace. You're the best!